Also by Peter Cawdron

RETRO

RETROGRADE

Peter Cawdron

A JOHN JOSEPH ADAMS BOOK
Houghton Mifflin Harcourt
Boston ▪ New York
2017

First Houghton Mifflin Harcourt Publishing Company edition 2017

www.hmhco.com

Library of Congress Cataloging-in-Publication Data is available.
ISBN 978-1-328-83455-3

Book design by Chrissy Kurpeski

Printed in the United States of America
DOC 10 9 8 7 6 5 4 3 2 1

MARS ENDEAVOUR MISSION
Principal Crew Manifest

Name	*Primary Position*
U.S. Module **(28 crew members)**	
Connor	Mission Commander
Harrison	U.S. Second in Command
Liz	Micropaleobiologist
James (Canada)	Robotics Engineer
Michelle (Puerto Rico)	Martian Geologist
Amira (Navajo Nation)	Imaging Specialist
McDonald	Chief of Agriculture
Manu (American Samoa)	Exo-environments Specialist
Danielle	Paleovolcanologist
Chinese Module **(27 crew members)**	
Wen	Chinese Commander
Su-shun	Chinese Second in Command
Jianyu	Surgeon

MARS ENDEAVOUR MISSION
Principal Crew Manifest (continued)

Name	*Primary Position*
Russian Module **(29 crew members)**	
Vlad	Russian Commander
Dimitri	Russian Second in Command
Anna	Medical Specialist
Eurasian Module **(36 crew members)**	
Max (United Kingdom)	Eurasian Commander
Adin (Israel)	Surface-Ops Controller
Prabhat (India)	Electron Microscopist
NASA (Houston)	
(John) Davies	Mission Controller

Solitude, isolation, are painful things,
and beyond human endurance.

— JULES VERNE

RETROGRADE

1

Devils

I'M GIDDY WITH RICE WINE.

"Okay, deal the cards again," James says, circling his hand around the table. "I get this. I can fool the landlord."

"It is *dou di zhu*," Su-shun replies. "'*Fight* the landlord,' not 'fool.'"

I laugh as Jianyu pours me another tiny glass. "Are you trying to get me drunk?" I ask.

Jianyu replies, but I can't hear him over the noise of the card game and James calling out, "To fool is to fight without being seen, my friend. To fool is as good as a fight. Sometimes, it's better."

"Sometimes it is," Su-shun admits, dealing cards around the table.

Jianyu smiles at me and then turns to James, saying, "You sound like Sun Tzu in *The Art of War*."

"Did he say that?" James asks with innocence in his voice.

"No," Su-shun replies, and everyone bursts out laughing.

"You've had too much to drink," I say to James, but I'm the one swaying under the influence of alcohol in the light Martian gravity. I hold on to the edge of the table with one hand, feeling as though I could float away. The rest of the Chinese crew gather around, yelling and placing bets — speaking so fast I find it hard to believe anyone can follow the conversation. All I can tell is that there's a lot of excitement around James and his grossly misplaced bravado, with the Chinese betting both for and against him, but I suspect it's mostly against.

Like smoke in some seedy Shanghai restaurant, water vapor drifts around us, rising up from humidifiers wafting homemade incense throughout the Chinese module. I love the ambience. For a Midwestern girl like me, immersing myself in another culture is as intoxicating as alcohol, and I find myself torn between staying and leaving. I've got thirty kilos of rock samples to sift through tomorrow — that's easily eight to ten hours of work.

"We should be going," I say, tapping James on the shoulder and pointing at the digital clock on the wall. It's showing 12:00 a.m., but the seconds counter has gone well beyond 60 — it's at 2,344 and climbing. I forget exactly how many seconds there are in the Martian time-slip, but a day on Mars is roughly forty minutes longer than it is on Earth, so our clocks are set to pause for the best part of an hour from 12:00 to 12:01. In theory, it means we can sleep in an extra half hour or so each day, but in practice, that gets channeled into our work. Our biological clocks are like those of drifters constantly traveling across time zones. The physiological effect is like driving around the world once a month — which is more crazy than it seems: around halfway through the month, noon starts to feel like midnight. I'm not sure I'll ever get used to it.

"Come on, Liz! I'm about to clean them out."

"Yeah, *that's* not happening," I say, gesturing toward the hatch leading out of the module. "Let's go."

Su-shun gives me a look like he's a cat with a mouse, giving James just enough freedom before swatting at him again with long, sharp claws. He smiles behind narrow, thin eyes. He's loving this.

I look to Jianyu, trying to get his attention as he moves behind James, but he's caught up in the fun.

Yelling echoes through the module. It's astonishingly loud inside the narrow, tubular mod. It's sometimes difficult to remember we're on another planet, millions of miles from home. We could be in a simulator on Earth, although things never got this wild back there. With no instructors critiquing our actions, life is a lot more free on Mars — or as free as it can be living inside a tin can.

Jianyu puts some money down on James, which surprises me — although "money" is too strong a term. Poker chips act as pseudo-currency in the informal economy that exists within the colony. Most people barter for anything they want beyond the basics, but chips are sometimes exchanged as well.

The sweet smell of spiced rice floats through the air. Thin strips of faux meat sizzle in a wok as the chef constantly turns over a suc-culent Asian dish, adding a small ladle of water every few seconds, causing steam to billow into the overly humid air. The chef is talking as rapidly as everyone else, though to whom I don't know — I'm not sure anyone's listening. Although the meal smells delicious, I can't imagine the crew wanting to eat at what equates to almost 1:00 a.m., but for the Chinese, the party is just getting started.

I love the Chinese mod. Technically, it's a mirror image of our own module, yet the Chinese have made it into a home. Somehow, they've transformed their mod into a back alley in Guangzhou — vibrant and full of life. Clothes hang from a line running across the back of the communal room, which is something Connor would never allow in the U.S. module. To my mind, the pieces of clothing act as pen-dants, colorful flags, festive decorations. I doubt anyone here gives them a second thought. They're a touch of life on Earth being trans-planted on Mars.

"*You* be the landlord," Su-shun yells, pointing at James as though he were fingering a murderer in a lineup.

"Oh, no, no, no, my friend," James says, wagging his finger. "I see what you're trying to do. *You* be the landlord!" Laughter erupts from around the crowded table.

Jianyu says, "Come on, Liz. Throw some chips into the pot." His hand runs down the back of my arm. Jianyu steps around me, but his hand lingers just long enough to express tenderness. He's normally guarded about our relationship. I don't think he's embarrassed about dating a foreigner, or intentionally secretive, he's just private about his feelings, and that's fine with me. Rural Chinese modesty is quaint to someone who lived in downtown Chicago for six years. Tonight, though, the rice wine is going to his head, and he sneaks a kiss on my cheek, adding, "You know you want to."

"No way," I say, laughing more at his impetuous public kiss than anything he said, yet I'm swept up in the euphoria. It's no longer a question of staying or leaving, but of betting or continuing to fiddle with the chips in my pocket. I'm tired. I performed an eight-hour surface op earlier today. My body yearns for bed, but my heart loves the explosion of life around me.

"Ah, ha ha," Su-shun says, this time pointing at me. "She's afraid he will lose!"

"She's too smart," Jianyu replies, winking at me, and more poker chips find themselves cast onto the pile in the middle of the table. How anyone keeps track of what's been bet and by whom, I have no idea, but the system seems to work. Deep down, I suspect no one really cares. The chips are like gold on a games night like this, even though they're little more than a novelty.

There are five players seated at the round dining table, with two dozen others cramped around them, all trying to get a good vantage point. That's pretty much everyone in the Chinese mod, but the commotion within the module gives the impression there are hundreds of people bustling through a crowded market.

Su-shun finishes dealing to the players, but before anyone can pick up their cards, Wen storms over, pulling people away so she can get to the table.

"Out. Out. Out!" she yells over the ruckus, reaching in and scooping up two piles of cards. "Americans must leave."

"What?" Su-shun has a look of disbelief on his face.

"You leave now!" Wen yells, looking me in the eye. This is a shift in persona. There's no banter, no friendly rivalry. I see anger in her eyes.

"James," I say, pulling on his shoulder. "We need to go."

"What? No way. I've got chips in that pot!"

Wen doesn't bother collecting the other cards. It's enough to simply toss them from the table. The other players are incensed.

"Leave!" she yells.

Wen doesn't stop with the cards. With a bat of her hand, the chips are scattered across the table. In the low Martian gravity, they skim through the air and bounce over the floor of the module. We've been on Mars for nine months building the main base, but the sight of objects being propelled under Martian gravity never gets old. It's jarring to see physical things obeying a rate other than the 1 g in which we were raised. It's as though the universe has betrayed us, and life on Mars never feels quite right.

"Wen!" Jianyu protests, but the old matriarch will not be pacified, and she screams again for us to leave.

Wen has her long hair pulled back into a ponytail. At sixty-four, she's the oldest person on Mars, but you'd never guess her age from her work rate or her physique. She's imposing, intimidating even the men.

James gets slowly to his feet. He sways a little under the influence of alcohol and strange gravity. At the best of times, it's easy to lose your footing on Mars. For James, this isn't the best of times. I take his arm. Wen grabs both of us, marching us toward the central hub at the end of the mod.

As we're in roughly one-third of Earth's gravity, even the most forceful march is stunted, but I can feel Wen pushing us on. Our feet bounce slightly between steps.

Most colonists struggle to retain 1 g fitness. It's easy to slack off and settle for less, but not Wen. She used to run marathons on Earth. I doubt she'd have any problem running several back-to-back up here. One of the Chinese men opens the hatch as we're marched out.

"We're just having a little fun!" James protests as we're thrust into the vast central hub connecting the various modules like spokes of a giant wheel. The Eurasians are in the process of closing their outer hatch. The outer hatch to the Russian module is already shut. It's normal to keep the inner hatches secure to control humidity and air-flow, but the heavy outer hatches are only ever closed during containment tests or depressurization drills. It's the middle of the night. This isn't about our game. Something else has happened, and not knowing why we're being treated like this is a little scary. My mind is dull with alcohol, and that thought passes like a bird on the breeze.

Wen yells, *"Zhànzhēng fànzi!"* as she shuts the hatch. I catch a glimpse of Jianyu behind her. He looks confused, bewildered. He tries to say something, mouthing a few words in English, but I don't understand.

Zhànzhēng fànzi. Jianyu has been teaching me Chinese. Although I struggle with the sheer complexity of the language, he's taught me some of the more common expressions, and I remember this one because to my ear it seems to rhyme. In Chinese, I'm pretty sure it means "warmonger."

I feel like a leper being shunned.

"What the hell?" James says, leaning against the railing of the walkway within the hub.

Starlight drifts down from above.

The four modules that make up the Martian colony are set deep underground within volcanic lava tubes to protect us from cosmic radiation. There's roughly thirty feet of basalt and regolith between us and the harsh, radiation-scorched surface of the planet.

The four mods have been built in two lava tunnels that converge in the shape of an X. At the center of the X, the roof of the tunnel has collapsed, probably millions of years ago, long before *Homo sapiens* existed as a species. That's the crazy thing about Mars: nothing's new. There's plenty of fine-dust erosion and the odd meteor strike, but the geological vistas we explore are hundreds of millions — if not billions — of years old. It's as though the planet has been frozen in time, waiting for explorers from Earth.

The collapsed section above the hub forms a natural skylight some forty feet across and easily visible from orbit. It took almost four months for our automated extrusion builder to create a glass dome over the skylight, forcing us to suit up when moving between mods for what felt like an eternity, but it was worth the wait. Once the dome was in place and the walls were sealed with thick plastic manufactured here on Mars, the hub tripled the usable space within the colony. The glass in the skylight is three feet thick and laced with lead, along with numerous layers of laminate to protect us from radiation. Near the edge, the glass distorts the light from outside, but on a clear night like tonight, you get a stunning view of the stars directly overhead.

Harrison comes bounding out of the U.S. module.

"Where the hell have you two been?" he yells across the hub with its crops of wheat and corn growing in layered fields beneath soft blue grow lights. The hub is huge, and not just because it's wider than the modules. It's naturally almost four stories deep. James and I are on a raised metal walkway above the top field, still feeling somewhat bewildered by Wen, somewhat jovial from being slightly drunk, and somewhat enchanted with Mars itself.

Harrison comes running along the walkway. He's not known for his subtlety. Harrison's a robotics engineer from landlocked Arizona, yet he swears like a sailor hitting his thumb with a hammer. One of the common misconceptions about life on Mars is that everyone's a scientist, but it takes mechanics, doctors, and engineers to make the colony work.

"Connor's been looking for you fuckers everywhere. You need to come with me. Now!"

"Whoa there, cowboy," James says in a thick drawl. "Just what the Sam Hill is going on?" James is from Canada, but he loves winding Harrison up with a fake Texas accent, even though Harrison's from Arizona. To James, the mysterious American Southwest is just one big muddle. Perhaps it's his blasé attitude that makes him so effective at annoying Harrison. I can't help but laugh.

I slur my words. "Yeah, cowboy. Slow down."

"Connor wants you back in the mod" is all Harrison will say, refusing to be baited. He grabs James by the wrist and pulls him on.

James snatches at my hand, and I fall in step behind the two men, laughing at the madness of such a rush on Mars. The rice wine has left me light-headed and as clumsy as a kid stepping off a spinning fairground ride. Running in Martian gravity is entirely counterintuitive. I lean into the run at an angle that would have me falling flat on my face on Earth, but on Mars it results in a gentle lope.

I can see Michelle standing by the hatch leading into the U.S. module, ready to close the heavy metal door behind us. We're the same age, but her dark skin is flawless and she usually looks much younger than me. Now, though, she looks exhausted. She's dressed in her pj's, barefoot, no bra beneath her top, hair disheveled. Why is she even awake?

"What's wrong with everyone?" I ask.

Michelle says, "They just nuked Chicago."

2

Chicago

THEY JUST NUKED CHICAGO. I don't hear anything after those four words.

Michelle's talking rapidly, rattling off details, but my mind is caught in a stupor, trying to shake off my alcohol-induced lethargy. Try as I may, I can't think straight. The moment seems to demand I switch seamlessly from one mind-set to another, but I can't. I'm numb, and those four words keep rattling around in my head.

They. Who the hell are "they"? Who would do this? And *why?*

Just. Any news we get is at least half an hour old by the time it's made its tortuous route to us. I have no idea what time it is in Chicago, as the Martian time-slip means we're constantly drifting out of sync with the various time zones on Earth.

Nuked. That's got to be a mistake. My mind cannot grasp how something like this could happen. Nuclear weapons are the stuff of nightmares.

Chicago. There are four million people in Chicago, including my parents, who live just outside of Joliet. I have dozens of friends in downtown apartments not more than half a mile from the waterfront. This must be a mistake. Please, this has to be a mistake.

My chest heaves as a knot forms deep inside. A knife seems to plunge through my heart, twisting as it's driven deeper.

Nuclear weapons are the harbingers of the much-feared Armageddon, but they're also relics of the long-forgotten Cold War. Perhaps I'm naive, but I thought nukes were little more than figurative displays of strength these days. Their only use is in saber rattling, not in actual combat, and certainly not against civilian targets. Not *Chicago.*

I'm hyperventilating, something that's easy to do in the low Martian gravity. Panic seizes me. I've got to calm down, but my mind's racing. I focus on my breathing, slowing my respiration. I try to take deep breaths. Looking down, I watch the rise and fall of my chest, blocking out everything other than the sound of air filling my lungs and the subsequent rush of breath fleeing my nostrils.

Nukes. They're localized, I tell myself, wanting to rationalize what's happened. Emotionally, it's too easy to imagine nothing but utter devastation everywhere, but rationally I know nuclear weapons cause less damage the further you move away from ground zero.

If ground zero was downtown Chicago — even if it was an airburst bomb — outlying suburbs could've survived. Either way, my old neighborhood would have been vaporized. Sophie, James, Hamid, Jules, Jacinta, the Uni crew — they wouldn't have felt anything, I tell myself. Nothing. For them, life would have been extinguished in a nanosecond, far quicker than anything the human mind can process as fear or pain. They wouldn't have had time to process the blinding flash of light around them. Death would have come so quickly, it wouldn't have been realized. Life would have simply stopped, like a lightbulb burning out, plunging the room into darkness, only my friends will never recognize the darkness. For a fraction of a second, temperatures akin to those in the heart of a giant star would have been unleashed in Chicago as hell descended on Earth.

My mind reels in shock.

Tears run down my cheeks.

I need something to hold on to, something to help me through the passage of time. My folks. Living further out, they might be okay. They *have* to be okay.

What was the yield? Nukes are deceptively powerful. A single 1.5 megaton thermonuclear warhead, barely the size of a motorbike, packs more punch than all the Allied bombs that fell on Germany throughout the entire Second World War.

I was a Greenpeace activist as a teen, walking the streets of downtown Chicago whenever a trade delegation from Russia or China came to town. We'd protest for disarmament every chance we got. That seems like a lifetime ago here on Mars, but it means I'm all too aware of the destruction these weapons bring. Was this a tactical nuke delivered by a cruise missile? Something in the kiloton range? Or was it from an intercontinental ballistic missile delivering one of several MIRV warheads ranging into the megatons? It surely couldn't be a Tsar, the class of weapons reaching into the tens of megatons, as those can only be delivered by aircraft. Such an attack would be impossible, I hope.

I'm assuming it was the Russians. Who else could it be? The Chinese have a nuclear arsenal, but it pales in comparison to U.S. and Russian stockpiles. And yet Wen was angry, torn with passion.

Mom and Dad live almost forty miles from downtown. I desperately try to convince myself they're going to be okay. I try not to think about explosive yield and compression waves, or prevailing winds and fallout.

"All right. Listen up. Find somewhere to sit down!" Connor yells. African American and built like a linebacker, Connor found that his biggest obstacle during selection wasn't his test scores or his intellect — as it was for most of us — it was his physical dimensions. I remember a reporter asking me why we all flew coach instead of business class when we traveled. It wasn't simply to keep costs down. NASA didn't want us getting too comfortable, given that our cockpit would make economy on easyJet look like first class. Flight seats, space suits, even sleeping pods here on Mars are all roughly identical. For Connor, they've always been a squeeze.

Connor climbs up on what looks like the table I was leaning over just minutes ago in the Chinese mod, only there aren't any playing cards or poker chips . . . no smell of ginger wafting through the air, no plumes of steam coming from a wok. Our mod is sterile. Lifeless.

Connor rubs his hand over the shaved, smooth skin on his head in much the same way I scratch my hair when lost in thought.

James slumps to the floor and leans against one of the storage cabinets. I join him, sliding rather than sitting down.

Harrison sits above us. His legs hang down beside my shoulder. He's mumbling, "This is fucked. This is so fucked." In a perverse way, it's nice to know I'm not the only one in shock.

"Listen!" Connor yells above the commotion. "I'll tell you what I know, but I need some quiet!"

The unrest dies. Most of the crew is bleary-eyed and wearing pajamas. They look scared. They huddle in small groups that represent working relationships rather than friendships. In a crisis, our professionalism as colonists and scientists comes to the forefront, and that's no surprise. We've been trained to be resilient.

"There's been a nuclear exchange."

"*Exchange?*" Harrison blurts out. "That's bullshit! We're not talking about swapping e-mail addresses. This is a goddamn nuclear war!" And with that, our collective professionalism collapses. Everyone talks over each other in an explosion of noise.

Connor signals for calm, gesturing for Harrison to give him some space. "We don't know much. We know cities around the world were hit, including several of our own. Please! Listen! Let me speak!"

"Who did this?" James asks with a head that's much clearer than mine.

"We don't know. We don't know who fired first, but once the missiles started flying, it doesn't look like there was much in the way of restraint."

Connor's head hangs low. His shoulders slump, which is alarming. This is a man who carries himself with physical gravitas. When Connor walks into a room, everyone notices. I doubt Connor has ever lost at anything, sporting or otherwise. He exudes confidence. Now, he looks defeated.

Connor was a sergeant in the Marine Corps, leading ground-assault troops in the Middle East before joining NASA. That has to be the most unlikely and torturous path ever to becoming an astronaut. Connor taught himself astrophysics in a foxhole. He studied online in every spare moment. He surprised everyone when he completed his PhD with honors while on deployment in Sudan. He submitted a research paper that caught the attention of NASA administrator Harold Darling — "Early European Exploration and Parallels with the Colonization of the Solar System."

Connor is as tough as Martian bedrock, yet now even he has tears in his eyes. "We lost New York, Chicago, and D.C."

Harrison mutters, "Fuck," and for once, I agree with his profane sentiments. I can see his knuckles turning white. He grips the edge of the bench as though he's ready to tear it apart.

"What about the West Coast?" Michelle asks. I hadn't noticed her before, but she's sitting up beside Harrison. There's a quiver in her voice that betrays her fears. "Have we heard anything about L.A.? San Diego? Seattle? The Bay Area?"

"There's a lot we don't know," Connor says. "What news services are running aren't helping. There are a lot of rumors — too much speculation. A large-scale electrical blackout has hit the Midwest. It's winter down there. Heavy snow makes everything worse. Communication with the West Coast is down."

"Down?" Michelle asks with surprise in her voice. "How can it be *down?* Surely, someone knows something. You can't cut off an entire region of the country, can you? Someone must know something."

"I'm sorry," Connor replies.

I feel incredulous. Is this a joke? This cannot be real. I'm slipping into denial. I shake my head. Am I dreaming? Is this a nightmare? Has the date clicked over to April first and this is all just some nasty, horrible prank?

Harrison asks a question that, in hindsight, seems obvious and of critical importance, but I would never have thought of it. "And out-side the U.S.?"

Connor speaks with a deathly slow cadence, reading from his tablet computer. "London, Paris, Bonn, Rome, Moscow, Saint Peters-burg, Tel Aviv, Karachi, New Delhi, Beijing, Shanghai, Tokyo."

No one speaks. The only sound is that of the vents circulating air through the mod. I'm not sure how, but my head sinks into my hands. My elbows rest on my knees as my hands pull at my hair, on the verge of tearing the fine strands from their roots. I don't remember moving my arms. Reality is a haze. I sob quietly, overcome by what I've heard.

"That's fifteen cities all around the globe," James mumbles. "And all in the Northern Hemisphere. What's the pattern? I don't see a pat-tern."

"This can't be right," someone calls out from the other side of the mod.

"Have they stopped?" Harrison asks, getting up and pacing around the module. He's manic, striding back and forth as he talks. "I mean — are they still lobbing nukes at each other? This isn't still go-ing on, right? Surely, reason has prevailed and they're not *still* punch-ing big red buttons and unleashing hell on each other?"

Connor gestures with his hands, signaling he doesn't know.

"This is insane," Michelle says. She slides from the counter, sink-ing to the floor beside me. "This is wrong. This can't be right."

Michelle and I were part of the same intake for the colony. We were both late additions to the U.S. team and have stuck by each other through the years of training as more than 90 percent of our class was slowly whittled away. Only four of us made the flight, and only two women.

I reach out and touch her thigh. Our eyes meet. Tears stream down her cheeks.

"This can't be real," Michelle says softly to me, and we hug. Touch is the only sense I trust. To touch someone else is to connect with re-ality, and I suspect the same realization holds for her. She buries her head in my shoulder. I can feel her frail body trembling.

Connor says, "I'm sorry," as though this is somehow his fault. "It's going to be a long night. There are a couple of news feeds coming through, but they're patchy and erratic. We're in retrograde. From here on out, our communication delays are only going to get worse. You know the drill—our downstream bandwidth is prioritized for monitoring metrics over research data, then data over text, text over images, and images over video, so be frugal with messages or you'll cause a logjam for everyone else. You're better off going to the cache server for news rather than making your own requests and waiting for a round-trip refresh that may never come. The primary relay mail server is down. I—I'll inform you of anything I hear from Houston."

He steps down from the table onto a chair and then slowly to the floor, saying, "Try to get some sleep."

Sleep? I almost laugh. I never want to sleep again. I know my body will overwhelm me at some point, but to sleep seems inhuman. Millions of people have died—been *murdered*. My parents, my friends —I don't want to think about what's happened to them. I only hope that somehow they've been spared.

A lump rises in my throat. Brothers, uncles, cousins, nephews, and nieces—most of my immediate family and my dad's family live in and around Greater Chicago. Mom's a Buckeye from Ohio. She had a falling-out with her folks, so I never really knew her side of the family. I spent my summers at my uncle's place near South Bend, Indiana, not more than an hour from Chicago, swimming in the numerous small lakes dotting the region. I've got good friends in Aurora, just outside Chicago.

How widespread is the damage?

How big was the bomb?

When did it detonate?

I have no idea what day of the week it is. I think it's a Thursday. I hope it's a Sunday, wishing the death toll to be as low as possible but knowing it has to be in the hundreds of thousands for Chicago alone. With time, it will grow into the millions in my hometown.

Who escaped?

I have to rationalize what happened. I have to compartmentalize the pain — it's the only way I can stand the uncertainty.

I'd like to think Mom and Dad survived, but survived to struggle through what? Last time I looked, it was –15°F in Chicago, with a blizzard blowing in over the lake. What would that do to a nuclear explosion? Probably nothing.

I try to recall what I know about nukes. They're weapons with layered kill zones within a high-density area. Depending on the yield of a particular bomb, there's an initial burst and a fireball that vaporizes everything within a few city blocks. Outside that, the blast wave flattens and scorches everything out to four or five miles, perhaps further, but beyond that the danger drops sharply as the distance increases. At twenty miles, the danger from flying debris is like that in any wild storm.

I shake the Hollywood images of an all-pervasive Armageddon from my head, knowing the destructive force of a nuclear explosion is largely in the blast wave, which equates roughly to an F5 tornado in its early phase, but it can't reach everywhere. It dies. It has to. It can't be as rampant and destructive as I imagine.

I tell myself this, trying to convince myself that, as bad as this calamity is, it's survivable at a distance. I'm shaking, desperately trying to hose down my initial hysteria. There's a sense of end-of-the-world apocalyptic doom that inevitably comes with such notions, and I do my best to talk myself out of the dire pessimism that floods my mind.

What else? The mushroom cloud will carry fine radioactive debris high into the atmosphere, dumping it on the countryside over hundreds of miles, but exactly where it goes is highly dependent on wind patterns. Radioactive fallout will appear like an elongated smudge on a map — it won't spread out in all directions. It's likely there's no increase in radiation around my folks' place, as the prevailing winds are to the southeast at this time of year.

With all of these weapons of mass destruction, though, the most devastating impact comes over time. Nukes are weapons of mass disruption. They kill and maim hundreds of thousands, perhaps millions, in the blink of an eye, but it's the problems they cause for tens of millions of survivors that will last for generations. And it's not just the obvious things, like radically increased cancer rates. There's economic shock and the impact on nearby food production, along with reduced access to major roads and collapsed bridges, that are likely to cripple large portions of the country for decades. Then there's the psychological impact of an entire nation reeling in shock — the mass hysteria, the fear and sense of vulnerability. The world will never be the same again.

I find myself strangely detached as I try to think about the ramifications of what has just happened. Removing myself from the moment and considering the implications objectively are a coping mechanism. It helps to think of faceless masses. If I think of my uncle Herm, or my brother Joe, I imagine the worst. As for my old neighbors, there's no comfort to be found. For them, life would have ceased in a blinding flash.

Dad's a survivor, I tell myself, wanting to cling to hope. He'll be rallying his neighbors, helping others in the retirement village. I can just see him assisting the caretaker, fixing one of the boilers or stripping down an engine to get it working again. He has to be alive. He has to be.

NASA prepared us for every possible contingency on Mars — but it never prepared us for what could happen on Earth.

"This is bullshit!" Harrison says, kicking a cabinet on the far side of the mod and snapping me out of my thoughts. Connor walks over to calm him down, but I guess we're each dealing with this in our own way.

Most of the other crew members are in a daze. They wander around like zombies. Michelle's coming apart. She's still crying, sobbing into my shoulder. Her arms are wrapped around me. I'm not sure why, but comforting her gives me strength. Perhaps I'm roleplaying, but I feel more able to deal with my own anguish by holding her, yet nothing's changed. Uncertainty, doubt, hurt, fear, sorrow — all of these emotions are there eating away at my heart, but they're not overwhelming me because I have an overriding concern for my dear friend. I guess I need Michelle as much as she needs me.

A hand rests gently on my shoulder.

James crouches beside us. "Hey," he says softly.

Michelle doesn't look up.

James and I make eye contact. There are tears in both our eyes. He must see that there are no words that can assuage the grief we all feel. He slumps cross-legged in front of us. His head bows, his arms rest on his knees. He must be uncomfortable sitting like that, but comfort is not a factor right now.

Someone dims the lights.

Several of the crew have tablets out. They're watching video clips from Earth. No real-time communication is possible.

Conversations with loved ones on Earth are impossible at the best of times. Even without all the emotion we're reeling beneath, talking to a camera is hard. That tiny, dark lens is too impersonal. I find I run out of things to say after about thirty seconds, which is silly when there's so much going on here, but it's the lack of feedback from another living, breathing human that makes it so difficult. Talking to someone face-to-face allows for so much more to be said than words alone convey. All we have is a black dot set into our smooth, colorful tablets.

I see Marie from the utilities crew sending a vid to Earth. She was in the first group selected for the mission, being named as part of the crew almost a year before my class. With so much other network traffic, it could take days before her message is transmitted in full and reassembled back there. She'd be better off sending a text message. As it is, she can barely speak through her tears. I hope there's someone there to receive her message and reply. I don't have the emotional strength to try. I'm afraid no one will answer. If no one responds, I'll fall apart.

I lean back on the storage cabinet with Michelle still clinging to me. She's five feet four while I'm almost six feet tall, so in some ways it's like comforting a teen.

Someone puts a news clip up on the wall screen. James turns to watch. He leans up against the cabinet beside us, looking as though he's in a trance. It's hard to believe that just moments ago we were laughing and yelling, playing cards and sipping rice wine. Michelle can't look. I feel her flinch as the audio starts. I rest my hand gently on the back of her head, stroking her soft hair. She knows what we're watching, and she's decided she doesn't want to see it. I'm sure she's listening intently.

A reporter stands on a third- or fourth-floor balcony looking out across a snow-covered city. There's a red glow in the sky directly behind him, almost like sunset, only the Sun is off to one side, casting long shadows through the seemingly dead winter trees. The clouds overhead are nothing more than gray mush.

"We're fifty miles from what's left of the Capitol," the reporter says. "You can hear the sirens behind me. There's a helicopter somewhere above us, and from the sound of it, a military jet, protecting us from who or what, I don't know. There's no one to chase. What can a fighter plane do against a ballistic missile? Nothing. But everyone's doing something, anything. It's chaos. No one knows what's going on. The country is paralyzed. There's been no official word on the fate of the president, the vice president, or Congress.

"What we do know is that before the attack, this was just another day in Washington, D.C. Congress was in session. President Carver was conducting bilateral talks with Indonesian president Yionoto at the White House.

"If there was any warning, it never made it to the media. The first we knew was when lightning seemed to break through the dark clouds hanging over the Capitol. For a moment, the Sun descended on Earth. A mushroom cloud pushed back the storm, but even that's gone now.

"Snow's falling. It melts, so it's not ash, but whether it's radioactive or not, no one knows. Fear has seized the nation.

"The roads are jammed with people leaving the city, but the damage has been done. There's no reason to flee. State police are urging people to stay in their homes and not to go out unless absolutely necessary. Clogging the freeways as a blizzard sweeps across the country is only going to lead to more heartache.

"Emergency services are stretched to the breaking point. If you need assistance and cannot get through to 911, you should make your way to your local police station, or the nearest hospital, but be prepared for a long wait.

"Back to you, Olivia."

The image switches to a view of an anchorwoman sitting at a news desk. Rather than being in a studio, she's seated at one end of an open-plan newsroom. Behind her, reporters look intently at computer screens. They type. They talk. They drink coffee. The rolling graphic at the bottom of the screen reads, WORLD WAR III . . . ESTIMATED 1.8 MILLION DEAD . . . AT LEAST 5 MILLION INJURED . . . AMERICA IS AT WAR . . .

"With who?" James asks.

"Hostilities have broken out on the Korean Peninsula," the anchor says, her face not betraying the terror she surely feels. "We have reports of U.S. troops mobilizing to stop the North Korean army short of Seoul, but the expectation is the city will fall before the weekend.

"Japanese defense forces have confirmed a Chinese naval blockade of the Korean Peninsula. There are unconfirmed reports the Chinese have taken the international airport at Inchon, effectively cutting off Seoul from the West."

James whispers, "They're certifiable — mad — insane," but I want him to be quiet. I don't want to miss a single word.

"In the Middle East, there's speculation of a large-scale counterattack being undertaken by the Israelis, using both conventional and nuclear forces against Syria, Iraq, and Iran. Any involvement by U.S. forces in theater is purely speculative at this point, but the assumption is Centcom will support the action. Those few military spokespeople we can reach will not comment. The sentiment around here is they simply do not know."

The anchor holds her finger to her ear, trying to hear a comment in her earpiece over the sound of talking behind her in the crowded newsroom.

"We're trying to take you to our correspondent just outside of Yonkers in New York. Just hold. Hold. Okay, we're transferring you now — live to the northern districts of what was once New York City."

The image doesn't change. The anchorwoman is a pretty brunette in her mid-twenties. She's petite, with flawless skin. She reaches below the desk and pulls out a plastic water bottle, unscrews the lid, and takes a sip. She's talking to someone off camera, but her lapel microphone has been switched off. I can just make out her voice mixed in with all the background noise coming in from the camera mic, but it's not distinct enough to pick up on what she's saying.

A young man comes over to her, handing her a few sheets of paper. She skims over them, again sipping at her water. It seems both she and the news crew are oblivious to their continued broadcast. Their cut to New York has failed, but they think New York is on the air.

Suddenly, the image shakes and the transmission goes black. The muffled audio still streams. It sounds as though we're hiding in a closet while there's a party going on in the lounge. A small test pattern appears in one corner of the screen, along with the station logo. No one in the module speaks. We all watch the test pattern, willing the news coverage to return, but it never does. Reluctantly, someone switches off the wall screen, and we find ourselves thrust back onto the red planet again.

Time is a blur.

One moment, I'm cradling Michelle's head in my lap as she drifts off to sleep, gently stroking her hair, the next I'm waking to the smell of synthetic coffee.

Rather than lying in my sleep pod upstairs, I find myself lying on the floor of the communal room just beyond the airlock. Someone's slipped a pillow under my head and wrapped me in a blanket. On Earth, sleeping on a hard floor would be absurdly uncomfortable. My hips would dig into the unforgiving tiles, but on Mars, the low gravity means I'm almost floating, just lightly touching the floor.

Harrison steps softly over someone sleeping next to me. It takes me a moment to realize it's Michelle. James is snoring, as are several other people.

A dim light over the kitchenette sink reveals dark silhouettes moving around the module. I sit up, running my hand through my hair. Nature is calling. There's a toilet in the hallway leading to the laboratories at the rear of the mod. I make my way there, stepping over dozens of sleeping colonists. It seems no one went to bed. A few people are awake. Connor and Harrison sit at one of the tables, talking in hushed tones.

Living space is at a premium on Mars, so our lavatories are like those on an airplane. The only difference is that the toilet seat can be folded away to make room for a shower barely large enough to turn around within. I relieve myself and then stare in the mirror, looking at bloodshot eyes and messy hair. Running cold water up over my face and through my hair, I try to compose myself, but the horror of the night comes flooding back and my hands tremble.

On returning to the communal room, I sit with Connor and Harrison.

"Coffee?" Harrison asks, gesturing to an empty cup in the middle of the table.

"Thanks," I reply as he pours me a cup from a thermally insulated carafe.

The coffee is black and lacks sweetener, but the bitter, burned taste seems somehow appropriate, so I sip at it without adding any artificial creamer or sucrose tablets.

"What time is it?"

"About five thirty," Harrison replies. "Dawn should be breaking up top."

"Have you heard any more from Earth?" I ask, directing my question to Connor, who's unusually quiet. He looks like he hasn't slept at all. Connor shakes his head.

"Remember that video clip?" Harrison asks.

"Yeah."

Harrison switches on his tablet and brings up a dark screen that shouldn't be familiar but is. A test pattern flickers in the bottom-right corner.

"So?" I say.

"Wait for it."

The screen flickers, and there's a reporter standing on a snow-covered balcony. "We're fifty miles from what's left of the Capitol . . ."

Harrison mutes the video, leaving it running on his tablet.

"I don't understand. I mean, that's the same broadcast."

"It's all we're receiving," Connor says, looking at me with blood-shot eyes. "They've got it on a loop."

I'm confused. Repeatedly sending the same video to Mars makes no sense, as it hogs precious bandwidth. A two-minute personal video to my folks can take anywhere from a couple of hours to a couple of days to reach Earth, depending on how it's broken up and the priority of other traffic. Looping the same video again and again is crazy.

"But why?" I ask.

"Maybe that's all they can send," Connor says.

"Maybe that's all they *want* to send," Harrison adds. Harrison's never been the most overly optimistic guy, and he tends to look for the worst in people and situations. He's wrong yet again, or so I think. I have no time for paranoia.

Connor says, "Our ground link has six general-purpose comms channels. This is the only one with anything on it. Everything else is static."

Harrison says, "The data link's active, but it's flooded with garbage. It looks encrypted, but it's probably junk."

Earth may enjoy lightning-fast broadband Internet spanning the globe, but even if you ignore the latency between Earth and Mars, our Internet access is like dial-up from the '90s. Our proxy servers constantly trim web pages, stripping out video or downgrading both the frame rate and image quality. Pictures are automatically converted into 256 colors, leaving most images looking like something from a cartoon. It's like using Windows 95. Most web pages are little more than text with a bit of markup, but at least we're connected.

"Why would they cut us off?" I ask, trying to keep my voice low, as the woman lying on the floor behind me is stirring.

"I don't think it's intentional," Connor says. "Not in that this is all they want to tell us here on Mars. I suspect this is all they're telling anyone."

"But that makes no sense," I say, sipping my coffee.

Harrison says, "Truth is the first casualty in war."

"This is war. America is under attack," Connor says. "My guess is, they're not giving anything away. There's just enough information in that clip to get a feel for the magnitude of the problem. Hopefully, there's enough to calm the population — make them think something is being done in response to the attack, but not enough info to give any insights to the enemy."

"Who is the enemy?"

Connor shrugs his shoulders.

Harrison says, "They mentioned China."

"But that was in the context of Korea," Connor says. "We have no idea what that means for the continental U.S. None of this makes any sense. If this is between China and the U.S., then why bomb Karachi? Why hit Moscow? Paris? No, I don't think there's anything accidental or haphazard about that video. I think it's staged."

"I don't understand."

"Not the attack," Connor says, clarifying his comment, "but our response — that video. It's as much a message to the American people as it is to our adversaries."

"Propaganda," Harrison adds, agreeing with Connor. "Disinformation."

Connor nods. I'd expect this kind of paranoia from Harrison, but not Connor. I'm surprised he's buying into this. Jumping to such a radical conclusion without any supporting evidence doesn't sit well with me. I'm alarmed by their reaction to the video. As shocking as it is to hear of this catastrophe, cool heads need to prevail. Now is not the time for conspiracy theories.

A soft chime sounds. A message flashes on Connor's tablet. He flicks the screen, unlocking it with his fingerprint. Although the screen is upside down relative to me, I catch a glimpse of the word "NASA" as Connor raises the device, clipping my view. His eyes dart back and forth as he reads a message. From the format, I can tell it's an automated transcript accompanying a video in case of signal degradation. I don't know about Harrison, but I'm holding my breath. I'm expecting Connor to get up and find somewhere private so he can absorb its contents.

"Well," Connor says as he finishes reading, "this concerns all of us. You're going to see it sooner or later, might as well be now."

A couple of the other scientists are awake. We gather around Connor as he sets his tablet upright, leaning it against the carafe. The screen is blinding in the dim light. Connor adjusts the brightness and the volume as the video starts playing. He's trying to find a setting we can hear without waking the others.

The video quality is poor. Mission controller John Davies sits at a desk on the screen. His hair is scruffy. Dark rings encircle his eyes. His skin is pale. Patches of stubble have grown around his lips, chin, and cheeks, which is uncharacteristic for this normally impeccably groomed man. We're used to seeing him wearing a shirt and tie, sometimes with a sports jacket, but in this clip he's wearing a torn T-shirt with dark stains on the collar. I'd like to think it's mud, but I suspect it's blood. I'm not sure where he's broadcasting from, but it's not Mission Control. The lighting's weak, casting soft shadows down his face, making him look like a zombie.

"Ah, we really screwed the pooch on this one," he begins, leaning on his elbows and running his fingers through his hair. For a few seconds, he can't bring himself to look at the camera, staring at the desk with his hands clutching at his head. "It's a mess down here. I—I don't know what you've heard. Latest count was twenty-two detonations around the globe, but there's no pattern. Everyone's gone crazy. Jameson said he got a message away to you before comms were cut. We still don't know what happened or why, only that we were hit hard — Chicago, Manhattan, D.C. Since then, there's been an almost total media blackout. There's panic on the streets. Even Twitter's fallen silent. Someone's taken down the Internet, the goddamn supposedly bulletproof Internet. Everything's off-line — national TV, cable, regional radio. The works. We get sporadic broadcasts on local stations, but they don't know shit.

"I don't know if this will reach you. We've powered the emergency uplink, but there's some serious cyber warfare going on down here following those nuclear strikes. I'm not sure how long we'll be able to stream information to you, but we'll do our best to keep you up to date.

"You've got *Prospect 28* undertaking aerobraking as she settles into orbit, with the landing scheduled for tomorrow. I — I wish I could . . . She's fully autonomous, so with a bit of luck you'll get your resupply regardless of what's happening back here."

In the video, Davies grips his hands in front of himself, wringing them together nervously. "We haven't forgotten you."

Harrison blurts out, "That's crap! He's lying. Look at him. He knows."

"They're not going to abandon us," Michelle says, talking over the top of Harrison.

Connor hits Pause on the video. He turns to face Harrison, gesturing for quiet and saying, "Just let the man speak."

"I'm telling you," Harrison says, ignoring Connor. "They've forgotten about us already. Look at the body language. Look at the way he's rubbing his hands. Davies is fighting for us, but whoever's above him has turned their back on us. And Davies. Davies isn't telling us the truth. He's not telling us everything he knows. He's telling us what we want to hear."

"You don't know that," Connor says, again gesturing with his hand for silence.

Harrison ignores him. "The world's got bigger problems than a bunch of scientists stuck on a rock millions of miles away!"

Connor starts the video again.

"*Prospect 29* was in final prep, with the vehicle on the pad, when hurricanes Louisa and Miles delayed deployment. As you know, we missed the window on the Hoffman transfer, but even before the war broke out, there was pressure on us to repurpose *29* for the team on Cruithne. That decision's been put on hold. We've got to see what unfolds down here once the dust settles but I — I'm pushing for a relief mission to Mars."

"See?" Harrison cries. "I told you. I fucking *told* you."

"We haven't forgotten you," Davies continues, repeating himself, but his voice doesn't sound convincing.

"Fucking liar!" Harrison says over the top of the mission controller. Harrison's erratic, becoming unhinged under the pressure we all feel. Connor pauses the video while Harrison vents. "Two years! They want us to wait another goddamn two years for Mars to reach opposition again before they send us a full resupply mission? What about the supposed contingency plan? Backup rockets on standby? High-burn short-duration flights, and all that bullshit?"

Connor plays the video. If he didn't, Harrison would keep going.

"You're going to have to make things last," Davies says. "Be frugal. We'll work something out, we've just got to figure out our priorities."

Harrison raises his voice again. "What other fucking priorities does NASA have?"

Michelle says, "They've spent a trillion dollars getting us here. They're not going to leave us here to die."

"Apparently, they are," Harrison replies, slamming his hand on the table.

"Harrison," Connor says, getting angry with the constant interruptions. Harrison finally falls silent.

Almost everyone's awake by now, having been woken by the yelling. They sit up, befuddled, still trying to come to grips with the new reality of life on Mars.

"I'm sorry," Davies says from well over fifty million miles away and at least five minutes removed, not counting transmission retries. "I wish there was more I could tell you. I wish there was more I could do for you. I don't know how long it's going to take for things to get back to normal, so be patient. For now, you're on your own."

"See? See, I told you," Harrison says, pointing at the screen.

Davies reaches out and switches off the camera without any attempt to say farewell. There's no warning, just the flick of his fingers and the screen fades to black.

"Fuck," Harrison mutters, but I think we all agree with his sentiment. The chaos on Earth had to affect us in some way, but I don't think anyone expected it to be so soon or so direct.

3

Breakfast

TIME IS AN ODDITY. One moment seems to drag, the next rushes by. Whether it's bewilderingly fast or deathly slow, time is painful. Everything that seemed so important yesterday is suddenly irrelevant — Mars, the mission, my research. I have no idea whether it's morning or afternoon, but someone gets hungry and breakfast starts to roll. The mood is sullen. Most of the crew have arrived at the same conclusion in hushed whispers with close friends — we've been abandoned.

I sit down next to Michelle and James with a bowl of cereal soaking in a white liquid that's supposed to approximate milk. I didn't think it was possible, but the milk tastes even more bland than usual. It's as though my taste buds have died.

Michelle sweeps her hair behind one ear. Knowing her as well as I do, I can tell something's on her mind, but she doesn't say anything.

James speaks softly. "What is it with our self-imposed isolation?" His eyes dart between mine and Michelle's, looking for our opinion. "We're all in this together. Why are we separating ourselves from the other mods?"

Michelle says, "I guess no one knows who they can trust."

I can't accept that, so I say, "But nothing's changed. I mean, not between us. Not up here. They may have lost their marbles down there, but we don't have to follow them."

Connor's listening. He's sitting a couple of seats away, but the way he's leaning over his bowl, stirring his cereal rather too methodically, suggests he hasn't missed a single word.

James speaks a little louder.

"Well, I know who I trust. I trust 120 scientists, doctors, and engineers handpicked from around the world."

Connor is silent.

Harrison glares at James, but either James is oblivious or he doesn't care.

James grows in his conviction, saying, "So what are we going to do? Sit here behind a closed airlock until they figure things out on Earth? Just how is that going to work when everything we need to survive is on the other side of that hatch?"

I'm angry. "I don't know about everyone else, but I came here to search for evidence of ancient microbial life. I intend to get on with my job, but I can't do that without the equipment the Russians have. And I need the long-range op kit maintained by the Eurasians. I need the data analytics provided by the Chinese. I'm not going to sit around here today. I'm going to work."

There's a mumble of assent from around the room.

"It's not that simple," Connor finally says. "Our countries are in a state of war."

"*We're* not," I say. I can't see Jianyu or Su-shun acting like this. I'm sure they'll put humanity before nationality, but I can imagine Wen reacting like Connor. I've got to see Jianyu. I'm sure he trusts me, and I trust him — hell, I *love* him. I'm not sure I've ever stated my feelings that bluntly to him, but it's the truth. I feel as though the two of us have been torn apart without reason in the midst of all this confusion. Rather than a single night, it feels as though it's been a month since we last laid eyes on each other. None of this is our doing. We can choose to ignore the paranoia.

James says, "We've got to stop thinking like Earthlings and start acting like Martians."

"Oh, I see what's going on here," Connor replies, resting his plastic spoon in his bowl. "You think this is just a little difference of opinion between us. You think we can divorce ourselves from what's going on back there on Earth. You might be right. The problem is, it's not just us."

He points at the airlock, adding, "There's nothing to say *they* will see things the same way."

Harrison speaks softly, which is out of character for him. As second in command, he has access to the same level of operational detail as Connor, and, given his soft voice, I'm wondering what he knows. "We have to think about the long term."

"We *need* each other," Michelle says with a surprising amount of emotion in her voice. "That's the testimony of history — united we stand, divided we fall."

James asks, "How are we supposed to start something new on Mars if we hold on to the fears and prejudices that dominate Earth?"

Connor shakes his head, stirring the soggy cereal in his bowl.

He looks up, saying, "You and I are separated by means, not intent. We all want the same thing, but we need to be pragmatic. The dynamics have changed."

"How?" I ask, surprising myself with how aggressive that one word sounds. It seems to explode from my lips and is more of a response to Harrison's cryptic comment than anything Connor has said. Harrison is hiding something, I'm sure of it. Connor knows. I suspect Connor knows precisely what has Harrison troubled. I'm not sure how many of the others realize this, but there's something the two men are keeping from us, something that's keeping Harrison unusually subdued. I feel like asking him straight, *What happened to all the cussing, Harry? Why aren't you your normal fucking obnoxious self?* I'd like to, but I'm too polite — too nice. I can't swear like Harrison. When he swears, it sounds natural, almost as though cusswords are the norm; for me, it would be crude and forced.

Connor purses his lips. He's censoring what he knows.

James picks up on it. "Nothing's changed up here, has it?"

Harrison looks at Connor.

Connor plays with his cereal, moving the sticky clumps around.

"It's a question of resources," Connor says without looking up from his bowl. "We can manufacture most of the mechanical parts we need using the 3-D printers, but we're limited by the quality of raw materials." Finally, he looks at us. "Recycling the *Prospect* resupply vessels was a stroke of genius by NASA. Essentially, *Prospect* is both a supply ship and a source of high-grade raw materials in itself — purified aluminum, fine-grade silicon, plastics, glass, copper . . . you name it. Saves us mining and refining these materials on Mars."

Harrison, the senior engineer for the mission, explains, "The mods are built on the principle of n-minus-2, meaning we have what we need to cover at least two missed resupply drops. With a mean time between failure of n-minus-2, we have a good buffer. Anything breaks and we have at least two derelict *Prospect* modules we can cannibalize, but not anymore."

Being a research scientist, I am vaguely aware of all this from our training, but I tend to ignore logistics. I don't have the bandwidth to keep up with the day-to-day running of the base. It's enough to be analyzing search results and planning new experiments.

Harrison continues. "We get one, maybe two major shipments every couple of years, when orbital conditions are right — along with high-burn runs for critical components in between, but those flights can't carry a decent payload. With the loss of *Prospect 29* during the hurricane season, we were down to n-minus-1. No big deal, we've got one bird in the air, one on the pad, but still I was nervous before all this went down. Moving into retrograde is a bitch. It's all about timing. Even without the war, *Prospect 29* was effectively lost when those hurricanes blew over Florida. The best anyone at NASA can do now is to strip *29* down to bare metal and send essentials. All we have left is *Prospect 28*."

"The bird in the air?" Michelle asks, seeking clarification.

Harrison nods.

"And that lands tomorrow, right?" I say, not seeing the point.

"Today," Harrison replies. "Davies recorded his message before midnight."

"Retro rockets failed to fire," Connor says coldly. "*28* sailed right by us."

Harrison lowers his voice. "Davies knew. He had to know. He had access to the same telemetry we have. The engines never came online."

"What?" James yells as more scientists gather around.

"Why would he lie to us?" Michelle calls out. She's holding back tears.

"'With a bit of luck,'" Connor replies, quoting Davies from Mission Control. "He was in denial. He was hoping they'd come online. He was hoping the problem lay in the telemetry readings. He must have known we'd be reeling in shock with all that's happened on Earth. He was probably still in shock himself."

"You can't blame him," Harrison says. "There's nothing he could do but hope the engines would fire. There was nothing anyone could do except wait, watch, and hope."

James says, "Fuck!" For once, it's nice to hear someone other than Harrison swearing. That one word carries an astonishing amount of weight.

"You can't be mad at Davies," Connor says. "It's not his fault."

"Like hell I can't," James says. "He shouldn't have lied to us!"

"And what would you have done in his place?" Connor yells in response, slamming his palm on the table. "Just what the hell could he have said that would have made any goddamn difference?"

"Watch the video again," Harrison says with far more calm than Connor. "Watch his eyes. I think he was reading from a script."

"Maybe. Maybe not," Connor says.

"Either way," Harrison says, "the video has been edited; at times it jumps — just marginally, but there are skips. I think he told us all he could."

"Sonofabitch!" James growls, pounding a fist on the table. All the testosterone flying around the module makes me nervous. In my experience, this kind of anger doesn't lead to good decision making.

I speak with a soft voice, asking what seems like an obvious question to me. "So . . . what's the impact? What can't we manufacture ourselves?"

Michelle picks up on what I mean. "Stuff like medicine? Electronics?"

"Like the man said," Connor replies, again turning his eyes down to his cereal, "be frugal." A sinking feeling hits my stomach. The reality of what it means to be isolated from Earth finally hits home. It's one thing to be abandoned in principle, but the enormity of what we face is only now sinking in. I always knew there were risks involved in signing up for a decade on Mars — now they've been realized. It seems that surviving a decade is wishful thinking.

"What about the others?" I ask, thinking of Jianyu and Su-shun. My mind is scrambling for possibilities. I guess that's the scientist in me, always looking for another angle. I'm not as close to the Eurasians, but Michelle is, and James gets on well with the Russians, although that might be primarily because he has a cast-iron stomach and can handle their homemade vodka. I want to know what Connor's proposing in relation to the other three modules, but all he does is shake his head.

Michelle says, "We can't just sit here and pretend nothing's happened. They're our colleagues. We need to talk with them."

Connor looks angry, but I can't think why. Our concerns aren't unreasonable.

Harrison listens intently and sounds thoughtful as he says, "We're going to have to figure out how we manage our shared resources." I'm surprised to see Harrison being more considerate than Connor, yet there's something in his voice that suggests he's downplaying our concerns. He's on the verge of being condescending but seems genuine, which is strange. It's almost as though he's hiding something.

I can read Connor, though. He thinks the colonists are going to start fighting each other. Rather than looking for cooperation between the mods, he's preparing for the worst.

"We have to talk to them," Michelle says.

"So talk," Connor says. "Good luck with that."

I push my bowl across the table and get up. I'm angry at Connor. This isn't leadership. This isn't why he was put in charge of our module. In my opinion, he's being petty and small-minded.

"Where are you going?" Michelle asks as I get to my feet.

"To talk," I say briskly. "There has to be someone on this rock who's still thinking straight."

James and Michelle follow me to the airlock. A green light shows there's equal pressure on the other side of the main hatch. Given that we've had the dome in place for a couple of months, I wasn't expecting anything else, but the uncertainty of the moment forces me to double-check. I really don't know what I'm going to face beyond the cold metal door, but I tell myself Connor's fears are unfounded. We're civilized. We were handpicked out of billions on planet Earth. If we can't make this work, what hope is there for humanity?

"We're scientists," Michelle says as I pull on the lever, unlocking the outer hatch. "We're better than this."

"Yes, we are," I say as Harrison catches up with us.

The hatch opens, revealing the hub at the center of the four modules. A raised metal walkway leads us over fields of wheat ready for harvest. A mechanical spider-harvester some six feet in diameter is perched on impossibly thin, spindly legs. It moves through the field, trimming dead stems and examining the stalks for fungal spores. Another robotic harvester clambers down from a storage bin on the roof with its blades already spinning, ready to move across the field. Our crops have been genetically modified to increase yield and reduce the time between harvests to a little over two weeks. It's reassuring to see the machinery of the colony continuing on, oblivious to the carnage on Earth.

I've always found the hub serene. There's something peaceful about watching crops grow. Nature has always set my heart at rest, and on this red planet, a splash of green soothes the soul. Grow lights hang from the ceiling of the sealed cavern, casting a diffuse light over the crops.

There's a pink haze visible overhead. A dust storm obscures the view through the dome, but there's a soft, ambient glow signaling the Sun is somewhere overhead. Like most of the colonists, I've become accustomed to interpreting the shadows within the hub as though they were a sundial. It's not the most accurate way of telling time, but it gives me a good idea of morning or afternoon. Today, though, the shadows are indistinct.

Even on a clear day, Mars is as dreary as a dull, overcast day on Earth. There's just not enough light this far from the Sun to have a bright, sunny day.

Beyond the dome, dust fines hang in the air like a pollen haze, giving the sky a pinkish-orange hue. Dust fines are particulate matter, like glass ground up so incredibly fine that the slightest breeze will leave it hanging in the air like cigarette smoke. Even if we could breathe the tenuously thin, toxic atmosphere on Mars, the dust fines would kill us. On Earth, similar types of particulate matter arising from air pollution cause everything from emphysema to cancer.

It's blustery outside, and the clouds come and go, allowing glimpses of sunlight to eke through and leaving me thinking, "Ten in the morning."

The circular walkway is suspended from the ceiling. The metal grating sways gently beneath us, rocking slightly with our motion. The odd wheat stalk pokes through the grating. The hatches to the other mods are still closed.

"Where are you going?" Michelle asks.

"Medical," I reply. "That's where Jianyu will be."

Jianyu is the senior doctor on the mission. Back on Earth, he worked as a cardiovascular surgeon. Before that, he was a trauma surgeon. Prior to that, he had a stint operating on spinal injuries in rural southern China.

Also — even though it's not his specialty — he's birthed dozens of children at country clinics throughout China, although he's modest about it — he says he enjoys watching the midwives do all the hard work. Whenever this comes up in conversation with other colonists, I remind him that, professional pride aside, "to enjoy watching" is probably not how he should describe seeing a woman give birth, but he's never really grasped why. For him, birth is a wonder of nature, a delight to behold.

"We'll talk to the Russians and the Eurasians," James says, leading Michelle on past the ladder I need to take to the lower levels. "The Chinese are all yours."

I start climbing down the side ladder, keeping three points of contact on the rungs at all times, as there's a little dew on the metal. There's an elevator to one side, but I'd rather climb. Physical exertion is important and somewhat habitual for us. In low gravity, it's important to stay mobile and keep muscle texture and bone density in a healthy range, and that comes only from exercise. Given all we've heard about the war on Earth, it would be easy to ignore the disciplines of life on Mars, but they're all we have.

"He means well," Harrison calls out from above. I look up. Michelle and James have continued on to the other modules, but Harrison follows me down to medical. It seems he feels compelled to make his point. "Connor's been in touch with the other module leaders via vidphone. They've talked."

"Huh" is all I can manage, not entirely convinced, wondering why Harrison feels obliged to tell me this . . . and wondering why he's following me.

On each landing, the position of the ladder changes, making it impossible for anyone to slip and fall more than one floor. In one-third the gravity we feel on Earth, a fall of ten feet is like tripping over a crack in the concrete and falling face-first on the pavement. It's nasty. It's going to hurt, but with a little luck, nothing will break — and up here on Mars, if you fall, you'll have slightly more time to brace and prepare yourself for the impact. In practice, it takes roughly only a second to fall to the ground, but it feels like an eternity compared to how rapidly we plummet back on Earth. One g applies a lot more force than we Earthlings ever really appreciate.

"They know what happened."

I don't reply. I'm hoping Harrison loses interest in me, so I deliberately avoid leading the conversation further.

I'm sure Connor is taking dozens of issues into consideration, but I don't agree with his isolationist approach. I can't see how open communication is a problem. Talking can't make things worse. Michelle is right. We need to be united.

Harrison's a good man — a little rough around the edges, but he means well. He wants to do what's right. He's loyal to Connor. I don't have a problem with that, but the scientist in me refuses to pander to authority. For me, loyalty is an affliction of the mind — subordinating reason for no good reason at all. In science, there's no absolute authority, only theories, evidence, predictions, and discoveries. I remind myself that, regardless of how good or smart or super-duper intelligent someone is, no one is above the scientific process. Einstein overturned Newton. One day, someone may do the same to Einstein. Who knows? And were he alive, Einstein would love to see that next step unfold in our understanding of the universe. Scientists don't care about being right or wrong, they care about learning. Loyalty is for soldiers, not scientists.

"They're as dazed and hurt as we are," Harrison continues, trying to elicit a response from me. I'm sure they are, but this is not a conversation I want to have with him — I want to hear from Jianyu. Harrison's saying this only to appease me, to talk me out of probing deeper into what the other mods are thinking.

I climb down the next ladder, descending below the hydroponic potato farm with its mesh of thin roots hanging down like vines. Water drips into collection channels. Fans circulate the air, extracting excess moisture and constantly moderating the balance of gases. Oxygen, nitrogen, carbon dioxide — they need to be carefully regulated in the various sections of the base. Grow lights illuminate lush green leaves. A mechanical gardener tends to the plants, trimming withered leaves and checking for mold or fungus on a crop of spinach. Despite our best efforts at sterilization, we've brought microbes to Mars, and they've adapted to life in the central hub surprisingly well. There are even a couple of researchers in the Eurasian mod specializing in studying them, wanting to stay one step ahead of their aggressively evolving traits. The lanky robotic gardener pays no attention to me. Its spidery appendages allow it to work efficiently regardless of whether it's upright, upside down, or climbing a metal trellis.

"There are no easy answers," Harrison says as I round another ladder and climb below the hydroponic rice paddies. Genetically modified rice is critical to our survival. It grows rapidly and is fortified with essential vitamins and minerals. There are numerous mini-layers within the rice farm, as with the potatoes and the leafy greens, all set beneath long grow lights that mimic daylight on Earth.

A few bees buzz around me, but they're stingless hybrids — a cross between the European honeybee and the Australian bush bee. Chickens cluck below on the lowest level of the hub. Down here, the hub seems more like a futuristic farm than a colony on Mars, but there's method to NASA's madness. Everything is recycled — absolutely everything — and NASA acknowledges that natural systems are far more efficient than mechanical ones, so we have a carefully regulated ecosystem to ensure the health of each component. I heard one estimate that said we avoided lifting five thousand tons into orbit with the inclusion of a few eggs, seeds, and larvae. Hydroponics are simple to build in situ. All the pipes, vats, and pumps were made here on Mars.

Worms break up organic waste in vast, carefully sealed, regulated vats before the intricate network of pipes feeds nutrients back into the plants via hydroponics. Bees provide honey and pollinate our various plant species, including herbs, along with the jasmine and frangipani Michelle had the foresight to request from Earth. Someone figured the trade-off of a few seeds for our olfactory welfare and psychological enrichment was worth it, I guess. The tiny flowers can be found all through the dorms, masking body odors. People like

Harrison might not think that's important, but their sweet, soothing smell keeps me from going insane.

Chickens eat our leftover scraps, providing us with eggs for protein. Every ten months, the laying hens are going to be replaced with a new generation, and I'm counting the days until chicken is on the menu. Between times, we get meat grown in vats, but it's bland.

The lowest level of the hub houses the repair shop with rows of spare hosing, isolation pumps, and hermetically sealed seed trays protecting our reserves. Even with all the exposed water in the hydroponics system, the air is dry, as the whole system is carefully regulated to limit microbial growth. We keep the inner hatch on each of the living modules closed intentionally, not just as a precaution against depressurization, but because we need to ensure precise climate control within the central hub. The growing racks are maintained in perpetual springtime, with temperatures at a pleasantly cool 70°F. Seeing the outer hatches on the individual mods closed following the outbreak of war was alarming but not unheard of, as each module is entirely self-contained and capable of sustaining its occupants for up to two years. Without the central hub, however, the quality of life would be poor.

I walk across the concrete floor and past a Japanese workbench. A humanoid robotic frame lies on a table beneath a plastic sheet. To my mind, it resembles a skeleton. From time to time, Harrison will scoff at the Japanese and their interest in humanlike robots, saying form follows function. He'd rather all the robots were designed for a specific purpose instead of aesthetics, and he's often down here swapping ideas with the Japanese, trying to talk them into his way of thinking.

I rush down a short flight of stairs leading to medical. I'm a micropaleobiologist, so Harrison's probably wondering why I'm obsessed with medical, as I don't think he knows about Jianyu and me. Is that what's making him nervous? That I'm going down to medical instead of to one of the other mods?

"We've got to be smart," Harrison says, catching up to me. "We won't get to make decisions twice. We need to make the right choice the first time."

At first, I thought Harrison followed me to tie up loose ends after the argument over breakfast, but he sounds worried. Is there something he doesn't want me to see down here?

The basement is divided in half, with the data center on one side and medical on the other, extending into a natural cavern beside the lowest level of the central hub. Thousands of tiny supercomputers hum behind smoky double-glazed glass. Billions of calculations are undertaken every second as our computer servers crunch through the findings of our various expeditions and analyze samples. The computers are located on a raised false floor. The room has a mini-airlock, keeping humidity out. On Mars, cooling supercomputers is easy. The bedrock this far down is a constant −40°F, making the interior more like a meat locker than a data center.

I push through the swinging doors leading into the medical suite and walk past the empty triage station. The lights in reception are in low-power mode, but there's a bright light on in the operating theater at the end of the hall. I walk past one of the storage rooms.

Its door is ajar. The lock has been broken.

I push cautiously on the door leading into the operating theater. "Jianyu?"

Jianyu turns to face me. He's carrying a clear plastic crate full of surgical equipment and medicine.

"What's going on?" I ask.

Harrison stands by the door as I walk into the theater.

"Why don't you ask him?" Jianyu snaps. He rests the box on a shelf and reaches through to the back of the cabinet, grabbing supplies.

"Harry?" I say, using Harrison's nickname rather than his first name — Jonathan. It's subtle, but calculated. Harry is an affectionate name. I'm trying to offer him the benefit of the doubt even though my gut tells me he doesn't deserve it. I'm hoping Harry is more honest than Harrison.

"This is bullshit," Harrison says. "Don't make me out to be the bad guy in all of this."

"What's going on?" I ask, feeling as though I already know but need confirmation.

Jianyu turns to me. His eyes are red. It's hard to know if that's from crying, lack of sleep, or perhaps a bit of both. "They cleaned us out, Liz."

I'm furious. "What the hell have you done, Harrison?"

"It wasn't just us," Harrison insists. "We weren't the first ones down here."

"Oh, well, that makes everything better," I reply, my words dripping with sarcasm.

"I don't like this crap any more than you do," Harrison says. "But we had to secure critical resources."

"From *who?* From the senior medical officer on the mission?" I ask, gesturing at Jianyu. "From one of the few people who actually knows how they should be used? What the hell is wrong with you?"

"I don't need to justify myself to you," Harrison says, finally looking me in the eye. Yet he's the one who followed me down here, knowing exactly what I would find.

"Yes, you do," I snap. "This isn't a military base, it's a research facility. You're here to ensure our collective survival, not to take sides in a war unfolding hundreds of millions of miles away."

Harrison shakes his finger at me, half pointing, half waving. "Choose your side carefully, Liz."

"What the fuck does that mean?" I snarl, relishing the use of profanity against Harrison and his foul mouth. "If I have to choose a side, I choose humanity."

Jianyu walks up behind me.

Harrison shakes his head, swearing under his breath as he turns and storms away. The swinging doors fly open as he thunders out of the medical suite.

A hand rests gently on my shoulder. Without turning, I rest my fingers on Jianyu's hand. His other hand presses softly on my waist as he stands behind me.

"Thank you," he says, kissing me gently on the side of my neck.

"What's going on?" I ask. "We're turning on each other. Everything's wrong. People are losing their minds. I mean, with all the suspicion and distrust between us, it's like we just went back to the 1950s."

"Well, we are in retrograde motion," Jianyu replies with a grin. I know what he means. Retrograde motion is counterintuitive. Technically, nothing has changed in our orbit of the Sun, but Earth just overtook us on the inside track.

The solar system is like one of those old coin funnels they use to collect for charity at the mall. Stick a quarter in and watch it spiral round and round as it slowly sinks into the hole in the middle — only the Sun is that hole, and thankfully, as there's no friction in space, Mercury, Venus, Earth, and Mars, along with all the other planets, just keep swirling round and around the funnel. And just like the funnel at the mall, those lower down, closer to the hole, travel faster.

The Babylonians were the first to recognize retrograde motion. The outer planets, like Mars, Jupiter, and Saturn, would slowly make their way across the night sky, shifting slightly from one evening to the next. But there would come a point where they seemed to reverse and move backward. It's an illusion, of course. Earth's whizzing around the Sun in 365 days, whereas Mars is crawling at 686 days. When Earth overtakes Mars on the inside, the red planet appears to drift backward against the stars.

Retrograde motion had astronomers scratching their heads for thousands of years until along came Copernicus, who realized there was a simple explanation for this complex phenomenon — Earth isn't at the center of the solar system, the Sun is — and with that, the scientific revolution was thrust onto center stage.

Retrograde motion is a mirage, an example of how our sight can deceive and mislead us. Yep, Jianyu's right. We're going backward.

We stand there facing each other, holding hands and looking into each other's eyes, but this isn't some teenage expression of puppy love. We're two equals connecting and understanding each other at a deeper level than words can convey. His lips quiver. I squeeze his fingers gently, wanting to express tenderness, to show that I care.

"My family," he says with trembling lips, and he stops himself.

Jianyu blinks rapidly for a few seconds, and I get a glimpse of the internal turmoil he's feeling, but he pushes on, asking, "Have you heard from your family?"

He's already thinking of others and not himself. It's typical of Jianyu, really — this is why I fell in love with him.

I cannot bring myself to say any more than "No."

I suspect it would sound cold and calloused if I told him I don't want to hear from my family, so I don't elaborate further. I care about them, of course, but I can't cope. Deep down, I know that anything I hear from Earth at this point would be a glimmer of reality at best. I doubt anyone really knows anything with much certainty — *Uncle Viv's unaccounted for, your mother's badly injured, the blast leveled Aurora.* My mind's already running to so many different possibilities, and gravitating to the worst outcomes. Somewhat paradoxically, I can handle the uncertainty that comes with distance. For me, knowing some of what's happened to my family would be worse than not knowing anything at all, as my mind would fill in the blanks. It's distressing not knowing, but to have a tiny glimpse and be left with unanswered questions would be torture.

Some people can't wait for Christmas to open their presents. I have no problem with that. I can wait. I want the whole story. For me, to know just a little of what's going on would amplify the anguish I already feel. My anxiety is crippling as it is. I couldn't stand any more. For now, I'd rather not know. I'd rather wait until I can hear with certainty what's happened, who's been hurt, who's been killed, who's escaped. Am I being selfish? Maybe. I prefer to think of it as self-preservation.

Standing with Jianyu, reality feels as though it's woven with little more than a thin strand of cotton. The slightest increase in tension and it'll break.

Jianyu seems to understand. He already knows what's happened to his family, and I can see in his eyes that he knows too much. I suspect he'd rather not know and still have hope.

"What happened here?" I ask, changing the subject and hiding from the pain we both feel.

"Fear," he replies. Jianyu tends to see beyond the moment. The ransacked medical quarters reveal desperation. "But they're guessing at what's important. They don't really know. I've salvaged a lot."

"And your people?" I ask, cringing as those words leave my mouth. My choice of term implies we're not the same. I don't mean to be divisive, and I stumble over a few more meaningless words trying to correct myself. "I mean, your mod. How's everyone coping?"

Jianyu is kind. I think he knows I'm not projecting my own fears onto him, but rather the paranoia I've seen in my own module.

"My people," he begins, pausing as he considers his response. "Our people are hurt. They don't understand how this could happen. Do you know? What have you heard?"

"Not much," I say, not trusting myself to let my mouth run any further. I don't want to bring up the news report of the Chinese blockade around the Korean Peninsula, or the attack on Seoul. Those are geopolitical events I can't begin to pretend to understand.

"Why would the U.S. fire on China?"

"Wh — What?" I ask, stammering as I blurt out, "We fired first?"

Jianyu nods.

I'm stunned.

I don't believe it.

The U.S. wouldn't start a nuclear war — that doesn't make sense.

Jianyu believes we did, and I find myself recalling Harrison's warning about picking sides. As much as I want us all to band together as survivors, that's naive.

I doubt anyone in the U.S. module would ever seriously consider

America firing first. During the Cold War, the U.S. maintained a defense policy that outlined how preemptive strikes could be justified if war was inevitable, but that was decades ago. I cannot fathom how any American could push that big red button knowing millions would die on both sides of the planet. Such a banal act should not lead to wholesale murder. This has to be a mistake.

I find myself wondering about Jianyu's source. Has he been misled? Has someone told him what they want him to believe? Is someone on Earth sowing discord on Mars? If so, why? For political reasons? When I consider what little they have to gain, I find myself wondering if it's true. Or perhaps Jianyu's source is the victim of propaganda, and is merely perpetuating a myth. Or perhaps I just don't want to face the truth.

I don't know what to think. All I can do is squeeze his hands and look deep into his eyes. I need him to see that I trust him, that I'm not afraid. I would take this position regardless of what we share, because I feel compelled to do what's right.

"We can't fight each other," I say. "We're in this together. All of us. All four mods."

Jianyu nods.

A tear rolls slowly down his cheek.

I reach up and wipe it away.

Jianyu is a complex individual. I expect him to say something meaningful, but he simply turns away, getting back to work.

"Help me with this," he says, handing me a box full of medical equipment. He finishes emptying a shelf into another box, carefully stacking small vials and sterile bandages. We carry the boxes out into the reception area. I'm expecting him to head for the elevator and up to the Chinese mod, but he keeps walking past the server room and into the maintenance section below hydroponics.

"Where are we going?"

"Somewhere where we can keep this safe. No one mod should have a monopoly on our medical supplies. Not even mine."

"And Anna?" I ask, referring to Anna Kolyma, the surgeon from the Russian module.

Every role in the Mars Endeavour colony has a primary and a secondary position. For critical services, such as medical and engineering, the roles are split between various mods for several reasons. Should a module suffer catastrophic failure, from fire, depressurization, or some other emergency, it's important that the other mods don't lose the critical roles they need to survive. Also, it's important to have a separation of duties between the modules to avoid groupthink, where people fall in step with prevailing attitudes in a closed environment. In hindsight, I find myself marveling at how prescient that decision was.

Anna's quiet and unassuming. I can't imagine she was involved in raiding medical, and I'm incensed to think Harrison couldn't trust the team to do what's in our collective best interest rather than thinking as Old World nationalists.

"She must know," he says. "She needs to know."

"I'll tell her," I say.

Jianyu lifts a sheet of plastic draped over a workbench and slides the box beneath it on one of the shelves raised off the ground. There are four other boxes there. I slide my box in beside his. He replaces the plastic, then rolls a barrel over, keeping it upright as he works it into place in front of the bench, blocking the lower shelves from sight.

"Su-shun will keep our secret," he says, and I nod.

4

Chinese

THE CHINESE MOD IS LIKE a funeral home. Gone is the hustle and bustle of the previous night. Scientists, engineers, and technicians eye me with suspicion as Jianyu leads me through the inner airlock.

The lights have been turned down. The temperature is stifling. If I didn't know the Chinese better, I'd wonder if something had gone wrong with their environmental controls. At a guess, no one cares. The contrast coming in from the hub, with its dry air and cool temperatures, and stepping into the warm, humid Chinese mod has me feeling as though I've stepped off an airplane at the Shanghai airport in the middle of a scorching Chinese summer.

"She should not be here," Su-shun says, but the tone in his voice is one of concern.

"She is one of us," Jianyu says in his soft-spoken voice, carefully selecting his words. I think this is what drew me to Jianyu. He doesn't say much, but when he does speak, he speaks from the heart, and his words carry depth. Unlike other men I've dated, he's not trying to impress me, or put on a show.

Dating is frowned upon within the Mars Endeavour colony. There's no official policy from NASA, ESA, or any of the other space agencies, but there's an undertone of professionalism that says we're here to do a job. And we are, but we're nothing if not human, and we function best when there's social cohesion. Science is a discipline of logic and reason, yet it cannot be divorced from human emotions. Contrary to what some may think, science *thrives* on emotion. Why do we invest so much in cancer research if it's not because we care?

I think the bigwigs back on Earth understand we're human. They know love is a healthy emotion, and they know we're mature enough to figure things out for ourselves, but from the content of our pre-flight briefings, I think they'd prefer we kept any romance within each mod. They're worried that cultural differences could be exacerbated on Mars, but I think they're wrong. For me, Jianyu is a breath of fresh air.

Harrison and I had a fling back in training, but there was too much pressure on us to be the perfect couple. For a while it was serious, and I thought it would go somewhere, but Harrison treated sex like an Olympic sport. Each encounter was going for gold. At first it was fun, but the pressure to outperform got to me. The media liaison officer heard we were dating and thought our lives were a 1960s *Life* magazine astronaut story ready-made for the public. Such romanticism might have been ideal for reality TV, but I felt there was too much attention on us. As much as I liked Harrison at the time, I felt we were a showboat. Perhaps that expectation was more from Harrison than the program; I'm not sure. Harrison has always been larger than life. When he swears, his words evoke a certain passion. Only Harrison can pull off such colorful language. For anyone else on Mars, swearing is vulgar, but for him, it's a flourish — a daub of brilliant green or bright yellow paint on an otherwise dull gray canvas. I don't know how he gets away with it, but he does. At a guess, his magnetic personality makes it seem cool.

With Harrison, I felt like a handbag — little more than a pretty accessory hung over his arm — but with Jianyu, I can be myself, and to hear Jianyu say, "She is one of us," melts my heart. I understand implicitly what he means. Not "us" as in the Chinese, but "us" as in colonists. Those few words carry a sense of trust and confidence.

"Wen will not agree," Su-shun says in a conspiratorial tone, as though he's betraying a friend.

Jianyu holds my hand and leads me farther into the common room. He doesn't have to hold my hand. It's not as though I don't know the layout, but he's speaking as much with his actions as with his words, making sure there's no doubt in anyone's mind that nothing has changed between us with all that's happened back on Earth. I can't help but love him all the more for the courage of his conviction.

"Tea?" he asks, as though I'm here on a social visit and we should sit and talk.

"Sure," I say, all too aware of the murmurs around me. Perhaps I am on show after all, but I don't feel under any pressure from Jianyu. I sit at the table as he fixes a pot of Chinese green tea from leaves grown here on Mars.

From the corridor leading to the laboratories at the rear of the mod, I hear Wen calling out, "No. No. No." I hope Jianyu is more prepared for this than I am, as it's clear she's still upset.

Wen storms into the common room, speaking in Chinese. Her words come at a rate so fast I can barely comprehend anything she says with my fledgling understanding of her language. Her words seem to blend together, making it impossible for me to distinguish between sentences, let alone individual words. I catch just the simplest of Chinese words, like "she" and "them." The other Chinese astronauts fall silent — watching, listening.

"In English," Jianyu says, refusing to respond to Wen in his native tongue. "There will be no secrets."

"She cannot be here," Wen says. "You know. You heard the edict from Sin-Sah."

Although Sin-Sah sounds like a Chinese word, it's an acronym that's morphed into a word out of necessity — CNSA, the China National Space Administration.

"I heard," Jianyu says, agreeing with her but unmoved by her challenge.

I start to get up. This is too soon. I wanted to come here to reach out a hand of friendship, but the wounds are still raw, and I understand that. There's an ache in my chest that won't go away. It's nothing medicine can cure. I lost dozens — perhaps hundreds — of friends and acquaintances, and possibly my parents. I know how grief works. Blame and anger, they're irrational, but they're active, not passive. They allow someone to feel as though they're doing something instead of being tossed around like a rag doll.

Jianyu stands behind me, gently resting his hand on my shoulder.

"It's okay," I say softly. "Perhaps we all need a bit more time."

"You should stay," Su-shun says, sitting down next to me. His act is innocuous enough, but it signals to the others his acceptance of my presence in the module. He's showing his support for both Jianyu and me. Such an act would be meaningless in America, but for the Chinese, it speaks volumes, identifying us as united in a common cause.

Jianyu pours green tea in a small cup that's almost a bowl, as there's no handle. He puts it in front of me and pours another cup for Su-shun.

"We need to talk," I say, looking at Wen. She looks as though she's about to explode, but both Jianyu and Su-shun are calm and relaxed, putting me at ease.

Jianyu pours a cup of tea for Wen, placing her cup opposite me on the table and inviting her to sit. "Please" is all he needs to say. Reluctantly, Wen sits. Jianyu places the teapot on the table after pouring himself a cup. He sits between Wen and me, almost as though he's acting as a mediator.

I've seen these cups before, but I've never truly noticed them or looked at them in any detail. Like almost everything on Mars, they're the result of 3-D printing. In the U.S. mod, everything's functional and utilitarian, serving a purpose — knives, forks, plates, cups; I've never given them a second thought. This teapot, though, and the matching tiny cups are works of art. They have ornate patterns painted in blue and faux gold. Someone has spent hours working on these cups, painstakingly reproducing traditional patterns in minute detail. There are several Chinese letters painted in ornate calligraphy, along with idealized images of birds and lilies. I don't know that I've ever appreciated the importance of tradition in Chinese culture before now. Suddenly, I realize no one's sipping their tea. They're waiting for me.

I cup my hands around the small bowl and raise it to my lips, sipping softly at the tea before slowly lowering the cup and setting it back on the table with a sense of reverence, wanting to show respect for the Chinese and their traditions.

Wen sips her tea, but her eyes never leave mine.

"So talk," she says, lowering her cup.

Neither Jianyu nor Su-shun says anything. They, along with everyone else in the common room, look at me as though I'm from another planet. I'm from the other side of the same planet, but even with all Jianyu and I have shared, I feel alien. I'm an intruder.

"We need each other," I say. "With all that has happened on Earth, we need each other now more than ever if we are to survive here on Mars."

Wen doesn't look impressed.

I continue. "We have all—"

Wen cuts me off. With brutish defiance, she asks, "What? What have you lost? You personally?"

"I—"

"I have lost everyone," Wen says with tears welling up in her eyes. "My two daughters. My son. My grandchildren. All of them killed by an American weapon of war fired without provocation at innocent civilians."

I can't speak. A knot forms in my throat.

Try as I may, I cannot maintain eye contact with Wen. My eyes fall, looking at her aged, leathery hands.

"They were prepared to lose me, their *mater,* but not I them."

The silence in the room is painful.

Wen is content to let her words resonate. She sips her cup of tea almost casually, hiding the anger welling up within, but I can see she can barely contain herself. Her hands are trembling—only slightly, but it's enough to betray the turmoil she feels inside.

"What have you lost?" she asks again.

It's a strange question. I don't think she means it in terms of keeping score, but it's clearly important to her, and I think I understand why. She needs to know I appreciate the gravity of the moment.

"I don't know," I say, still unable to meet her eyes. I raise my hand, not sure what I'm trying to signal but wanting to convey the frustration I feel. "I—I can't bring myself to ask."

Jianyu rests his hand gently on my forearm, giving me strength. Tears flood my eyes, but I fight to hold them back. I don't want Wen's pity, I want her understanding. I want her allegiance.

"I had dozens of friends living in downtown Chicago. My parents—"

I have to breathe deeply before continuing. "My parents live in one of the outer suburbs, but I can't ask after them. You probably think I'm weak. I hope for the best, but I fear the worst. But to ask, to know for sure—that would break my heart."

Sniffing, I wipe tears from the corner of my eyes, saying, "Right now, I need to be here. There will be time for mourning later. For now, it's important that I'm here on Mars. I need to be here mentally as well as physically. I cannot allow my heart to wander back to Earth. I need to be here—now."

Su-shun nods softly.

"We cannot trust her," Wen says, looking at him.

I feel robbed.

I've laid my heart bare, but it's not enough for Wen. I don't know what else I can say to persuade her about my genuine concern for the colony, and I'm wondering if being here in the Chinese mod is a lost cause. Maybe Connor was right. It's one thing to set our own attitudes in order, but no one can do that for anyone else — and culture runs far deeper than most realize.

"We can trust her," Jianyu says in his soft voice.

"She is one of *them*," Wen protests. "Blood is thicker than water. If it comes to it, she will side with the Americans."

Jianyu says, "She will side with the Martians."

Martians? That's the second time such a concept has been floated, and he's right. James said the same thing. We're no longer bound by arbitrary lines on a map, or cultural ties to the land on which we were born. There are no countries on Mars. There is but a single colony.

Wen's gaze seems to pierce his soul, and, like me, he can't maintain eye contact. His eyes drop to the table.

"Do not be fooled," she says to him. "Such notions are dangerous. You would be naive to think the Eurasians or the Americans will side with us. It is not just our hatch that is closed."

"We can't do this," I say. "We can't survive on our own. Sooner or later, we have to work together or we'll all perish."

As much as I want to, I can't bring myself to say "or we'll all die," and I wonder what that says about me. Is the lack of that admission a weakness? Wen knows all this, yet she and Connor and the other mod leaders persist in isolating their crews.

"Why did you lie?" Wen asks. I'm intensely aware of dozens of eyes focusing on me as everyone listens in on our conversation, but I don't know what she means. I don't want to say that, though, as such an admission will sound as if I'm denying her allegation.

"Why did you fire first?" Wen asks, and the look on my face must tell her everything she needs to know. Jianyu said the same thing, but it's still shocking to hear. I can't believe America would start a world war with nuclear weapons. That makes no sense, and perhaps my reaction is what Wen was expecting all along — denial.

If I say, "I don't know what happened down there — let's focus on what we're doing up here," I will come across as dismissive. If I point out that "I didn't fire first, not me personally," any subsequent words will be meaningless. If I say, "It's too early to tell what happened," she'll interpret that as well-meaning and sincere but ultimately a deceptive position. I dare not suggest her information might not be accurate, even though that's a valid concern, or, again, I'll be seen as beguiling her with cunning words.

I wonder what lie she's referring to. What did Connor tell her? He must have said something that was contradicted by CNSA, and that raises another question — did he know otherwise? Or was he being fed misinformation as well?

Ultimately, I say the only thing I can. "I'm sorry."

Wen sips her tea. Outwardly, she looks calm, but I know she's thinking deeply about all that's happened and what I've said. I drink as well, but more to hide for a moment. Su-shun and Jianyu sip their tea without saying a word.

I breathe deeply, trying to compose myself. I can't remember how many times people asked me what life on Mars would be like. It must have occurred hundreds, if not thousands, of times prior to launch, and my reply was always to describe some variation of our training. I'd tell them, "We'll be conducting expeditions, analyzing samples, raising crops, repairing suits and mods." I must have described every possible scenario, but I never imagined sitting with the Chinese, drinking tea while struggling with the ramifications of a nuclear war on Earth.

For the Chinese, drinking tea is part of a bonding process that reaches beyond a physical act, and that all four of us have sipped at roughly the same time seems to be significant.

I find the hierarchy in the Chinese module fascinating. The U.S. mod has a chain of command, but it's imposed, being the result of crew selection and training. For the Chinese, though, Wen's leadership is based on years of respect. They trust her with their lives. That Jianyu and Su-shun are siding with me must be far more controversial than I realize, and I appreciate their trust. I don't want to see war on Mars. The colony is frail. We could tear ourselves apart all too easily, and from what I've seen in medical, it's already begun. I hope

James and Michelle are faring better with the Eurasians and the Russians, although if we really did fire first, I doubt they're gaining any ground.

Wen asks, "Connor? Did he send you?"

"No," I reply, looking her in the eye.

"Harrison?"

"No."

"But they know you're here?"

"They know, but they don't approve."

Gaining formal approval is important for the Chinese, so I'm sure to let them know my visit is not sanctioned or in any way a ruse on Connor's part.

"Hmmm," Wen says, rubbing her hand on her chin. Damn, she'd be good at poker, or whatever that landlord game was we were playing last night, as I have no idea what she's thinking.

Jianyu says, "We need to trust those outside our mod."

As usual, his words are precise. He's not just talking about the U.S. contingent. He's referring to the Russians and the Eurasians as well — and he's right. Wen must know that, but the complexity of all that's transpired is not lost on her. She's not one to oversimplify a response. In the six years we've trained together, Wen has always been reserved. "Conservative" is too strong a term, but she's always been measured in her responses. She's hurt, but she's not acting out of hurt. She's finding some deeper motivation, balancing her priorities. She's conflicted. I can see that.

"The problem is time and context," she says. I have no idea what she's talking about, but I suspect there's more to her position than what has been said so far. Wen addresses Jianyu, saying, "You trust her here and now, but no one can make assurances about the future. Trust must reach beyond sincerity. She may be genuine in her desire to help, but a slip of the tongue could betray us. We cannot afford to make mistakes."

They know something.

I can't help but straighten in my chair as the realization sinks in.

They know something we don't in the U.S. module, and it's something big.

"Double-blind," Su-shun says, confirming my suspicion. Although I don't know what he's talking about, I understand what he means. If I don't know their secret, I can't screw things up. It's a classic scientific principle — divorce the experimenter from any bias in collecting results. But why is this necessary for me?

"Yes," Wen says. "It is not trust that is the problem. Just for her to know would place us in danger. It is better if she doesn't understand."

I feel as though my head is about to explode. All this time, I thought they were talking about the war on Earth.

But something has happened on Mars.

"He does not know," Jianyu says.

"He"? For a second, I'm not sure I heard Jianyu correctly. Did Jianyu mean "she"? No. Jianyu *must* be referring to Harrison, as he confronted him down in medical.

"How can you be sure?" Wen asks. "At the very least, Connor knows. If Connor knows, Harrison must know."

Wen must have seen Harrison following me down to medical on one of the numerous closed-circuit-TV cameras.

"I am sure," Jianyu replies, not actually answering Wen's question, but that doesn't seem to bother her. I doubt that my facial expression has gone unnoticed. They must think I'm dumb. I am.

"She can help," Su-shun says. "She is on the inside."

"It's a big risk," Wen says.

"It is," Jianyu replies, and just for once, I wish he were verbose, as I'm desperately trying to read between the lines.

Wen sips her tea. I copy her, noting my tea has cooled. I have no idea what I've got myself into. Su-shun is suggesting they tell me their secret even though that would set me against the U.S. contingent. I feel distinctly uncomfortable with that notion. I'm no traitor, and my allegiance isn't with a nation. I came to Mars for the science.

No goddamn nuclear war is going to steal that from me. I feel compelled to speak.

"You can't tell me what you know. I understand that. I accept that. You can't ask me to take sides without telling me why, but telling me why forces me one way or the other. I get it. I do."

I'm clutching at straws. "I don't know what's going on, and I don't care. What I care about is us. We've got to stop thinking like Earthlings and start thinking like Martians.

"I don't know what the hell happened back on Earth, but I'll be damned if I'm going to sit by and watch the same madness unfold here on Mars.

"I mean, think about why we're here. We're here because we dared to make a difference, because we're venturing out from Earth, because we're looking to establish *Homo sapiens* on another world."

Wen looks at me as though I'm a child. I can't help myself. I have to respond to her glare.

"And you're right. I am naive. But I don't care. We thought the colony was important before all this happened. I think it's more important now."

Typical American. I've said more than everyone else combined. Ha. Oh well, nothing like reinforcing stereotypes, but I had to say something.

Wen looks deep into my eyes as she says, "They lied about *Prospect.*"

"*What?*"

She holds her hand out and someone steps up beside her, handing her a computer tablet. Wen flicks through a few screens before turning the tablet around and handing it to me.

The tablet shows an image of the Martian surface stretching out into the distance. The zoom has been increased so much that the picture has lost the normal, crisp high definition I'm used to seeing. Grainy mountains line the horizon, bathed by a pinkish sky. There are three slightly dark blotches off to one side. They're small, but they're out of place in the cloudless sky. Almost directly below them is an indistinguishable silver blob.

"Prospect?" I say.

"Three miles outside the landing ellipse," Su-shun says. "But she made it down intact."

"Why would they lie?" I ask.

Jianyu asks, "Why would they raid medical?"

Wen speaks with solemn authority. "They are afraid."

5

Russians

JAMES KNOCKS ON THE INSIDE of the hatch leading into the Chinese mod even though it's wide open. He's already closed the outer hatch behind him and is standing alongside Su-shun in the cylindrical airlock extending between the hatches, tacitly requesting permission to approach. Yesterday, such a notion would have been preposterous.

I excuse myself and walk over to him.

The internal airlocks within the colony are anachronistic now that the central hub is pressurized. It's strangely bizarre, and a little disquieting, to walk past space suits hanging on the wall, complete with helmets, gloves, and boots readily available in the unlikely event that the hub loses its integrity. The metal grating on the raised floor is designed to whisk away dust during the decontamination process. Whenever we conducted egress or ingress during the construction of the hub, the airlock cycled to prevent cross-contamination. A jet of high-pressure air would envelop the airlock, swirling around us like a cyclone. In some ways, it was like being stuck inside a vacuum cleaner. But now that the hub is complete, the airlocks are peculiar — out of place. God forbid they're ever needed again. Now, the main points of exit and entry onto the surface of Mars are through airlocks built into the central hub itself.

James whispers, "The Russians are refusing entry." Given what Wen has told me, I think I know why.

I'm about to say something to James when Jianyu walks up behind me, saying, "I will go with you to the other mods — to talk to the Russians, the Eurasians, and the Americans." Jianyu's just come from a hurried conversation with Wen. The dynamics of life on Mars are changing, shifting like a sand dune in the wind. He looks at me, saying, "We all need answers."

Jianyu's speech patterns are characteristic of someone who learned English later in life. To me, it makes his words sound measured, dignified.

That he wants to visit the U.S. mod is a surprise, but I note we're last on the list. I guess he wants to show Connor and Harrison that the Chinese haven't gone into hiding. Sparks are going to fly when he asks for the missing medical supplies, and, knowing him, he will. Jianyu may be soft-spoken and gentle, but he's no coward.

We exit the Chinese airlock. Su-shun closes the outer hatch behind us as we walk around the raised gantry toward the Russian module. There's an eerie silence within the hub. I can't shake the feeling we're being watched.

On any given day, there are dozens of people in here, mostly in transit, but some of them work on the fields. Today, the only motion is mechanical. Even McDonald is absent. As the primary agricultural specialist in the colony, he's always caring for his crops. His absence speaks of his own personal loss. It seems everyone's grieving for someone. A robotic gardener moves slowly across the wheat, spraying a fine mist of fortified water onto the crops ready for harvest.

The outer hatch on the Russian mod opens as we approach. Vlad stands inside the airlock. Vlad's the commander of the Russian module and is from the rugged Ural Mountains — the Russian equivalent of the Rockies. He always looks angry. I've never known him to smile or laugh — even back in training. Today, he looks like an undertaker.

There's little in the way of greeting. To my surprise, Jianyu darts inside before us. It's unlike him to be so physically assertive, and I get the feeling there's more going on between the Chinese and the Russians than either James or I realize.

"Come," Vlad says coldly. He runs his hands over his full beard. Vlad's in his late fifties, and has probably been growing his beard since his early twenties, as its straggly ends reach down to just above where I imagine his belly button must be. Given how impractical a beard is in space, I'm surprised he didn't shave it off before we launched. I guess it speaks of his stubborn character. Vlad wouldn't look out of place in Mississippi, although I can't imagine him enjoying the heat, or the humidity. He's bald, with just a few thin strands of hair at the back of his head set in stark contrast to the thick gray hair of his beard.

"We didn't want this," Vlad says, pacing back and forth through the common room inside the Russian mod. Unlike the U.S. and Chinese mods, the Russian common area is deserted. Anna sits on a bench watching us, but she and Vlad are the only colonists in sight. A red light blinks softly on top of a camera mounted above the kitchen, and I wonder who's watching. Vlad is agitated. He repeats his point. "We did not want it to come to this."

Somehow, I get the feeling Vlad isn't talking about the war on Earth. He's addressing Jianyu.

"You trust them?" Vlad asks as we walk into the deserted mod. Vlad's voice carries both anger and exasperation.

Jianyu takes my hand. Ordinarily, I'd appreciate a public statement like this, but in this context I'm sure Vlad sees our relationship as compromising Jianyu's judgment. I don't mean to offend Jianyu, but I let go of his hand, gesturing with both of my hands as I reply to Vlad. Jianyu may be content to let his actions speak, but I need to say something aloud. "We have to trust each other. We can't let what happened on Earth destroy the life we're building up here. Nations don't exist on Mars."

Vlad doesn't look impressed. He mumbles his dissent, but I don't catch his words. I doubt they're in English.

Jianyu and I sit at the central table as James walks over to Anna. She's not pleased to see him, which is surprising, given how close they are, and I wonder if she's putting on a front for Vlad. Anna is the secondary surgeon on Mars. Anna and Jianyu aren't allowed to travel together in the same rover on surface missions, even in an emergency, for fear of losing both surgeons at the same time. On paper, Anna's more qualified than Jianyu. She has a broader range of experience, having worked in everything from military field hospitals to private European clinics, specializing in thoracic trauma.

There was considerable horse trading when the final roster for Mars was developed, and I can't help wondering if Anna was overlooked for political reasons. I know the U.S. mod was pushing for its own senior surgeon, but as leadership roles within the colony were carefully balanced between modules, the U.S. would have had to surrender Harrison's position to accommodate another senior role, while the Russians were scrambling to retain Dimitri as chief communications officer. Rumor has it, the selection of Jianyu from the Chinese mod was a compromise between the Russians and the Americans, but Anna has never let that affect her attitude or professionalism.

James says, "We have to work together."

"Yet we are split into different modules," Anna replies. "Segregated by country and culture."

"The Eurasians are united," I say.

Vlad glares at me, not saying what he's thinking.

"Does someone want to tell me what all this is about?" James asks, standing beside Anna. Like me, he must pick up on the underlying current. The Russians are upset about something other than the war. Whatever their concern, it must be related to the war on Earth, but it clearly concerns life on Mars, and I wonder if this is the fallout from Connor's lying about the *Prospect* mission.

Anna is from the Russian steppes, but she could just as well be from Milan or Paris. Even without makeup, she's stunning — a natural blond with long, flowing locks that gleam in the downlights. Most of us Martian women are quite plain. As much as we try to divorce ourselves from sexist stereotypes, the men on Mars like to work out, and the women try to keep up their appearances. As for me, I look ordinary, for lack of a better word. My cheeks lack any natural ruddy coloration, and my chin is quite pronounced. I'd kill for an hourglass figure like Anna's. My thin lips suffer for a lack of lipstick. I can't help but feel a little intimidated whenever I'm around her. She's beautiful — ridiculously intelligent as well. It's not hard to see why James is attracted to her.

Anna turns to James, resting her hand affectionately on his forearm as she says, "You must realize. Trust does not come easily to us."

"But we have to work together," James says.

No one answers.

James tightens his lips. He's been around the Russians long enough to understand their cultural idiosyncrasies. He must know this is nothing personal, particularly as Anna is openly displaying her affection for him as she continues. She speaks softly. "You say 'we.' But do not underestimate the impact of history on your psyche. When you say 'we,' you refer to Americans, not the rest of the world." I'm left wondering if Anna's been spending too much time with Max, the mission psychiatrist from the Eurasian mod.

"You Americans have only ever known victory. Even losses such as Vietnam and Iraq, or Afghanistan, have been whitewashed as mistaken ventures with unclear outcomes, not defeats. We Russians, we know the meaning of both victory and defeat. But you — you have not had armies raze your villages. You have not seen them besiege your cities for years on end. You do not know what it means to be truly free, as you have never really known oppression."

For a freedom-loving American like James, these are hard words to hear. If there's a cornerstone of American life, it's the freedoms we enjoy, yet I understand what she means. Our forefathers fought for freedom in the Revolutionary War, but the Russians have never stopped fighting for their freedom. For thousands of years, their country has been a battleground. Communism fell, and then they were enslaved by a succession of dictators. Even the simplest of freedoms we take for granted is hard-won by them. Hundreds, if not thousands, of news reporters have been killed trying to expose corruption in Russia. In the U.S. that could never happen — I hope.

"I . . ." James is lost for words. Like me back in the Chinese mod, he's been taken by surprise. I feel for him, yet I understand this is something he has to work through.

To his credit, James doesn't let his mouth run. He must see the look in my eyes, the resignation I have in the moment. We Americans are so used to leading the charge. We want to be out in front, directing traffic. It's hard to take a backseat and let someone else drive, but knowing what I do about the *Prospect* resupply mission, I'm aware that now is the time to listen. I want to blurt out an explanation, but there are no shortcuts.

Anna leads James over, and they sit beside us. James is unusually subdued. I understand what he's going through. I felt the same way with Wen. With all we've been through over the past day, reacting to the news of war on Earth, we still have a U.S.-centric view of the world. We can't see this any other way, but we must. We need to see this from the perspective of humanity as a whole.

"Do you know why Russians make such good scientists?" Vlad asks, pouring vodka into shot glasses and setting them on the table in front of us. No one is going to hazard a guess, so he continues, laughing as he says, "We trust no one, especially not our own government."

"Liz?" James asks, turning to me, but I'm quiet. This isn't my news to break — it's theirs. Both the Chinese and the Russians are struggling with the need to trust us as Americans. I may not agree with that, but I understand why. As an American, it's difficult for me to accept, but given the deception around the *Prospect* spacecraft, I can see their reasoning is valid.

"Land of the free," I say to James, but with no real sense of resolve, just resignation. "Home of the brave. Perhaps sometimes we trust each other too much."

It's nigh on impossible for us to see our foreign policy through the lens of another culture. I don't know that the Chinese or the Russians are afraid of Americans so much as weary of the clash between our ideology and our actions. I'd like to think America is the greatest nation on Earth, but most people think that of their country regardless of where they live.

Vlad reads my mind as he says, "Hah. Yes. Home of the brave. Yes. But no one smells their own shit."

Good old Vlad. He never was one to dance around an issue.

He screws the cap on the vodka bottle, setting it down in the middle of the table as he says, "We all shit, but our shit never stinks quite as bad as the guy in the stall next to us. Ha ha."

"Vlad," I say, feeling James is at a disadvantage, and being more than a little uncomfortable with his defecation metaphor. "James is right. We're all in this together. We have to trust each other. I understand you have reservations, but please . . . you know us. We would never do anything to betray the colony."

"And yet Connor lies."

James looks at me with wide eyes. I stare at the table and nod. I can't look either Vlad or James in the eye.

Vlad addresses Jianyu, scolding him as he says, "You should not have told her — not without asking us. We shared that information with you. We trusted you."

James grinds his teeth. I can see him clenching his jaw. He's dying to know what's going on, but he's letting this play out between the Russians and the Chinese.

"They are not all the same," Jianyu says. "It would be a mistake to think so."

Vlad picks up a shot glass, raising it in front of us as though he's about to propose a toast.

"Ah, don't you think it's a bit early?" I ask, still feeling a little dusty after the rice wine last night.

"Nonsense," Vlad replies. "Drink. Drink."

James and I exchange glances. He doesn't hesitate. Like Vlad, he knocks back his shot in a single, swift motion. What the hell. If Vlad needs to bond over vodka, then so be it. When in Moscow, and all that crap. I grab the glass and tip my head back, opening my throat and waiting for the inevitable sting of high-proof alcohol to lash at the soft tissue inside my mouth. To my surprise, it's water.

"Ha ha ha!" Vlad says, slapping his shot glass down on the table and waving his finger at us. "See? You trust too much, you Americans. Trust will be your undoing."

For someone who never laughs, Vlad's making up for lost time.

"Very funny," James says, gently returning his empty glass to the table.

Anna grips his arm, sliding her hand under his bicep.

"They can help us secure a rover," Jianyu says.

Vlad nods.

"It's *Prospect*," I say to James, realizing the others have forgotten he's still in the dark. "*Prospect* landed."

"But Connor . . . ?"

I nod.

"He *lied?*" James asks as the realization sinks in.

"Yes, yes," Vlad replies as though he's affirming the obvious. He pours himself another tiny shot glass full of water and gestures to the rest of us to see if we'd like any more. I wave him away. One shot was enough.

"Why would he lie?" James asks.

Vlad slaps James on the back, saying, "Because everyone lies, my friend. Russian. American. Chinese. We are all liars. Is that not written in the Bible?"

I can't help but look sideways at Vlad. I would never have taken him for a religious man, but I know he was raised in the Russian Orthodox Church.

Vlad says, "To deny such logic is to reinforce that it's true."

It's a circular argument, but okay, whatever — and the Russians think *we're* crazy?

He continues. "We lie because it's easy, because we have something to hide, because lies are more convenient than truth."

Jianyu grins.

For me, this is a surprising realization. As an American, I'd never admit to sanctioned lies, as the concept seems too conspiratorial — like something from *The X-Files*. On one level, I know it happens, but as an official policy, I'd never believe it. The Russians and the Chinese, though, have no problem believing their leaders would lie to them if it served a purpose.

Anna looks relieved. It must have hurt her to keep this secret from James, and had Jianyu not told me, I doubt she would have said anything to him. Her loyalty to Vlad is absolute.

James asks the question I'm thinking: "So if *Prospect* landed, *where is it?* Why isn't anyone going out to retrieve it?"

Anna says, "An automated rover was dispatched last night."

"Last night?" I say, surprised.

"Before the attack," Vlad says, and I feel the fine hairs on the back of my neck prick up.

"Wait a minute. That makes no sense. Why would Connor do that?"

Normally, resupply drops are retrieved by a crew of four, as the automated rovers can only grab the cargo modules, not the entire craft. The implication is that Connor planned this ruse before the war began and then lied about it afterward, when we were reeling in shock. I cannot for a moment imagine he knew about the horror that was to unfold on Earth, but to have dispatched an automated rover and then to have lied about *Prospect* is cold.

"Maybe he was expecting it to land safely and was simply preparing ahead of time," James says. "Maybe there were perishables on the manifest and he had to get there before the landing batteries ran dry."

"But he told you *Prospect* sailed by Mars," Vlad says. "And he told us the same thing."

Anna says, "He never recalled the rover."

"Trust," Vlad says. "Trust only what you can prove. Not what people tell you." I have to admit, he's right. Like James, I want to find some alternative that explains this away without assuming Connor lied, but there are no other possibilities. I feel dirty, filthy, soiled, as though I'm guilty by mere association with him.

"So what do we do?" James asks.

Vlad says, "An automated rover can retrieve the cargo pods, but not the craft itself. At some point, Connor is going to have to send a team out to reclaim the craft. For now, he's only after supplies, not raw materials. He's amassing a stockpile for the U.S. mod."

"Medical was raided," I say. "We confronted Harrison. He admitted to taking supplies."

If Vlad's surprised by this revelation, it doesn't show.

"What was on the manifest for this run?" Jianyu asks.

If anyone knows, it's James. He's an engineer. Although he has a master's degree in physics, his mission specialty is life-support systems. He works in mechanical, in one of the pods opposite the computer servers.

"Ah," James says, casting his mind back. "This particular *Prospect* mission was mainly backfilling redundant parts, resupplying electronic equipment. There wasn't much in the way of medical, from memory, but there were some perishables. There were grow lights, backup storage units, extra fusion cells, along with servo components for the harvesters. I can't imagine what use any of this stuff is to Connor. Oh, there was also an experimental 3-D printer."

Vlad says, "We already have two printers."

"We do, but this one's different. Our regular printers are construction-grade. They're good for coating walls and building chairs, but this one is smaller, barely the size of a trash can. It's capable of printing down to twenty-two nanometers. That's small enough that we can make our own CPUs and computer memory. It's not quite as good as the eleven-nanometer wafers we get from Intel, but still far better than anything we had at the turn of the century. And it's not like medical fabrication, where you need exotic organic material to start with. Mars is essentially a big desert. There are plenty of silicates, iron oxide, magnesium, aluminum, you name it. Feed this thing rocks and it'll pump out solar panels, semiconductors."

"Doesn't make sense," Anna says. "What would Connor want with a 3-D printer?"

Vlad says, "Control resources, and you control the colony."

"You think that's what he wants? To take over the colony?" I ask, surprised by the notion. Connor and I may not agree on much, but he's no tin-pot dictator.

"Not overtly," Anna replies. "But he doesn't want anyone dictating terms to him. America is . . . Well, we're all equal, but some are more equal than others."

"Orwell," I say, noting this is a quote from *Animal Farm* and recognizing the irony in hearing a Russian quote from a book that exposed the flaws of Communism. Under any other circumstance, I'd call bullshit on the abysmal human rights record of Russia, but as Vlad said, we all shit, and it never smells like roses.

Anna smiles. I don't.

Vlad says, "Connor wants to deal from a position of strength. We Russians — we respect that. We may not agree, but we understand."

I feel dirty. I'd like to think America is better than this. My America is driven by principle rather than power. But Vlad's pragmatic. America is an ideal, yet I have to admit the ideal is rarely realized. Our foreign policy is a litany of sincere but self-centered acts that have had, at best, dubious results. Reluctantly, I nod. I don't want to agree with Vlad's jaded perspective, but history is on the side of his interpretation.

"So what do we do?" James asks.

"We're all in this together," I say, throwing a little more of that American idealism into the melting pot, yet I find myself wondering if Connor and Harrison have a point. Do the Russians, the Chinese, and the Eurasians see things the same way we do? Can we count on them to make rational choices in the best interests of the colony as a whole? To be fair, Connor has failed that test himself. By acting alone, he's caused the very schism he was trying to avoid.

Jianyu says, "Our enemy is human nature, not any one person or culture. When threatened, everyone is defensive."

If Jianyu were running for president, he'd get my vote.

"We cannot tell the Europeans what we know," Anna says.

"Ah, our special relationship," James says, and she nods. Anything that gets to the British will get back to the Americans.

Am I a traitor? Am I betraying my own country? Maybe I am, but I'm determined to do what's right, and standing idly by while Connor lies to the colony is wrong.

"What are you going to do?" James asks. It's a good question, harking back to something Jianyu alluded to earlier. The Russians and the Chinese have clearly not only been talking about the *Prospect* landing — they've been planning a response. I can't imagine they're going to sit by passively as Connor claims the payload, particularly if it has a high-fidelity 3-D printer. It hurts me to think we're already resorting to fighting among ourselves on Day One, squabbling like children over a toy we could easily share. Earth is littered with corpses — millions have died — their bodies have barely cooled, and already we're returning to our baser instincts.

"We need that printer," Vlad says. "It belongs to the colony as a whole, and not any one module."

Anna says, "Connor won't bring it in through the main airlock — that would raise too many questions."

"One of the research stations?" I ask, referring to the outposts that have been built to allow for refuge while exploring.

Vlad nods.

There are fourteen stations dotted around the colony out to a range of a hundred miles, built to allow the colonists refuge while exploring the planet's surface. Like the hub at the heart of our base, they're essentially spray-coated caves and lava tubes, with the weight of the regolith above supporting their internal air pressure. A few surface stations have been built, but regulations don't allow surface activity for more than forty-eight hours at a time, due to the way radiation damage accumulates — think suntan, but skip the tan bit and go straight for the cellular damage. As sexy as bronze skin may seem to ghostly white folk, fusing base pairs within your DNA is a lousy way to die. On frigid Mars, it's not a burn so much as a slow roast. As it is, just by being on Mars, we're already playing with fire when it comes to the risk of cancer, raising our odds of developing a whole host of cellular diseases well beyond what anyone on Earth would consider acceptable. Shelter is important. Most of the remote stations are barely more than a room with an airlock. They're sparse — desk, cot, toilet, comms unit, and, if you're lucky, potable water.

The lava tubes in which the colony was built extend for hundreds of miles in either direction, leading to a labyrinth of caves and caverns, some carved out by ancient watercourses, others the result of volcanic gases and lava flows. I've been to most of them collecting samples, but even I haven't been to some of the more remote stations.

"How would you know which one?" James asks.

"Mars Recon," Vlad replies, pointing at the roof and gesturing to the satellite tasked with watching us from above. Mars Recon passes overhead every hour or so, constantly winding its way around the planet and taking high-resolution photographs of everything from weather patterns to target sites for future exploration. Recon can resolve images down to half a foot, which is impressive. I had my photo taken one day on a rare journey outside the tunnels. My dark shadow was more obvious than my white suit, but the computer software picked me out in an instant — or rather, not me personally, but the algorithm detected something foreign on the surface and marked it for investigation. A comparison with surface logs confirmed it was me.

One of the Russians must have been watching the Recon feed and picked up on the descent of *Prospect* on its three massive parachutes. I wouldn't have looked. I would have taken Connor's word for the loss of the spacecraft. If *Prospect* had sailed past Mars, why bother looking at satellite imagery for the landing? As Vlad said, we Americans trust too much.

Has Connor anticipated this? He must realize there's a chance someone will look at the Recon footage. Everyone knows the landing ellipse is on the plains of the tableland to our west. The resupply ships always come down there. I want to confront him. I feel that's the only way to get some clarity, but the mood among the Russians and the Chinese is to let this play out. They seem content to know. Perhaps they're thinking more strategically, not wanting to play their cards until they have to.

"So we follow the automated rover," James says. "Find out where it took the cargo."

Vlad says, "There's a dust storm moving in from the south, obscuring Recon."

I say, "I was scheduled to retrieve core samples from the permafrost in the northern section of the Hadfield branch. It's a subterranean excavation site, but I need a surface rover to get to the entrance of the lava tube — a collapsed section about four miles from here."

Vlad exchanges looks with Jianyu. Neither man says anything.

"How far is it from there to the landing zone?" I ask. "It can't be more than a few miles due west."

Vlad brings up a surface map on his tablet, turning it around so I can see the landmarks clearly. I recognize most of them. Even though archaeobiologists like me spend most of our times spelunking, following ancient subsurface erosion and dried-up riverbeds, few of these areas are directly accessible from the colony. Most sites require some overland travel, and I can take advantage of that to check out the landing zone.

Vlad says, "If Connor looks, he'll see your homing beacon well outside the planned route."

"I'll tell him I'm looking for new access points, following leads from the satellite imagery."

"In the *Prospect* landing ellipse?" James asks.

I shrug my shoulders in response. We don't have too many other options. "Once I'm out there, what can he do?"

"And what will you do out there?" Jianyu asks, with typical foresight. I hadn't thought of doing anything beyond verifying the landing and seeing if the automated rover had retrieved the cargo.

Vlad says, "She can follow the tracks south to wherever Connor is hiding the modules."

"Has anyone checked the extension?" Anna asks, referring to Phase II of the colony, expanding through the network of lava tubes leading away from the central X housing the hub. It's a good point. Most of the construction is undertaken by robotic serfs. Unlike the anthropomorphic robots of science fiction — made in the image of muscle-bound men — our serfs are purpose-built and resemble equipment from the old robotic assembly lines found in car factories. They're anything but humanoid.

James says, "If I were going to hide supplies, that's where I'd put them. No one goes down there."

"I'm not so sure," Vlad says. "It's a dead end. The tunnel walls are sealed, but there's no secondary airlock. You can get in there easily enough from horticulture, but the whole tube has to be evacuated if you want to use the far hatch. I just can't see it as a viable option. There's really only one way in or out. Connor isn't going to be able to hide the 3-D printer down there. He certainly won't bring it in through the hub. And depressurizing the entire tunnel isn't an option without carting a bunch of suits down there, which would raise too many questions."

Jianyu says, "He could have hidden the medical supplies in there."

Vlad nods, agreeing with him. "But nothing from *Prospect*. It's too difficult, too risky."

"So he must be using one of the outlying research posts," James says.

"Well," I say. "There's only one way we're going to find out."

6

Eurasians

AS WE EXIT THE RUSSIAN MOD, I spot Harrison waiting on the circular walkway suspended above the crops. He's halfway between the Eurasian module and the hatch leading into the U.S. mod, looking at something on a computer tablet. He's trying to look disinterested, but he's not. It's a pretense, a sham — a lie.

Jianyu hangs back beside me as James leads the way.

"Are you sure you want to do this?" Jianyu asks quietly, seeing Harrison and sensing the tension between us.

"Yes."

I refuse to be intimidated by Harrison. He's living in his own little world, with everything fitting into his carefully prescribed, predefined delusions. Strange how it took this crisis for me to see him clearly. I don't doubt his sincerity. I don't doubt for a moment that he means well, only "well" is poorly defined and heavily influenced by his sense of patriotism. His interests are myopic — shortsighted.

James ignores him, pressing the intercom button on the hatch leading into the Eurasian module. A familiar face comes up on the screen.

"Hey, Adin," James says. "Can we come in?"

"Of course. Of course," is the reply, and the hatch opens almost immediately. Adin is standing inside the airlock. He had to be there before we called. Perhaps he saw us approaching on the closed-circuit cameras and made the effort to come and greet us. A warm welcome is a pleasant surprise.

James steps over the rim of the hatch, followed by Jianyu. Adin steps the other way, coming out into the hub. Quietly, he says, "Can we talk?" From his body language, it's clear this is a question for me alone. Rather than going on with James, Jianyu waits inside the hatch. He looks worried, although to be fair, Jianyu always looks a little worried, and I suspect he's concerned about seeing Harrison on the warpath.

"Sure," I say to Adin, although I'd rather not stand on the walkway with Harrison loitering thirty feet away. I suspect Harrison's ire is directed at me following our confrontation in medical. He's clearly keeping tabs on us restless few Americans wandering between modules. Harrison is leaning against one of the railings, peering over the edge at the crops stacked below us, making as though he's inspecting the fittings or the hydroponics.

Adin and I couldn't be more different, but we're great friends. Adin's gay, and from Israel. He's from a devout Jewish Orthodox family with deeply conservative views — to me that's some serious cognitive dissonance, but he makes it work and is happy.

We were buddied together on a two-month-long expedition to the Atacama Desert in Chile. Daytime temperatures hit a pleasant 80°F, but the nights dropped well below freezing. It was Exploration Training 301 — but it was torture. When you're stuck in a high-altitude desert, nothing is easy. Even simple chores, like boiling water for coffee, would sap my strength. The air was so thin, the Sun so intense — and, somewhat surprisingly, the cold so piercing — it took constant focus to accomplish even menial tasks. We were gathering samples and conducting field analysis. Fixing guide ropes on the tents, or digging a latrine pit, was exhausting, yet the real work was in hiking to remote outcrops, selecting samples for analysis, avoiding contamination during collection, setting up solar cells for the computers and satellite relay, and then dragging everything back down the mountain again. I don't think I would have made it without Adin.

In Israel, military service is compulsory, which means everyone's exposed to physical hardship at some point in their lives, and Adin soaks up pressure like a sponge. I'd be dead on my feet, dragging my boots over the rough scoria on the steep side of an active volcano, and he'd hang back with me, telling me I could do this, just keep going, put one foot in front of the other. Somehow, his voice carried me through. Well, that and the fact that he carried most of my equipment. I may not understand the quirks of Orthodox Jewish culture, but to me, "Adin" is Hebrew for "Atlas."

Adin sees Harrison and turns away from him, speaking to me in soft tones.

"You've spoken to them? The Russians and the Chinese?"

"Yes," I reply, unsure why he's raising this with me.

"And the Russians. They didn't care, right?"

"Care?"

"The Chinese are torn up about the attack on Earth, but the Russians?"

He's right. I remember Connor mentioning both Moscow and Saint Petersburg being hit, but neither Vlad nor Anna brought that up. They were focused on what happened to *Prospect.*

"Don't you think that's unusual?" he asks in his distinct Israeli accent. "Don't you wonder why?"

Well, now that he's pointed it out, I do.

"I don't think there was an attack."

"What?" I say, raising my voice. Adin gestures for quiet, glancing back over his shoulder toward Harrison. I match Adin's conspiratorial tone, whispering as I ask, "Are you serious?"

"Think about it," Adin replies. "What proof is there? We'd believe anything up here — anything they tell us."

My mind immediately jumps to the question, Who does he think "they" are? Who would concoct such a fabrication? And *why?* Adin has a slight smile. His eyes are glassy. He's in denial. As much as I'd like to believe him, belief is not at issue here — accepting reality is. Like all conspiracy theories, his central conceit revolves around one unusual fact at the expense of an abundance of contradictory evidence. Yes, I have no proof, but what proof is there for anything in life? I've never been to Paris, but I'm sure there's a stunning tower rising above the rooftops. I've never been to Stonehenge, or seen the pyramids of Egypt either — sure, the stones that were used to build them are stupidly heavy, but these artifacts were built by people, not aliens. When it comes to war on Earth, all I have is the testimony of news reports and the NASA flight director. It would be easy to believe it's fake simply because that's an outcome I could accept, but that wouldn't be right. Reality is a bitter pill.

"Adin," I say, resting my hand on his shoulder. "It's okay."

Tears well up in his eyes. He knows. He hopes otherwise, as we all do, but deep inside he knows it's true. My heart breaks as his lower lip trembles.

"All we have is each other," I say, pulling him close and holding him tight. Adin buries his head into my shoulder and cries, which for a man his size must be humbling.

There's silence for almost a minute as we comfort each other, both reeling from the unimaginable loss suffered on Earth.

"Yeah," Adin says, pulling back. He wipes his eyes, saying, "Thanks, Liz."

As one of only a few gay men among the predominantly hetero colony, Adin's always been on the outside of the social structures of the group — not because of any conscious decision or bias on anyone's part — it's just been hard for him to fit into our overtly heterosexual microcosm.

Most colonists make an effort to be inclusive, but the very act of being inclusive implies that Adin isn't included in the first place, which is tough on him. I've seen this before — back at base camp in the Atacama Desert. I think that's why Adin was so determined to help me during that training run. It was his way of breaking down barriers. Acceptance shouldn't take effort. If it does, there's no real acceptance to begin with. To me, Adin's family.

Back on Atacama, I was the one in a tailspin. I was suffering badly from altitude sickness high in the Chilean desert, at sixteen thousand feet. As with most of our training, the instructors saw my struggle as an opportunity to assess how I'd handle adversity on Mars. Actual suffering in the present was immaterial. As far as they were concerned, it was better to flush out problems on Earth than on Mars, and that had me in a panic about being dropped. I was convinced I was on the RTR list — Return to Research, which meant staying on Earth. The fact that altitude sickness is serious but somewhat whimsical and arbitrary in who it affects didn't seem to matter. Adin wasn't affected, and neither was the tiny stick figure of a woman Amira, or Harrison. Connor, though, couldn't get out of his cot. He should have been evac'd down to the airfield, but, like me, he insisted he was fine. Physically, I looked okay but felt like I was perpetually hungover. The crunch of gravel underfoot was like a jackhammer starting up at six in the morning after I'd gone to bed at four.

Adin and I were paired up and sent out to conduct surveys, collect volcanic samples, and look for evidence of microbial life. To say Adin did most of the work in our team would be an understatement. I shuffled along like a zombie — or perhaps a vampire, as I was wearing a hood low over my forehead and dark shades to protect my eyes from the glare. My recollection is that I was a real bitch to him. Adin, though, didn't seem to notice. I'm sure he did, but he didn't care. He had the maturity to see beyond my gruff exterior and recognize that fatigue makes whining, grumpy assholes of us all. My dad would have kicked my butt down the side of that mountain, but Adin was patient to a fault. If it hadn't been for his work ethic, and how he covered for me, I don't think I would have made it to Mars.

"We'd best be —"

"Hey," I say, cutting him off. "We're here for each other, right? You and me, just like in the desert?"

He smiles. "Just like in the desert."

I turn and make eye contact with Harrison. Mistake, bad mistake. He looks pissed. He mouths something at me. I'm not sure what he said, but I can't let it slide. Call me pigheaded, but I cannot ignore the challenge. Already, my blood is boiling.

"I'll be right in," I say, excusing myself. "I just need to catch up with Harrison."

"No problem," Adin says, pulling on the heavy outer hatch.

Jianyu is seated inside the airlock. He must have seen Harrison out here and hung back, clearly still concerned after the argument in medical. James has already disappeared into the module to talk to the Eurasians. Jianyu looks at me knowingly. That Adin is entering the mod and I'm not is akin to me shouting my intentions at the ever-perceptive Jianyu. I turn my head slightly, glancing in the direction of the U.S. module. No words need to be exchanged. Jianyu looks back at me as if to say, "Is that wise?" I'm not sure what the expression on my face conveys, but I hope it's something along the lines of "Hell, no."

Jianyu raises an eyebrow. I lift my hand, pressing gently at the air in front of me, gesturing that he should go on without me. His eyes pierce my soul, but I push the hatch shut, making it clear I want to go on alone. I don't mean to shut Jianyu out, but this is something I need to do on my own. I can't hide behind anyone when it comes to Harrison — there's history between us that needs to be aired. Unresolved tension has been building between us for months, and it's been made worse by all that's transpired on Earth.

Harrison stares at his tablet. He's such a faker. I know him well enough to know when he's seething inside and struggling to contain himself.

"What's the problem, Harry?" I ask, walking over to him and wondering where he's been since we tangled in medical. No doubt, he's seen us talking to the Chinese and the Russians. In his mind, such contact would be treasonous, and I'm not expecting much in the way of rational thinking. Fireworks are in order.

"You can't do this, Liz."

"Do what? Talk with our fellow colonists?"

"You know what I mean. This is not — you need to fall in line with Connor."

"With Connor?" I ask, hoping that by mirroring his words back to him, he can hear how preposterous they sound. For all his zeal, I doubt even Connor would condone this kind of bullish attitude. "I don't —"

"Where does your loyalty lie?" Harrison asks, cutting me off. "Are you with us?"

Harrison doesn't say as much, but his choice of phrase is telling. *You're either with us or against us.* I just can't think in such shallow, trite terms.

"'With you'?" I reply, in utter disbelief that such tribal notions have made it to Mars. "Not if being 'with you' means being against anyone else."

"You're one of us, Liz."

"Only if by 'us' you mean humanity," I say, refusing to be bullied. I can't believe I dated this jerk.

"Things are complicated," he says, and I can see he's trying to rationalize his reasoning. He has to justify his position, but I'll have no part of it, and I'll be damned if I'm going to let him dictate my stance. He must sense that, as he says, "We're Americans, Liz," as though that's an explanation.

"So all this is about patriotism?" I ask, staring him in the eye. "And here I was under the illusion we cared about right and wrong regardless of which shitty patch of dirt we were born on."

"Come on, Liz," he says. "You know what I mean."

"Oh, I know precisely what you mean. It must be quite convenient to find that patriotism aligns perfectly with your paranoid agenda. I'm sure it's inspiring to live in your fictional little Paul Revere universe — with bluecoats pitted against red."

Harrison isn't baited by my comments. I expect him to react, to fight back verbally, but he isn't some dumb redneck, even if his drawl makes him sound that way at times. He's intensely intelligent. But that's the surprising thing about smart people: they tend to be so smart, they're easily fooled. "Fooled" isn't the right word — lulled into complacency, perhaps. A preconceived agenda might as well be a blindfold — pin the tail on the donkey, only we're the ass. I guess familiarity breeds an acceptance of even the wackiest ideas over time, and so otherwise intelligent people like Harrison tend to see problems everywhere but at home. For him, American pride is on the line, and it's all too easy for him to see me as un-American when what's really important is doing what's right.

Harrison doesn't miss a trick. If one approach fails, he'll try another. Harrison has a photogenic smile. He relaxes, gesturing with his arms as though he wants to welcome me home with a warm, friendly hug — me — the prodigal daughter forgiven.

"Liz."

I edge away from him, making it clear from my body language that I'm not playing.

I'd like to think the crew was picked on the basis of their qualifications alone, but I'm not naive enough to believe that. No one in mission planning would ever admit to filling quotas, yet the split of men to women and various forms of American ethnicity, such as being of Native American descent, or Italian, or Irish, or Hispanic, all played a part in crew selection. Token gestures toward the major religions are visible, but there was a bias toward the Christian God. (Allah and Buddha had to hitch a ride with some of the other nations.) I can't help but wonder if some of our brightest never made the cut so that someone like Harrison could represent a key electoral demographic — all-American Anglo-Saxon quarterbacks are always popular in front of the cameras.

Harrison was one of the early celebronauts, as we affectionately called them. He's an extrovert. When he wants to, he can draw a room full of people into his own personal orbit and make them feel like they're flying among the stars. With his charm, he made it onto the late-night talk shows and White House dinner lists.

Things were pretty serious between us: weekend ski trips, aligning schedules so we were posted overseas together. We even managed a few days in Hawaii while returning from a research seminar in Australia. I found myself drawn to him, but it didn't work out. At the time, I was hard-pressed to understand why, and I blamed myself for the erratic arguments over crazy little things, but now I know. Harrison's slick exterior hides deep-seated opinions that override the principles I value.

He grins, putting on a show. He chooses his words with cold, calculated precision hidden behind a warm smile. Pearly white teeth and puppy-dog eyes paint a friendly persona.

"Why the hostility?"

He's gaslighting our differences, trivializing my position, making it seem as though we're arguing over something minor, like what color to paint the lounge. I have to remind myself what's actually happening here — the colony is being broken up into fiefdoms. Medical supplies have been stolen. *Prospect* is being pilfered for the benefit of one team. Lies are being peddled as truth.

"You need to stop with the charade," I say.

"Come with me."

"No."

"You *have* to come with me. There are things you don't understand."

"No way in hell," I say, feeling my fists clench by my side.

"If you —"

"Don't even think about threatening me," I say, cutting him off.

"Damn it, Liz," Harrison yells, slamming his open palm against the railing. "Work *with* me, not against me!" I'm not sure if Harrison intends this to be a veiled threat of violence, but to me it is. To him, it's frustration playing out, but I think the meaning is clear — *I'm big and strong, and if I can't get my way with words, I'll use force.* The entire walkway shakes under his blow, but Harrison doesn't care. He looks at me with eyes that seem to pierce my soul, but I will not be intimidated. I hold his gaze, refusing to back down. Finally, he storms off.

I'm trembling. I don't think it was apparent at the time, but I'm quivering like a leaf in the wind. I stood up to him. I can't believe I faced off against Harrison and came out ahead. Whatever animosity there was between us before, it's now a fiery pit. The battle lines have been drawn.

For all my bravado, I'm left feeling as though I've betrayed my country, so perhaps it was Harrison who won after all. I breathe deeply, steeling myself and trying to put on a brave face as I turn back to the Eurasian module, but I have to hold on to the railing as I walk. My legs are weak, drained of strength. I hate to think what will happen the next time Harrison and I meet.

I wait by the hatch, shaking my hands as though I'm flicking water from them, trying to shift my mind away from the adrenaline surging through my body. I need to appear calm before the Eurasians. Fat chance.

Adin must have been watching on the monitor. "Don't worry about him. We're in retrograde," he says, as though that offers some kind of explanation. "It's like winter. Long nights are replaced by long delays in talking to Earth — makes everyone a little edgy." I don't think that's Harrison's problem, but I appreciate Adin's concern. Max stands behind him, looking shell-shocked, which, for the leader of the Eurasian module, is not a good look. He's taken the war on Earth hard. Max is the mission psychiatrist. I thought he'd be switching into overdrive after all that's happened, but he's human like the rest of us. He's hurt.

"Please, come in," Adin says. I doubt he overheard the confrontation with Harrison, but he must realize the tension's rising between us. They seem relieved to have me enter their module.

Prabhat gestures to the table, offering me some tea. I don't want any, but I accept to be polite. Prabhat is from New Delhi. Her eyelids are swollen from too many tears, but her cultural upbringing demands courtesy. Etiquette wins over grief, and she shows genuine care for James, Jianyu, and me, drawing attention away from herself.

"We heard from Connor, but we weren't expecting to see anyone — not yet."

I nod, acknowledging her point. Prabhat has a soft Indian accent. Her gentle cadence reflects an air of regal pride. Prabhat's extraordinarily intelligent, holding two doctorates — one in physics and the other in applied chemistry. She's subtle, but she's letting me know she understands we're here of our own accord. There's no judgment in her words. She's not siding with anyone, but I suspect she realizes there are schisms in the American camp.

"We're all in shock," I say, still refocusing my mind after the confrontation with Harrison.

"It is good to see you," she replies. "We need each other now, more than ever."

Jianyu nods slowly, and she responds in kind, giving me a glimpse of these two ancient cultures communicating on a level that eclipses anything I've seen in Western civilization. America is some four hundred years old, whereas the Chinese and the Indians predate the Babylonians, perhaps even the Egyptians. They seem to relate to each other at a deeper level.

Max clutches his hands on top of the table. The British are normally reserved, keeping a stiff upper lip and all that crap, but Max looks like he's about to have a nervous breakdown. I rest my hand gently on his.

"It's okay," I say, surprised to see how hard the war has hit the Eurasians. The Russians, Chinese, and Americans can consolidate and double down in their modules, but for the Eurasians, there's nowhere to retreat to, as they're all lumped together.

I recognize a couple of the scientists from Italy and Spain, and become aware of the strange dynamic that exists within the Eurasian module. For them, this is tragic but not personal, and it's easy to see Max's struggling with that distinction. He's from Soho, in central London, which must be little more than a radioactive wasteland by now, and he's feeling very much alone in the crowd.

"What have you heard?" he asks as a couple of the Japanese astronauts join us at the table. Japan lobbied hard for its own module, but it simply didn't have the resources. In the end, the physical selection of the intersection between two lava tubes forced a simple decision — there would only be four modules. With the U.S., China, and Russia dominating the Mars program, everyone else got lumped together. The Japanese are silent, but their reaction is more than a cultural idiosyncrasy — like the rest of us, they're still in shock.

"Not much," I reply, playing catch-up mentally. My mind is still outside on the walkway, screaming at Harrison. I have to be here — now. "We received a broadcast from the outskirts of D.C., but that's all. It repeats over and over."

"We've seen that too."

I spot Michelle talking to one of the Australians in the lab at the rear of the module.

James asks, "Any word from ESA or the other space agencies?"

Max shakes his head. I'm tempted to tell him what we heard from NASA, but I don't think there's anything significant, and I don't want to bring up *Prospect*. That the European Space Agency hasn't made contact with its team is alarming, heightening the isolation they must feel. I hate Connor for closing ranks. We should be embracing our companions, not hiding away behind metal doors.

"I'm going to work," I say, breaking ranks with the gloomy mood.

Prabhat looks stunned.

I say, "That's why we're here, right? To expand the reach of humanity on another world? I — I don't mean to belittle what's happened back there, and I've yet to hear from my parents outside Chicago, but I can't sit around here on Mars waiting for a message that may never come."

Max nods.

"I'm going to collect the core drill results from H7."

Prabhat shakes her head, but in her culture this is a gesture of support, not disagreement. Looking down at the table, she says, "Me too. I've got a backlog of samples to run through the scanning electron microscope. Can't afford any downtime."

I squeeze her shoulder, knowing how difficult this is for her.

"I'll prep your rover," Adin says with his trademark enthusiasm.

"Thanks."

Max breathes deeply, steeling himself before saying, "Action is good. It's good to engage in meaningful work."

"Let's get this party started," I say, taking a final sip of tea and getting to my feet. Adin has already disappeared out the back of the mod, heading for the maintenance hatch.

I slip into the bathroom. Peeing in an adult diaper while wedged into a space suit is unpleasant to say the least. I'd rather clear out the plumbing now, and hopefully make it through the entire journey without any nature calls.

Jianyu waits for me, which is a little out of character for him. Outwardly, he's always so relaxed, but I think he's rattled by the pace at which events are unfolding — nuclear war on Earth, schisms on Mars, and now me running off into the Martian desert. Technically, we're supposed to travel in pairs during surface ops, but I'm not game to include anyone else in this little conspiracy, and taking either James or Jianyu would raise too many questions: what interest do they have in core samples?

"I'll be fine," I say, stepping out of the bathroom, even though Jianyu hasn't said anything. I feel a little awkward and want to break the silence between us as we head to the rear of the module, but Jianyu doesn't respond. He's lost in thought.

We climb up the ladder leading to the maintenance area. Regardless of the gloomy emotions suppressing Prabhat and Max, and the confrontation I had with Harrison, I am delighted to feel a spring in my stride. Perhaps I've talked myself out of the lethargy I felt this morning. In the light Martian gravity, I make short work of the thirty-odd ladder rungs in the claustrophobic tunnel leading to mechanical. There are other routes, but this is the most direct.

Jianyu is hard on my heels.

"Are you sure you're okay with this?" I ask, watching as he steps off the ladder and into the prep room.

"Yes."

Liar. But I don't say anything to him. Some lies are for the best, spoken only because we care.

Like most of the free-form rooms in the colony, the prep room is a reclaimed cavern, part of a lava chamber near the surface, and although it's only ten feet in diameter, the ceiling reaches up over forty feet. Mini half-floors wrap around the walls, providing spare workbenches for the mechanics and allowing light to seep in from a smoky skylight in the ceiling. A glass viewport on the wall gives us a view of the rovers outside. As usual, they're parked under an over-hang, but not to protect them from the elements, as the thin Martian atmosphere doesn't pose much of a risk to our equipment. The roof of the cave provides the mechanics with protection from the harsh cosmic radiation scorching the surface of the planet. Mechanics like Adin venture outside most days, while scientists like me generally make only two or three surface trips a month. It may not be physi-cally hot on Mars, but the lack of a global magnetic field means solar winds and cosmic rays lash the surface.

"Be careful," Jianyu finally says.

"Always."

I think it's sweet that he's suddenly concerned about my going on a surface mission. It's like he's seeing me off on my inaugural run, but I've lost count of the number of times I've been topside. I kiss him briskly on the lips before pulling back and adding, "Don't worry. It's just another day on the fourth planet from Sol."

We sit opposite each other in the inner airlock, and I pull off my shoes, stowing them in a locker before whipping off my shirt and stripping down to my underwear. As far as I'm concerned, wearing a bra and underpants is like wearing a bikini, or gym gear, but Jianyu averts his eyes. He's seen more, but I guess this is different. I think he's blushing. I ruffle his hair playfully, and he smiles, amused that I'm teasing him.

I pull out a female adult diaper, and he looks briefly at the ceiling as I slip my underwear off and slip the diaper on. He's a doctor—a surgeon—but I guess my brash approach takes him off guard.

My inner pressure suit resembles an Arctic wetsuit, but with a metal ring collar. The fabric is a smart material. The fine weave and thick padding comprise a variety of synthetic polymers and SMAs, or shape memory alloys — tiny strands that will contract and tighten with a single pulse of electricity, sealing me in the suit and simulating the pressure of an atmosphere around me.

I slip my legs into the suit.

"Four hours," I say. "Two out, two back. Piece of cake."

I wriggle my feet in the built-in soft, spongy boots, wanting to get the soles in exactly the right spot. Tiny filaments woven into the insulation will provide me with heating once I connect to the bulky life-support pack. One-piece pressure suits like these are used as undergarments during surface operations on Mars to protect us from the cold and to simulate pressure around the body. Down in the tunnels, they're all I wear. Once there's some bedrock protecting me from cosmic radiation, all I need is to stay warm and supported, so the pressure suits are ideal for spelunking, and much easier to move around in than a full surface suit.

I finish squeezing into the suit. The trouser legs aren't quite in position. Skintight is an understatement, especially when it comes to my broad hips, and I dance back and forth, working the thick, spongy material around my thighs so the seams align properly. I don't have to be quite so rigorous, but on a long haul, I find the suit more comfortable if I am.

Jianyu laughs.

"Is my dance amusing you?" I ask, mocking him in a formal tone. "Or do you think I'm fat?"

"No, no, no." Jianyu's eyes widen, horrified by the notion. I'm not sure whether he thinks I'm being serious or not, so I accentuate my motion, something that's easy to do in Martian gravity, and rock from one leg to the other, dancing around as I work at the material. Finally, I slip my arms into the suit and then work my head through the snug opening in the collar. Other than my hands, the only exposed skin is a small oval framing my forehead, cheeks, and chin. I tuck a few loose strands of hair behind the stretchy neoprene. At a guess, right about now I look like a space nun in a gymnast's leotard, or perhaps Catwoman from *Batman*.

"That looks awkward," Jianyu says as I close two sets of parallel zippers to seal myself in the suit. Although it's difficult and everything's tight, it's an ingenious design, with a thin flap of rubber sandwiched between the zippers to form an airtight seal wedged in place.

I run my hands over the thick foam clinging to my body, saying, "Maybe you think I'm sexy?"

Jianyu bursts out laughing. I think we both need this — to release the emotional pressure of the last twelve hours.

Jianyu helps me with my gloves, which wouldn't be out of place on a deep-sea dive. They overlap the padding on my arms by about four inches, slowly tapering until they're flush with my sleeves.

The actual surface suit is loose-fitting, hanging off my frame. The boots and gloves are hilariously oversized and always leave me feeling a little like She-Hulk, only in white rather than green.

The helmet is a large dome with a clear glass faceplate and a glare visor. It attaches to the ring collar on the inner pressure suit rather than the surface suit. Jianyu helps me fit it in place, twisting the locking rings together. A final ring collar fits around the neck of my pressure suit, sealing the surface suit. Oxygen begins to flow from the backpack into the helmet.

Our suits operate at a lower pressure than the base, so I need to acclimatize. It's a bit like going from sunbathing by the ocean to climbing in the Rockies after less than an hour. As much as I want to simply switch gears and get on with the op, there's a physiological change that can't be ignored. Rush, and I'll be left with a migraine, aching joints, and cramping muscles. From here on out, I slow my movements.

"Please be careful out there," Jianyu says. I smile. He sounds like my dad, always worrying, but the suit is extremely well-designed. Even something static like the helmet is a marvel of engineering. This is no motorcycle helmet; it has been tested to withstand every potential scenario on Mars. NASA is paranoid about falls. They've done everything possible to avoid damage to the helmet by weaving a honeycomb structure into the various layers of plastic, and I understand why. Everything about life on Mars changes once I'm wearing a surface suit and backpack — my sense of balance, my freedom of motion, the mass I'm dragging around, my center of gravity, even my physical dimensions such as width and height. It takes four or five ops to get used to the physical limitations of wearing a full suit.

"You look great," Jianyu says, stepping back and surveying my outfit.

"I look like an ad for Michelin Tires," I say from behind the glass. "Or the Stay Puft Marshmallow Man." I'm assuming he knows what I mean, but I don't know for sure if either of those cultural references made it over to China. He smiles, but I get the feeling he's being polite. I tap on my wrist computer, and a single pulse of electricity activates the smart material within the inner garment, causing it to contract and provide a mechanical counterpressure simulating the weight of the atmosphere we take for granted around us back on Earth. It's as though King Kong has just grabbed me. An invisible giant squeezes my entire body at once. It's not painful, just firm and formfitting. I've been shrink-wrapped.

"You be —"

"Careful," I say from behind my visor. I reach out and squeeze his arm with thick-gloved hands. "Will do."

7

Prospect

STEPPING INTO THE MAIN AIRLOCK, I close the thick metal door behind me. Jianyu peers through the glass window set into the hatch, and I don't know why, but I have an ominous feeling. It's as though this is the last time I'll see him alive. I shake that irrational thought from my mind. The soft hiss of oxygen and my own breathing are my only companions. Breathing pure oxygen prior to the pressure drop helps extract nitrogen from the blood and prevent the bends. Adin will be watching the gas-exchange rates remotely. He won't allow me to leave the airlock until I'm in the green zone.

I lower my external sun visor to protect the internal glass dome, and stand in the spread-eagle position so typical of full-body security scanners at the airport, with my arms raised slightly above my head. A rush of air scrubs my suit. A series of spotlights come on, slowly rotating around me. High-intensity ultraviolet light does its best to kill any microbes clinging to the outside of my suit. Much to the horror of scientists back on Earth, we've managed to revive a whole host of microbes from various suits *after* conducting surface ops.

There's no indication these bugs can survive and thrive beyond the base, but that they journey with us on our treks across the planet is a concern, as we could contaminate Mars. There was even consideration given to scrubbing the colony because we couldn't contain errant microbes, but the general consensus is that even if they can survive dormant on the surface for any length of time, they're starved of an ecosystem. At best, they'll lie in a suspended state until they're so soaked with radiation they're no longer viable as organisms. Su-shun's testing that theory under controlled conditions in his lab, and so far it seems to hold.

After the sterilization procedure is complete, I sit on the bench seat and go through the prep list on my wristpad computer, checking suit integrity, battery strength, air reserves, suit communication, GPS navigation, and environmental controls. There are eight satellites providing GPS for the colony, but only to a resolution of a hundred yards, so it's still easy to become disoriented out on the surface.

There's nothing to do in the airlock but wait. It takes up to forty minutes to acclimatize, depending on a variety of factors, including things as simple as how long ago I last had a cup of coffee. As I sit there patiently, my eyes rest on a spare surface suit hanging on the rack opposite me, waiting to be cleaned. A light coating of red dust hides dangerous perchlorates clinging to the material. It needs a chem bath.

The colony logo on the shoulder patch was a point of controversy prior to our launch. Around the outside of the logo are the four modules — USA, Eurasia, Russia, and China, but no mention of the other contributing nations, like India, Italy, Canada, Japan, and Australia.

Then there's the name — Endeavour. It was supposed to be a neutral name with broad meaning — a bold undertaking to colonize Mars. Given that the project was originally a U.S. initiative, "Endeavour" was a gesture at openness, and was supposed to be a more internationally inclusive name. If Congress had had its way, the colony would have been called Columbus, or The Lewis and Clark.

The HMS *Endeavour* was the British research vessel that explored the South Pacific in the 1700s — Lt. James Cook discovered Australia and New Zealand, and conducted scientific measurements of the transit of Venus across the surface of the Sun from the island of Ta-hiti. *Endeavour* was also the name of one of the U.S. space shuttles, so it seemed like a good idea, but once the name was promoted in the media, the backlash began. The HMS *Endeavour* wasn't quite as popular as NASA assumed. In New Zealand, European settlers started the Maori wars, while Australia was invaded by Europeans without any recognition of the Aborigines, who had lived there for easily forty thousand years.

I felt bad for the design committee. They had good intentions, and now that we're here, the controversy has blown over, but at the time, it seemed as though the mere choice of name could be enough to derail the entire project. It's not like the colony was being called Hades.

Then there's the logo itself. They kept that simple to avoid controversy — a stylized, retro-1950s silhouette of an astronaut's head and shoulders. I like it. To me, it looks like it was inspired by *Flash Gordon,* but the helmet is an entirely clear fishbowl dome, and several prominent atheists complained that it looked like a halo, while the bulging backpack appears to be a folded wing. I guess someone thought we were angels. Sheesh. The media picked up on that angle and complained about idolizing astronauts, saying, "They think they're better than us," which was absurd.

The governor of Ohio complained the logo was too "science-fic-tiony," as though that's a thing. Apparently, in his mind science fiction belittles science — which, of course, it doesn't.

Just when I thought the controversy was over, someone pointed out that the astronaut was male, and the circus began again.

As a woman, I was quizzed almost constantly about how I felt playing second fiddle to men. I thought it was silly. The ratio of women to men in the colony is 61 to 59, so it was absurd to claim that the patriarchy was being established on Mars. But, they'd say, there's only one woman leading a module. Yes, but most of the menial jobs have gone to the men, so it balances out.

Don McMillan from the U.S. mod does the laundry for the entire colony. At first, it was a little disconcerting having a guy fold my underwear and bras and iron my shirts, but he does it for everyone and never mixes up garments with the wrong owners. Don takes supreme pride in his work, as he should. Mars is nothing if not a level playing field.

After all this time, the controversy seems crazy — splitting hairs. I'm quite proud of our little colony, and as for the logo on the mission patch, I agree with Shakespeare — it's much ado about nothing.

Adin talks to me over the radio. "I've got you stable at seventeen minutes," he says, monitoring my biometrics and tracking how my body is acclimatizing to the changing pressure in both the suit and the airlock. I'm halfway. "You're go on Rover Four. That's R4. Over."

"Copy that," I reply. "R4."

I have my eyes closed, resting my hands in my lap and meditating quietly. There are a bunch of different techniques for making the transition to surface ops, but for me, a little time spent clearing my mind is the key. If I'm relaxed and peaceful, my body tends to go easy on me.

Warmth radiates through my suit, and I'm so relaxed I could drift off to sleep when Adin says, "You're at twenty-eight minutes and showing good internals. You are clear for egress."

"Roger."

The airlock is equalized and flushed with Martian atmosphere. As much as I love life in the colony, it's only at times like this that I feel like I'm really on Mars and not just caught up in yet another long-term simulation run. When the outer hatch opens and the desert rocks, dust, and sand appear bathed in a soft, ruddy light, I can't help feeling overcome with a sense of euphoria. Mars is unmoved by the affairs of Earth, and has been for billions of years. Looking out at the ancient landscape, it's hard to accept that life on Earth has been rocked by nuclear explosions detonating around the globe. Everything here is so sedate.

Tiny pebbles crunch beneath my boots. Fine dust is kicked up with even the softest of steps, swirling around my boots before settling. The exhilaration of being on Mars never gets old.

The surface rovers are lined up, ready for deployment, facing the opening of the broad cave. The ceiling is low, reaching to barely a foot above the roll bar on each rover. Although most of our base has been built around natural formations, the maintenance cave has been carved from solid rock. Grooves and cuts line the ceiling like the scratchings of some Paleolithic tribe marking its territory.

"You're going solo?" Adin asks from the control room overlooking the rovers, only now realizing I'm alone, even though I spent half an hour in the airlock by myself.

"No one else wanted to go," I reply, walking up to R4. That's not a valid reason for going out alone. Surface ops are supposed to be conducted using a buddy system, but given the uncertainty of the last day, it's hardly a surprise. Knowing the range and life-support capabilities of the rovers, it's not really a concern. Besides, all the critical systems are monitored remotely.

Adin's silent. I suspect he's kicking himself for responding to my request without really thinking things through. Too late.

I climb up into the cab of R4. A fine coating of dust covers the controls. Most of the electronics are sealed in plastic to protect them from various corrosives and volatiles in the Martian environment, but inevitably the dust gets everywhere. Dust on Mars is different from anything I've experienced on Earth. Back home, dust is soft and more of a nuisance than a problem. Up here, it's as fine as cigarette smoke. Roll some between your fingers and you'd swear it was oily, with the consistency of graphene.

Dust represents a serious health concern for us, and there have been times when I've been stuck in an airlock for hours waiting on a broken clean cycle to run. If even a nominal amount of dust circulates through the base, it could cause serious health problems. Perchlorates in the dust are highly reactive when they come in contact with moisture — they're chemical time bombs waiting to go off in our lungs, and on returning to base it's important not to handle the outside of the suit until the techs have given it a chemical shower.

Some of the dust is akin to glass particles ground up so fine they hang in the air for up to several minutes. This dust can be easily sucked into our lungs when breathing. Ingesting sandpaper would do less tissue damage than Martian dust, as the fines are so small they can breach cell membranes. Back on Earth, similar fine-grain particulate material, like cigarette smoke and asbestos fibers, can cause cancer, and the general view is there's no safe level of exposure, so we're fastidious when it comes to dust management.

We were supposed to have self-contained, pressurized rovers like those depicted in blockbuster movies, but reality falls short of Hollywood. The plans are still there, and there's a prototype kept on standby for use in emergencies. But daily surface activity takes place in rovers that are close cousins to the lunar vehicles of the Apollo program. We get a little more comfort and a higher ride, but not much else. I don't complain, though, as not everyone gets to go on surface ops, and, being lightweight, the rovers are good for long distance. They're like the Jeeps of World War II — as tough as an old boot, and dependable in rain, hail, or shine — or, as the case may be on Mars, in dust storms, fog, or temperatures dropping more than a hundred degrees in just a few hours.

Like the Curiosity rover of old, R4 is a six-wheel-drive vehicle set on spindly aluminum wheels, raised up on a spidery rocker-bogie suspension. The first time I heard that phrase, I thought Connor was teasing me. *Rocker-bogie* — it was April first, and we were touring the build plant in Tennessee. I was sure Connor was pranking me, but it's a legitimate term describing how the various wheels move in complementary ways to negotiate rough terrain, and it works beautifully. The rovers are a smooth ride on a planet without roads.

"Pre-op check," I say, knowing Adin is listening from the control room. Jianyu is probably up there as well. "Fuel cells: 96 percent. Comms: good. Backup power: 92 percent. Oil pressure: 15 PSI. Hydraulics: 42 PSI. Oxygen reserves: 8 hours. Primary computer:

15 percent CPU, 20 percent memory. Secondary: online at 1 percent CPU and 10 percent memory." I'm not telling Adin anything he doesn't already know from his telemetry readouts, but it's standard procedure to confirm readings.

"R4, you're clear for departure."

"Thanks, Adin."

I engage the automatic transmission, and the rover pulls out of the cave into the morning light. Dust clouds hide the mountains to the south, leaving them nothing more than a blur. Turning north, the autonomous nav unit engages, following the tracks of previous rovers that have compressed the dust and rocks into an impromptu road. Our computers are insanely smart, making decisions with far more finesse than a human. Occasionally, there's a slight detour of a few feet as machine learning allows the nav unit to analyze every route taken by the rover fleet over the past month so as to plot the optimum path and avoid excess wear and tear.

The Romans may have advocated straight lines, but our roads follow the contours of the land, picking the leeward slopes where possible and taking advantage of the soft dust and sand that has settled in those regions. With so little water cycling on Mars over the last billion or so years, there's been nothing to take the edge off jagged rocks. Even small rocks can be unforgiving, damaging the lightweight aluminum wheels on the rovers — they can be as sharp as a kitchen knife. Inflated wheels aren't an option; intense UV coupled with cosmic radiation causes complex rubber molecules to break down in short order, but the rover has good suspension, and I bounce lightly with the rocking of the cabin.

Cliff tops tower above me. I'm following an ancient riverbed. Hard bedrock gives way to sand dunes rippling through the canyon. Rocks lie scattered at various intervals. Sometimes, it's as though a drunk truck driver dumped a load of gravel in the middle of the road, and then there's nothing but smooth sand for a few hundred yards.

Mars has a strange hierarchy of rocks that goes unnoticed by most. There are far more small, splintered fragments of stone littering the ground than there are rocks, and far more rocks than boulders, and more boulders than collapsed cliffs or canyon walls and craters. It's a confused sense of order amid the utter chaos. In some places, erosion has exposed layered, sedimentary rock set down shortly after the solar system formed, during what we call the Wet Mars geological era, but most of these layers are buried in mounds of fine debris.

Contrary to the claims of conspiracy theorists who think we're cohabiting with aliens, there are no squirrels or Mayan statues on Mars, no oblique faces, miniature stone people, or even extraterrestrials hiding behind the rocks, although there's no shortage of pareidolia; I haven't seen the Lion King in the clouds, but the human mind is a hive of imagination, and when starved of stimulus, it's easy to see things that aren't there. As I round a bend, following the ancient riverbed, I swear I see an astronaut watching me from the shadows on the far side of the canyon. But I blink, and he's gone.

"Adin?" I say, quickly remembering radio protocol and correcting myself with, "Base, is there anyone else out here?"

"Negative."

I bring the rover to a halt. I'm tempted to climb down out of the open cab and head over the ridge to look. Seeing funny shapes is one thing, but seeing a fellow astronaut almost two miles from base near one of the collapsed sections of the lava tube is entirely another. Given all that's happened, I feel unsettled.

"Did you see something?"

Adin's asking about pareidolia. As EVA controller, he's responsible for monitoring my vitals remotely, as well as monitoring the rover's health, position, bearing, and mission profile — not that there is one in this case. He will have noticed that the rover has come to a halt. He's probably watching my heart rate and respiration spike as well. If he gets edgy, he can call an abort and force me to return to base. Going against the wishes of a controller is a surefire way to never go topside again, and all of us trail monkeys know that. Controllers like Adin don't abuse their power, but they take their position seriously. I've known Adin to agonize over a dodgy wheel bearing for days, analyzing logs and trying to understand how he could miss a fault I thought was minor and unavoidable. But it's this kind of attitude that keeps us alive on Mars. Nothing is left to chance. Chance may occur, but when it does, it's scolded as an impostor and sent packing.

"No," I say. "Nothing."

I put the rover back in drive, shaking off the feeling I'm being watched.

The rover is semiautonomous and can be set to automatically avoid obstacles, trace old tracks, and find its way home in the event that an astronaut becomes incapacitated. Adin can take control remotely if needed, but he doesn't have full access to all the subsystems.

I leave the rover on its current route, following the trail, and stand in the open cabin, turning around and looking back at the ridge on the far side of the vast canyon. Nothing. The cab of the rover sways gently on its rocker-bogie suspension. I steady myself, holding on to the roll bar. I can't take my eyes off the distant rubble, straining to make out any shapes or movement. Who would be out this far on foot? And why?

Pareidolia. Maybe I'm seeing what I want to see — catching a fleeting glimpse of a vaguely familiar shape and mentally filling in the gaps, fabricating my own reality.

"R4, I'm getting some jitter on your instrumentation readings. Can you check the main bus broadcast unit?"

"Copy that," I say, turning back and sitting down. Jitter is the term for intermittent interruption of transmission. Depending on the location of the satellites in orbit, atmospheric conditions, and our position within geological formations like canyons, telemetry can spike and give false readings. Repeater stations mounted on the walls of the canyon help to reduce the uncertainty in transmission, but they're not foolproof. Adin's asking me to double-check that I'm broadcasting clearly, which means any problem is a phantom in the convoluted network processes that unfold between us.

"Main bus clear," I say. The mind is a funny thing. I could swear I saw something — someone — but it was my brain fooling itself. "All systems nominal."

"Copy that," Adin says, and, knowing him, he's settling in for the long haul. Transits are dull. Watching a dozen screens with tiny peaks and troughs on a bazillion metrics feeding in from both the rover and my suit is boring as hell. Adin will have a cup of coffee in hand by now. In the past, I've dropped in on him while other scientists have been out on the surface, and he'd have a bunch of monitoring alerts set up and be leaning back in his chair, reading an e-book. Not exactly standard operating procedure, but understandable.

A quarter of a mile farther on, the track divides. I'm supposed to head on through the valley, but I take the controls for a moment, steering toward the highlands.

Martian geology is similar to the U.S. Southwest in that there are vast, sweeping vistas, canyons, and ravines everywhere. While the Grand Canyon on Earth was carved out over twenty million years, the erosion on Mars is the product of billions of years of minuscule change. For a planet that's roughly a third the size of Earth, Martian geology is extreme. Olympus Mons makes Mount Everest look like a sand castle. Olympus is so tall that it reaches beyond the bulk of the atmosphere. It would be a wonderful location for an astronomical observatory. If Valles Marineris were on Earth, it would be as though the Grand Canyon extended from New York to Los Angeles, consuming most of the U.S. along the way.

Lost somewhere deep in time is a period when Mars was far more geologically active than Earth, with volcanoes that buried the land in lava, and floods that would make Noah quake in his boots.

The track I'm following winds its way up the steep side of the canyon, tracing several U-shaped bends that extend for easily a quarter mile each. The ascent to the tableland is slow.

"R4," is the call over the radio, and I'm surprised it took Adin this long to realize I've deviated from my original target. "Confirm your route. Over."

"Roger, Command," I reply, steeling myself to lie my ass off. "Going for a scenic drive . . . No rush. Taking the time to check out some interesting formations on the tableland. I've been wanting to get up here for a while . . . The view is breathtaking."

"Copy that."

Adin sounds worried; is he going to panic and abort? He shouldn't. It's no big deal. It's not unheard of for surface ops to check out potential sites for future exploration when there's time to spare. As I'm broadcasting on an open channel and there's no encryption, anyone can listen in. If Connor or Harrison is listening, he'll know precisely where I'm going, and why. I'm half expecting to be subjected to a rant from Harrison trying to talk me down again. After the confrontation in the hub, he would see this act as openly hostile and defiant.

There's silence for the next few minutes. Once I'm satisfied I got away with the deviation, I turn on some music. Again, the automated driver follows the trail, leaving me to relax and enjoy the view. Roughly a thousand feet up the side of the slope, I get a glimpse of the colony. As I close on the rim of the canyon, I'm surprised to see how small and insignificant our base actually is. If I didn't know what I was looking for, I'd miss the dome stretching over the subsurface hub. The colony itself is set in what was once an ancient spillway at the base of a broad canyon opening out onto the lower plains. Only one of the lava tubes is visible, snaking beneath the surface of Mars like a cat crawling under a rug. Erosion has exposed the roof of the lava tube, but the thick metamorphic rock has withstood the weather better than the sedimentary layers in the canyon, remaining intact. Humanity finally makes it to Mars, and the god of war barely notices.

The sides of the canyon are covered in loose rocks and layers of dust that have accumulated on the slopes for millions of years. The approach to the tableland reveals distinct dark patches bleeding out onto the sloping rock pile, marking points where subsurface water is leaching through the canyon walls. These were some of our first targets for samples when we arrived on Mars. There were no organics, much to my disappointment. There's no life on Mars — not now. Apart from us, Mars is a dead planet.

The rover emerges onto the tableland as a dust storm looms tens of thousands of feet overhead, making me feel small. Fluffy dice hang from the center of the windshield in roughly the position they would be if the rover had a rearview mirror. I'm not sure who dragged them here from Earth, but I love their sense of humor. I'd like to have heard the rationalization behind that inclusion. We were all allowed a personal carry of five pounds, so I guess they came with that, or some industrious engineer with a sense of nostalgia shoved them into a spare spot as padding.

My GPS map indicates I'm a mile from the point of touchdown, just north of the official landing ellipse, which covers an area of forty square miles. I punch the coordinates into the automated rover nav unit, and the computer leads me across the desolate plain. Ancient craters litter the land, with ejecta scattered across the desert. Most of the craters are old and have suffered so much erosion that they appear as little more than mounds until the rover gets close enough that I can see over the lip into the bowl. The rover negotiates the terrain automatically, calculating the optimum path through the rubble, avoiding boulders and exposed bedrock to protect the wheels.

I'm confused. I should be able to see something by now. Parachutes catching in the wind. Scorch marks from the landing rockets. *Prospect* is bigger than my rover. It should be easily visible on the plain, but there's nothing here.

8

Landslide

"WHAT CAN YOU SEE?" Vlad asks over the radio. He must be in the control room with Adin. As I've moved beyond the line of sight of the colony, it's not possible to transmit directly. Everything is routed through a low-bandwidth satellite, limiting coverage to audio and still images rather than video.

"Not much," I say, not wanting to be too chatty with the potential for anyone to listen in — although if anyone from the U.S. mod *is* listening, the game is up. Even Adin must have figured it out by now. Why would a biologist come up to the tableland and head out toward the landing ellipse rather than trace the edge of the canyon? There's only one reason I'd be out here. I'll bet Adin's standing beside Vlad talking about *Prospect*.

"Visibility's dropping," I say as the dust storm descends. Unlike the movies, a dust storm on Mars is barely a breeze. There are no hurricane-force winds throwing rocks around, but the low Martian gravity causes fine dust to hang in the air, obscuring my view. This is what Vlad was worried about in the satellite imagery. Dust hides everything. Storms like these can be gone in a few hours or hang around for months, obscuring the view from space.

"You should be right on it," Vlad says. The GPS unit agrees, but I don't see any sign of *Prospect*. Even with the dust, I should catch a glimpse of the huge parachutes lying on the surface of the planet. The cabin of the rover is raised almost ten feet in the air, being more like the skeleton of a monster truck than a car, and affording me a good view across the plain. Even with the dust, I can see at least a hundred yards in all directions.

"I'm not seeing anything. No tracks. No parachutes. No space-craft. No engine scorch. Nothing but rocks."

"Circle the area, see what you can pick up," Vlad says.

With thick-gloved fingers, I plot a course on the touch screen, slowly moving outward, keeping the spot identified by Vlad in the center as I circle at a hundred yards. This will give me an effective view over several hundred yards around the landing site.

"Could it have come down in a crater?" Vlad asks.

"Negative," I reply. "Nothing over about twenty feet in this region. Visibility is falling, but I'm able to see into the surrounding craters."

An alarm comes up on the console of the rover, but I wave it away with my fingers gliding over the touch screen, wanting to focus on the search. The rover rides up on a mound, giving me good visibility on either side.

"Nothing."

"Keep looking."

"Could an automated rover have picked up the whole craft?" I ask.

"Not without a crane. Besides, you should see the chutes. They would have detached after landing."

Another alarm sounds, but I silence it. The light continues to flash, but I ignore it.

"Switching on range radar," I say, knowing the navigation ra-dar will light up anything made from metal up to a mile away. "And you've double-checked the coordinates?"

"Yes," Vlad says. "I've overlaid the satellite imagery on top of your route. It appears as though you've already passed the landing site."

"There's nothing here," I say, desperately wanting to see something in the gloomy half-light. I stand in the cabin, trying to increase my visibility. "We're in the wrong spot. We have to be."

"Perhaps —"

"R4, comms check," Adin says, sending a formal request over the top of Vlad.

"Comms good. R4 out," I reply, dropping back into my seat, unsure why Adin would interrupt the conversation with a communications check — we were communicating clearly. I bring up the maintenance console, shifting the map and navigation to one side of the screen with a flick of my glove.

"R4," Adin continues, taking the channel from Vlad. "I'm show-ing inconsistent telemetry readings. Request full status check. Over."

"Copy that," I reply. "Fuel cells — fuel cells: 6 percent. *What?* How is that possible?"

In the moment, I'm overwhelmed by the readout in front of me. My hands shake. Everything's wrong, but Adin's voice helps calm my nerves.

"I'm reading hydraulics and engine pressure well within toler-ance," he says, "but I have concerns about fuel and air. Over."

My voice quivers. "Thirty minutes," I say, reading the gauge for breathable air and realizing I'm easily two hours away from the col-ony. As long as I'm within fifty yards of the rover, my suit metrics are picked up by the rover and relayed back to base. According to the readout in front of me, I have half an hour's air in my backpack. But I started with eight hours. I should have six left.

"Ah, this is R4 requesting clarification on life-support metrics and fuel cells," I say, trying to stay calm by following the standard operat-ing procedure.

"Copy that, I confirm your readings. Recommend immediate re-turn, over."

"Base," I say, with my voice shaking. I pause, considering my op-tions carefully. My life hangs in the balance of the decisions made in the next few minutes. "This is R4. I am declaring an emergency, over."

"Copy that."

To anyone listening in, our conversation sounds overly relaxed and repetitive, but in reality, by declaring a formal emergency, I've requested that Adin initiate the colony's SEP, or surface emergency protocol. In the silence that follows, I know Adin is raising the leaders of the four mods on a priority conference call to inform them of the situation, and alerting the rapid-response team. From here on out, all communication will be automatically relayed to Earth, not that there's anything they can do in real time. So much for a quiet excursion.

It takes less than thirty seconds before Adin is back on the air, but the silence feels like a lifetime. He speaks with distinct clarity as by now the colony leadership will be listening in the background — Max, Vlad, Wen, and Connor. They'll have a separate channel so they can talk among themselves, but they'll hear every word that's spoken for the duration of the emergency.

"R4. Let's work the problem. I want you to do a full reboot of the primary computer. Backup will take over and refresh the monitoring metrics, resetting alarm states. That will give us an independent reading. Do you copy?"

"I copy."

My heart is thumping inside my chest.

"We're going to get you through this," Adin says. He must be watching my vitals spiking on his monitor. "Deep breaths."

I shut down the main computer, and the rover comes to a halt as control switches from the primary to the secondary computer system.

"Recommend you plot an immediate return," Adin says, repeating his earlier suggestion. The console flickers back to life.

"On it."

It seems obvious in hindsight, but in my panicked state, I hadn't given my current direction any thought. With thick-gloved fingers, I punch in the retrace mode, which instructs the secondary computer to follow the outbound path back to base.

The rover turns. Dust swirls around the cab of the rover.

"Ah, base," I say. "Can you confirm my heading? I'm blind up here. I've got partial restoration of controls. No maps. No GPS. Limited visibility. Over."

"You're good," Adin says. "You are tracking east toward the canyon."

"Copy that," I say. "And the metric refresh?"

I'm desperately hoping for some good news — hoping the secondary computer has picked up on a glitch in the original readings, revealing that I have plenty of reserves.

"I'm still showing you low on oxygen, with what appears to be a leaking fuel cell. You're carrying six cells, but number two has shorted and may have leaked onto the servo controls, taking the other cells off-line."

"R4 is sluggish," I reply, noting that the rover is struggling to climb a rise.

This is the same rover I took out yesterday. It should have been automatically restocked on return to base, but a quick glance in the rear of the cabin confirms my suspicion — the racks are empty. There should be at least one spare life-support pack back there.

"You said R4 was good to go," I say.

"I know, I know," Adin replies with a hint of frustration in his voice. Out of habit, he's sent me out in my usual rover, but it hasn't been prepped with spare O_2 after yesterday's journey.

This is the third leaking fuel cell we've had on Mars. In the past, the results haven't been so dire, and the affected rovers have limped back to base. "Pre-ops showed healthy cells and resupply."

I saw that too. I'm confused. I should have visually checked the racks instead of being so eager to get moving, but I was worried about Adin scrubbing the mission when he realized I was going solo. I rushed the departure — not in a frantic manner, but I wasn't my usual methodical self. Jianyu, Harrison, Adin, the war back on Earth — I allowed myself to get distracted, and that innocent mistake may cost me my life.

"We're chasing down a technical glitch," Adin says, and I struggle not to hyperventilate at the thought that a computer bug is going to kill me. "Inventory check shows you're carrying a medi-kit. I want you to open the medi-kit. There should be a small oxygen canister in there. It will be on the right. Beneath the major trauma pack."

I don't know that I've ever moved this fast on Mars before — I'm out of my seat and scrambling to get to the cabinets at the rear of the rover. I rifle through the drawers.

"Got it," I say, checking a mechanical pressure gauge on the side of the outlet valve. "It's at 98 percent of capacity."

"Okay, that's a one-hour supply. I need you to calm down and slow your breathing. You're burning through your O_2."

Easier said than done.

Adin continues, saying, "James and Su-shun are prepping a second rover. Just relax. Everything's going to be fine."

Of course he'd say that — that's his job — to keep us surface monkeys calm in an emergency.

"Roger that," I say, feeling the rover ride up a steep incline and then rock forward, plummeting into a crater. I rush back to the driver's seat, knowing I didn't cross any craters on the outbound route. Something's wrong.

"Base. Course check. Over," I say, grabbing the controls as the rover begins sinking in the soft dust that's accumulated over eons in the heart of the crater. I pull the steering column to one side, directing the rover toward a collapsed section of the crater wall. "I am off course. Repeat. Off course."

The computerized drive display is blank — nothing but a black screen with a single green cursor blinking in the top left corner.

"I've lost both computers. Repeat. Both systems off-line. Over."

"Copy that" is the reply from Adin, which is disconcerting, as he's not telling me what I want to hear. He should be telling me my bearing. On Mars, we use north, south, east, and west for basic directions, and a simple 360-degree circle with zero pointing north for more precise headings. All he needs to do is say "one-eighty" for south, or "two-seventy" for due west, and I'll be able to undertake at least a rough course correction, but he's preoccupied with something else, and it's all I can do not to yell at him. Dust billows around me. I have no idea which way I'm going, as visibility is down to fifty yards. Without my onboard computers, I'm blind. Their sophistication is too easy to take for granted. It's only now I realize how helpless I am without them.

I resist the temptation to panic. It's clear from Adin's terse voice that he's fighting some other battle on my behalf. I need to focus on getting the hell out of this crater while he figures out whatever's got me in a tailspin. I suspect he's lost me on satellite. That's the only reason he wouldn't have warned me about veering off course.

A glance at my wrist computer reveals the time in formal notation — 14:02 — early afternoon. It's the middle of the Martian spring here in the southern hemisphere. The colony is located roughly 5 degrees below the equator. Noon at this time of year should put the Sun almost directly overhead. By 2:00 p.m., I'm guesstimating the Sun will be tracking slightly west. I lean back, craning my neck to see the faint blur of the Sun through the dust storm. The Sun is on my left, so I must be facing north. I turn the rover until the soft shadow of the windshield is roughly equal on both sides and the Sun is at my back. Sailors of old navigated by the stars for thousands of years — all I have is a single, obscured star, but it's close enough to cut through the haze. That shadow gives me a rough bearing east. It's hardly the kind of precision needed to get me back onto the track leading down to the colony, but it will ensure I intersect the canyon instead of driving endlessly across the open plain.

"I'm good. I'm good," I say, celebrating a little victory and letting Adin and the others know that I'm not freaking out. "Heading due east."

"Copy that."

Again, Adin's lack of communication tells me he's up to his armpits in alligators. Deep breaths, Liz. Slow things down.

My wristpad computer starts blinking, flashing a warning that my air supply has dwindled to a mere ten minutes. The rover slows.

It's running out of juice. If there's one small mercy, it's that the storm is drifting away from me. I'm on the edge of the vast, billowing dust cloud, but visibility is clearing. The storm must be drifting northwest. I grab the oxygen cylinder, hugging it under my arm like a teddy bear, and quietly note the minutes passing as the rough terrain disappears beneath my wheels. I'll wait as long as I can before hooking up the spare cylinder to my suit.

After about five minutes of trundling along in silence, I say, "Sure would be nice to hear something from you guys," followed by a nervous laugh.

"Sorry," Adin says. "We've got two rovers out of commission. A third is like yours, having failed prep checks. I've got R7 outbound toward you now."

"ETA?"

There's silence. This is not something they want to tell me.

Reluctantly, Adin says, "Under normal conditions, just under two hours. James thinks he can trim that to an hour and a half."

I'm dead, and they know it. My heart sinks. This is a recovery mission, not a rescue. My rover slows to a crawl, but I can see the sharp edge of the tableland ahead. A jagged line marks the rim of the canyon, but there's no sign of the trail winding down to the canyon floor. I'm lost — not as lost as I was ten minutes ago, but lost nonetheless.

"Halfway," I mumble. "I've reached the canyon."

"Listen," Adin says. "I want you to conserve your oxygen. I need you to lower your respiration rate — buy yourself as much time as you can. Jianyu recommends you lie down with your feet raised. Slow things down. I'm with you. I'm going to stay with you the whole way, but I need you to relax."

I'm not dumb. I know what he's doing. Death never comes easy, but acceptance makes it more bearable.

I can't lie down and give up.

A steady beep every five seconds marks the five-minute alarm on my primary pack. R4 comes to a halt, having lost too much charge to drive the electric engine.

Everything is difficult in a space suit. For astronauts in orbit, wearing a space suit is tiring, as even in a weightless environment, flexing against the pressure within a suit takes effort. In a gravity well like Mars, it's like running a marathon.

I climb out of my seat, taking hold of a rail on the edge of the rover, and slowly swing around so I can work my way backward down the steps to the surface. Within seconds, I'm breathing heavily. I push off the last step and jump, gliding to the surface like the Apollo astronauts of old. I leave the rover roughly thirty feet from the edge of the cliff.

"I have to see," I say, struggling for breath but determined to drain every last ounce of oxygen from my backpack before switching to the medical cylinder.

"Liz."

Jianyu's voice seems to cut right through me. My legs falter.

"Please. We are doing all we can. We need you to rest. Conserve your strength."

Tears roll down my cheeks, but I keep walking.

"I can see you," I say. I doubt I'm telling Jianyu and Adin anything they don't already know, as they should have acquired the rover again from one of the satellites, but I add, "I'm maybe two miles south of the track, on a ridge overlooking the colony . . . I can see the dome . . . So close. Little more than a mile away."

I sit cross-legged less than two feet from the edge of the cliff, far closer than regulations dictate, but when you're dying, who cares? The maintenance yard carved into the hillside is invisible from here, but I know precisely where it is from the nearby landmarks and the bumps formed by the subsurface lava tubes. The dome over the hub appears black and out of place in the otherwise pristine ruddy desert.

I feel light-headed. Dots dance before my eyes. With slow, deliberate motions, I connect the spare oxygen cylinder to a buddy-breathing valve on the front of my suit collar. I purge the valve of dust and start the flow. Breathing deeply, I enjoy the rush provided by 100 percent oxygen. The scrubber on my pack will clean excess CO_2 out of the air to prevent a buildup, but the only oxygen I have is coming from the medical cylinder, so I ease back on the flow. I'm determined to make it last as long as possible.

"We're coming for you," Jianyu says.

"You won't make it in time," I reply, but I'm not distressed. I'm quietly resigned to my fate. There are worse ways to die than looking out across a valley on Mars. The vista is majestic — breathtaking. Peaceful. Unmoved after billions of years orbiting Sol.

"I'll miss this," I say. "I'll miss you ... I'm so close ... If I had wings ... If I could fly, I'd be down there already."

"I love you," Jianyu says.

At first, I'm not sure why, but I let out a soft laugh. Perhaps it's that those three words seemed to explode out of nowhere. Jianyu's never said that before. I guess he wanted to make sure it was said, and I appreciate that.

"I love you too," I say, not sure who's listening in — not giving a damn who'll listen to this in the future. Incidents like this tend to be overanalyzed for years. A wry smile comes to my face as I realize I'm going to be in a training video, but for all the wrong reasons. I'll probably get a high school named after me — poor kids — and I wonder which photo they'll hang in the reception area.

Each of us had dozens of studio photographs taken before we left for Mars. Although the shots are all smiles, everyone knew what they were really for — the obituary. As long as we're alive, they're stored on a hard drive somewhere, perhaps with a copy on Wikipedia. As soon as we're dead, they're front-page news — well, maybe not with a full-scale nuclear war in progress. Have the bombs stopped falling? The devastation and destruction wrought in a fraction of a second are going to take generations to repair. Construction of my high school might have to wait.

I still remember the photographer's flash going off, the optimism of the guy with the camera, the "Just one more, a little to the left. That's it. And smile." Dozens and dozens of photos . . . only to be remembered for the one with the cheesiest grin.

"Do you want to talk?" Jianyu asks after what seems like an eternity. The wind gently buffets my helmet. "There's only me. Connor took everyone else off-line. If you want to talk, you can."

I guess this is the Martian equivalent of a confessional booth — last rites and all that crap. Say something sweet for Mom. Hi to Dad. This is madness. I don't want to talk. I don't want to die. What I want is to live.

I get to my feet and look out over the edge of the cliff. There's a thirty-foot drop immediately below me, then the classic steep Martian slope runs at a sharp angle for easily half a mile to the canyon floor below. Rocks and boulders have accumulated here over hundreds of millions of years of near-constant gradual erosion, forming a slope not unlike the side of one of the great pyramids when seen from afar. A few dark stains mark subsurface salt brines leaking out of the water table, running down the exposed surface.

"Tell James to turn back."

"I don't understand," Jianyu says, but I'm too busy to reply. I unclip the protective ring collar sealing me in the surface suit and begin loosening the waistband so I can shed the leggings. As I sit in the dust, my outer gloves and boots are the first things to be tossed to one side.

"Have him meet me at the bottom," I say, switching off the oxygen and removing the cylinder so I can take off the upper portion of the suit.

"What are you doing?" Jianyu asks.

"Taking off my suit," I reply, as if such a conclusion should be obvious.

If anyone could see me, they'd think I've gone mad. Maybe I have. The bulky surface suit lies abandoned on the sand beside me. I reconnect the oxygen, wearing only my black, formfitting pressure suit.

The spare oxygen cylinder has roughly two feet of hosing, so I can hold the handle comfortably in one hand.

"Liz."

"If you can't make it here in time, then I need to come to you."

"Don't do anything stupid, Liz."

"Hah," I laugh. "Look out the window. I'm coming straight at you."

With the heating elements disconnected from the battery in my backpack, the cold seeps through my thermal-pressure suit. The mechanical counterpressure provided by the smart material will protect me from the extremely low pressure in the Martian atmosphere, but any tears in the suit material will result in vacuum bruising beneath my skin.

It might be spring on Mars, but the temperature is still −40°F and dropping fast as the afternoon wears on. I can hear Jianyu calling for Adin in the background, but if I'm going to do this, I need to act now, while I still have a good supply of oxygen. Without the CO_2 scrubber in my primary backpack, I'm going to have to manually vent excess carbon dioxide, but there's an emergency valve designed specifically for this scenario. I love the engineers at NASA — they thought of every possible contingency. I'll lose oxygen during the vent, but CO_2 buildup is a far worse problem than a lack of O_2. For now, it feels liberating to stand on the surface of Mars in what amounts to barely more than a wetsuit.

After a brief glimpse over the edge to ensure I'm not going to come down on any boulders, I move back and take a good, long run-up, charging at the rim of the canyon. Unlike runners on Earth, I don't maintain an upright stance; rather, I lean into the run, driving as hard as I can against the loose rocks. Back home, I'd fall flat on my face, but up here, the angle allows me to get good traction on the sandy, rocky ground.

At the last second, I leap — launching myself out into the thin Martian atmosphere, sailing over the edge of the cliff. In one-third gravity, I arc through the air, soaring like a gymnast. My momentum carries me well away from the cliff face, but within roughly a second, I begin plummeting toward the rocks and debris below. Regardless of whether it's on Earth or on Mars, gravity always obliges, and I accelerate toward the rocks. The planet comes rushing up to greet me all too quickly, and my feet plunge into the soft dirt and loose stones.

Jianyu is yelling something over the radio, but I can't hear him clearly as the emergency comms built into my helmet are relayed through the rover. By now, given the angle, there are probably a dozen metric tons of Martian bedrock between me and the rover, and the radio cuts out.

Instinctively, I crouch as I land, sinking up to my knees in the loose rubble. The whole surface begins to move, having been given impetus by my motion. I scramble, wanting to stay on top of the ensuing landslide. Rocks, stones, grit, and dust swirl about me as an avalanche forms. The whole topside of the slope collapses, shifting forward in unison across roughly fifty feet on either side of me, sliding toward the canyon floor. I flail around, leaning back and trying to spread my weight, wanting to ride the wave of grit and stones cascading down the slope. I may well have dug my own grave. If I end up buried by even just a few feet of Martian rubble, I won't be able to free myself, and it'll be impossible for anyone to find me.

Rocks pelt my helmet. I should have kept the outer suit, but I felt I had to reduce my overall weight to avoid being buried alive.

With my legs out in front of me, I can kind of steer. I push against the stream of rocks thundering down the side of the canyon. The noise is akin to a jet engine screaming in my ears. I can barely see where I'm going, but down is good. I only hope there aren't any drop-offs or ledges ahead. So much dust is being kicked up, the sky darkens around me.

I try to catch myself with my arms, wanting to slow my descent, but I'm careful not to lose my grip on the oxygen cylinder. Sharp stones tear at my pressure suit, carving chunks out of the thermal insulation. I might as well be sliding down a cheese grater. The swirling dust obscures my view of the valley, cloaking me in a reddish haze.

I'm sinking. For all my efforts to stay above the rush of rocks and stones, the dust and debris bury me, and I find myself twisting, tumbling, being flung around within the avalanche. A large rock careens into my back, knocking the breath out of me.

My thick-gloved hands grab at the surface as I sink beneath the rubble. Even though I'm still in motion, I try to claw my way out of the landslide. Rocks crush my fingers, slamming into my arms and battering my wrists. Thousands of stones compact themselves against my body, making it hard to breathe. With my left hand, I keep the oxygen cylinder from being torn away and carried down the slope. If I lose that, I'll be dead within seconds.

The flow of rocks slows. I come to a halt upside down, buried in rubble, but my legs are free. Slowly, painfully, I drag myself out of the landslide. Cracks line my helmet. I sweep the dust away, clearing the respiration valve to vent CO_2 and breathing deeply from the oxygen cylinder. For the moment, I'm content to lie on my back with my legs spread, wanting to remain stable and avoid sliding further. Pebbles roll past, pelting my helmet.

I try to get to my feet but find myself sinking in the soft debris. It's an effort to stand. At a guess, I'm a third of the way down the slope, and I haven't killed myself. Yet. Aches and pains aside, I'm pleased with my progress. The rush of adrenaline sure beats waiting to die from asphyxiation.

The mound slopes away for hundreds of yards below me. With a few lunges, I free myself from the loose rocks and find myself riding a gentle, rolling landslide down the hill. By continually stepping forward, I'm carried on a carpet of what feels like loose scoria. Having grown up in Indiana, I loved cross-country skiing in winter. I find I can emulate that same motion, dragging my legs through the rocks and establishing a rhythm that allows me to skate with the rockslide. At a guess, I'm hitting maybe twenty miles an hour. It's as though I'm on a moving sidewalk rushing through an airport, and now that I have some control, my heart rate slows and I find myself in the peculiar situation where I'm enjoying the ride.

I laugh.

I was about to die almost a mile from safety. Now, I'm barely a hundred yards from the canyon floor.

I feel light-headed, so I vent the air in my helmet, purging excess CO_2.

In the distance, a rover races along the ancient waterway lining the canyon, bouncing high in the air as it flies over dunes. I've never seen a rover move so fast. The tiny vehicle kicks up a massive dust cloud behind it.

Blood bubbles from a cut on my forearm, seething and spitting as it evaporates in the frigid, thin atmosphere. Within seconds, a goopy brown sludge seals the wound as my blood coagulates. Tiny bubbles still appear, fascinating me, and I stumble, almost falling into the swell of rocks dragging me on. Shock is a strange sensation. I'm only vaguely aware that the sense of detachment I feel is a physiological response to the trauma of being crushed and torn up by the avalanche.

As I approach the base of the slope, the landslide slows, impeded by the canyon floor, and by the time I reach the ground, I'm able to step off at a walking pace. Once I'm free of the rockfall, I wobble like a newborn calf. I'm surprised by how much stability the rocks clamped around my legs gave me, as now it's all I can do not to collapse. Bits of torn insulation hang from my legs, exposing my skin to the frigid Martian atmosphere.

"So beautiful" is all I can say as the surface of Mars rushes up and slams into the side of my helmet. I swear, I didn't fall. The planet jumped out at me, and with those few thoughts, darkness washes over me.

9

Jianyu

"HEY," A FAMILIAR VOICE SAYS, gently sweeping the hair from my face. I try to move and Jianyu says, "Easy."

I'm in the recovery room inside medical, down in the basement of the hub.

"You gave us quite a scare out there."

"W — water," I say from beneath an oxygen mask.

"Here," he says, gently moving the mask to one side and handing me a plastic bottle with a long, curved straw built into the top. I squeeze the bottle, but my hand is so weak no water comes out. I suck on the straw instead, and Jianyu pops a valve on top to ease the flow.

"Just relax," he says.

I'm wearing a paper-thin surgical gown, but other than that I'm naked. I feel exposed. Jianyu seems to sense I'm uncomfortable dressed like this and pulls a blanket over me, resting the top of it across my chest.

"Thank you."

He nods with his usual understated modesty.

"How bad?" I ask.

"You're going to be fine. Sore, but fine. You've got extensive bruis-ing on your lower back and legs, multiple cuts and abrasions on your arms, but you're in one piece. I think you may have even knocked some sense into that head of yours."

He smiles.

"Your suit lost its integrity. When James reached you, it was only maintaining partial pressure."

"The cracks in my helmet," I say.

"You were venting oxygen."

I knew I'd come close to dying, but I had no idea just how close.

"Your lungs — with the pressure falling, they began reversing the gas exchange, drawing oxygen out of your bloodstream and damag-ing the fine cilia lining. Given time, it'll heal, but you may feel a little short of breath."

He squeezes my hand.

"I — I feel —"

"High?" he asks. "You should. I've got you on a concoction of drugs that would have a street value of 10,000 yuan in Shanghai."

"Great," I say, completing my sentence rather than commenting on his drug cocktail. I trust Jianyu. Right now, I'd trust anyone. Any-thing you want? Take it. Couldn't care. I'm loving these drugs.

My arms are heavily bandaged, and there's a compression ban-dage wrapped around my head. I touch softly at my forehead, feeling a pronounced lump.

"You have a concussion — some mild bruising around the brain. I'm going to keep you here under observation."

"You can observe me," I say in what feels like a drunken slur. "I don't mind."

I really don't know what I'm saying or what I'm agreeing to, but I feel happy.

I'm *alive*.

"You should rest."

"So should you," I say, noticing his bloodshot eyes. My bladder feels like it's about to burst. "I need to —"

I try to get up, but there's a Velcro strap in place to stop me from rolling off the narrow bed. Pulling at the strap, I free myself.

"Not too fast," Jianyu says, taking my arm and steadying me. He removes the oxygen mask, stops the flow of gas, and lays the mask to one side.

"Just need to go to the bathroom."

"I can get you a bedpan," he says, and I give him a look that signals my immense displeasure at such a notion. Even though I feel woozy, I'm sure I'm perfectly capable of waddling to the bathroom. Jianyu helps me down and guides me to the adjacent toilet.

"Don't lock the door," he says, as I close the door behind me. I wonder if it's just me. I doubt he's this overprotective with anyone else, although, to be fair, we haven't had any serious injuries since we arrived on Mars, and no fatalities. For highly experienced surgeons like Jianyu and Anna, staffing the Mars colony must be like caring for kindergartners.

After relieving myself, I try to straighten my hair in the mirror with a bit of water.

"Is everything okay?"

"I'm fine," I tell him, but somehow I succeed in making my hair worse than it was. Sweet moves, Liz. What's more, now my hair is damp, making my feeble efforts obvious. I need a shower, but given the miles of bandage wrapped around me, that's not happening anytime soon.

I shuffle back into the recovery room, feeling weak and out of breath. Jianyu looks as though he's ready to catch me should I fall. I'm tired, but I feel much better than I look. Getting up and walking around has helped clear my head.

I sit on the edge of the bed with my hands clasped in my lap. "There was nothing out there."

"I believe you."

Typical Jianyu. I swear, he can read minds. That's my concern — not that I didn't find the *Prospect* spacecraft, but that no one will believe that it wasn't out there. I didn't miss anything. There was nothing to miss. I've been on enough surface ops to know I was on-target, even with dodgy GPS.

The vidphone beside my bed has a small red flashing light, signaling there's at least one stored message waiting for me. Jianyu follows my gaze, saying, "You're our most popular patient."

"I'm your *only* patient," I say with a laugh.

I reach out and play the messages.

"Hey, Liz. Hope you're feeling better. Get well soon," Michelle says from the U.S. module. She blows me a kiss as the screen flickers, automatically moving on to the next message.

"*Dou di zhu,* remember? We have a card game to finish," Su-shun says with his usual deadpan expression, which makes me smile. "Seriously, no more gravel surfing, okay? Catch you later."

"Don't ever do that again," James says with a grin on his face. "You're one crazy lady. Get well soon, babe."

Jianyu interjects, "He broke the suspension on his rover, driving like a maniac to reach you."

I'm glad he didn't crash. I hate to think I put both our lives in jeopardy.

Connor appears next on the vidphone. His message is equally short but lacks compassion. "We need to talk. Come and see me."

I shake my head. It's not that I won't talk to him, but that he reminds me of everything that's wrong with this crisis. Cold, sterile calculations instead of the warmth that comes from shared humanity.

"Hey, sweetie," Anna says. "You gave us all a scare out there, but you're in good hands. I'm sure Jai will pamper you, but if there's anything you need—anything—let me know. Anytime. Even if you just want to talk. Okay? Bye."

Jianyu goes by Jai in English, even though the two names are pronounced differently and have different meanings. Most of the Chinese contingent have English names. Su-shun goes by George, not that anyone calls him that, as his Chinese name is sewn onto his uniform using English characters. Names are funny things, assigned to us by our parents without any input from us, but the Chinese get to choose their own English names. I'm not sure what name I'd choose if I had a choice. I guess Liz has grown on me.

"I'm so sorry," Adin says, his face nervous on the tiny screen. His eyes dart around as though he's wary of someone peering over his shoulder. "Your computers. They shouldn't have failed—they're designed to be redundant. Listen, I can't talk. Come and see me. Soon. Please. I—I don't know. I hope I'm wrong. I really do."

Adin rubs the stubble on his chin, adding, "If this—," only to be cut off abruptly.

I'm confused. Adin's message is garbled. He feels guilty about what happened to me out on the surface. I'm about to say something to Jianyu when another light flashes, signaling an incoming call arriving in real time. With a flick of my fingers across the touch screen, I answer the call.

"Liz."

It's Harrison.

"What the hell were you doing out there?"

Jianyu reaches for the button to terminate the call. I shake my head, whispering, "No."

"Is Jianyu down there with you? Talk some sense into her, Jai. Please. She could have died out there."

As repulsed as I am by Harrison, I know he cares—in his own messed-up way. For all our differences, he's not some crazed demon. He's human. Something like this happens, and it has an effect on him. Harrison is an übermale. He can't help himself. Everything has to be ordered and under control—his control. Only I doubt he realizes how rough and brutish he is when he's passionate about something. The irony is, all his efforts to wrest control of life are a clear sign of a life out of control. As for me, I despise what he's become, but not with unbound rage. I simply wish he could see himself for who he really is; I wish he would change, out of a desire to do what's right.

"You shouldn't have been out there alone, Liz."

In hindsight, I agree. Perhaps I would have picked up on the telemetry discrepancy earlier if I had a partner with me. If nothing else, we could have used buddy breathing until the cavalry arrived.

"Did you find it? Did you find the Russian rover?" Harrison asks.

I look at Jianyu. He's as surprised as I am.

"What?" Harrison says, picking up on my confusion. "Let me guess. They told you it was one of ours? Ha. Typical Russians."

Harrison looks at the ceiling for a moment. I'm silent. I have nothing to say to this man. I'm still furious at his arrogance the last time we spoke, but Harrison seems to have forgotten about that. Convenient.

"Poor Liz," he says. "You still haven't figured it out yet, have you? You still don't know who's lying to you . . . Don't you know, Liz? *Everyone's* lying."

I slam my hand down on the vidphone, hitting the Disconnect button.

"Hey," Jianyu says, taking my arm gently. "It's okay."

"No," I say with tears streaming down my cheeks. "No, it's not." I bury my head in his shoulder and sob.

"Easy. Easy," Jianyu says, stroking my back and holding me tight as I sit on the edge of the bed.

"What's going on?" I ask. "Why are we tearing ourselves apart? This is crazy. This is madness. Are we at war on Mars? At least, back on Earth, they have an excuse. Here, we have nothing. We should know better. We should *be* better."

"I know," Jianyu says, stroking my damp hair as I rest my head on his shoulder. "It's going to be okay. I promise you. We will get to the bottom of this. You and me. We'll figure this out."

That's precisely what I need to hear. I need to know that I'm not in this alone. I'm upset. I'm shaking, trembling in his arms, but I'm not alone, and that's a relief.

"I'm going to give you a sedative," he says.

"No. I don't want to —"

"It's okay," Jianyu says, leaning back so he can look at me. He wipes the tears from my eyes, adding, "You need to rest. Your body has to heal. All this . . . all this madness. It can wait. It will still be here when you wake."

I laugh, sniffing and holding back more tears as I say, "Well, that's not quite the consolation I was after, but, okay. I'll take it." Like I really don't want to miss out on all the fun.

Jianyu hands me a couple of tablets. I don't ask what they are. I wouldn't know the medical terms anyway, and besides, I trust him.

"Thank you," I say, swallowing them with a sip of water.

Jianyu lays me back on the pillow. He's gentle, fixing the oxygen mask in place and starting the flow of gas again. He kisses my forehead softly. My eyelids feel heavy. Jianyu wraps the Velcro strap loosely around my waist and pulls the blanket up, covering me and keeping me warm.

"Get some sleep," he says, squeezing my hand. One of the nurses waves a brief hello as he collects some equipment, carrying it out of the room. Jianyu turns out the light, saying, "Sweet dreams."

I don't dream, but my sleep is deep, refreshing, and revitalizing.

I'm not sure what time it is when I wake, but the lights in the hallway outside are low, so I'm guessing it's night.

The drugs are wearing off. My body aches. Time for a top-up. In the dim light, I can see Jianyu collapsed on a chair beside me. His figure is barely a silhouette in the darkness. He must be exhausted. He could have left me in the care of the nurse, but not Jianyu. He's fallen asleep in an upright position, with his arm lying across the back of a second chair, outstretched toward me, and his head resting on his shoulder.

"Hey," I say softly from beneath my oxygen mask. He looks awfully uncomfortable. There's another bed beside mine in the recovery room. He could have curled up on that, but he's ever the professional.

Jianyu doesn't respond. The soft hiss of oxygen is the only sound in the medical center. A thin plastic tube winds its way from the mask, passing loosely across my chest and down to a set of oxygen cylinders mounted below the bed. As I move to one side, rolling over so I can reach Jianyu, I notice a dark figure lying on the floor in the corridor. Something's horribly wrong.

"Jai?" I say, feeling my heart beat a little faster.

Jianyu is motionless. I tap his fingers, wanting to get his attention. "Jianyu, please."

His hand is cold. His fingers rebound softly in response to my touch, but he doesn't wake.

Panic seizes me. I start to get up, but the Velcro strap holds me in place. I pull at the strap, tearing it violently from my waist. Still, Jianyu lies motionless when the sound should have woken him.

"Oh, Jianyu," I whisper, swinging my legs around and over the edge of the bed. I shove rather than push his arm, striking him forcibly, scared by what's happening, desperately wanting him to wake. His arm falls from the back of the chair. To my horror, his head rolls back, leaving him staring blindly at the ceiling.

"No. No. No," I moan, pulling the oxygen mask from my face.

Dots appear before my eyes. I'm breathing, but I feel as though I'm trapped below the surface of a lake, with my lungs screaming for air. My steps are unsure. I'm giddy. Even in the weak Martian gravity, my legs can't support me, and I collapse, falling to the floor. I gasp for breath, confused, sucking in huge volumes of air but not finding any oxygen. I stretch for the mask hanging limp beside the bed, hissing softly in the shadows, but it's just out of reach. A pitch-black darkness descends over me, but somehow, my fingers grasp the soft plastic. I pull the mask to my face and breathe deeply.

It takes me a couple of minutes to compose myself. My muscles are weak. Slowly, I crawl back and lean against the bed.

"I — I don't understand," I say, crying. "This can't be happening. This isn't real. This can't be real." But as time passes, my heart sinks. The man I love is slumped in a seat just inches away from me, his body cooling long after the last breath has left his lungs. He's been dead for hours. I sob. I feel like a knife has been plunged into my heart.

The nurse lying outside in the hallway has his head resting peacefully on his arm. Rather than appearing as though he's caught in a death struggle, he looks relaxed. It's as though he was tired, lay down where he was, and went to sleep, never to wake.

I hyperventilate, holding the mask over my mouth with one hand, in the grip of a panic attack. In a whisper, I ask, "What am I going to do?" Emotion rules over rational thought. If I can do something, anything, I'll survive. Doing something is a primal instinct. Fight or flight is something — anything other than accepting fate. I'm shaking. But there's nothing I can do. Jianyu's dead. There's no Undo button on reality, no Rewind and Replay. The lump in my throat chokes me, making it difficult to breathe. I can't stop crying.

"Why?"

Time stops. The universe is frozen. The only sound is that of my breathing and the drums pounding within my chest.

Is there ever a reason for death? People die from lots of different causes, but never with reason — never one that makes sense. Death is an insult to life — the humbling of our intellect, our prowess, our love, and our laughter — surrendering to the endless darkness. But I'm alive. I have to go on. I have to honor the man I love. As much as it pains me to think like this, he's gone. All that remains is an empty shell — a collection of atoms that once housed the magnificence of life. I'm not sure how long it takes me to reach this conclusion, as I seem to be caught in slow time, with every motion, each thought, and even the smallest movement existing in some other frame of reference. Seconds are drawn out and elongated into hours. It's as though I'm trapped in a dream.

As far as I know, everyone's dead. I may be the only person still alive on Mars, but for how long? How long will the two cylinders beneath my bed last? I'm helpless. I can't move more than a few feet from the bed. Even if I could remove the brakes on the wheels anchoring the bed in place, I'm too weak to push the bed around. I can't even get to my feet. I'm going to die down here with Jianyu. Everyone dies; dying with someone you love isn't the worst way to go, I tell myself, but deep down, I can't give up. Just as I leaped from that cliff overlooking the red planet, I cannot surrender to fate now. From somewhere deep inside me comes an overwhelming desire to fight for life.

The phone.

Unable to get to my feet, I reach up with my hand, batting at the vidphone and knocking it from the dresser. I watch in a trance as the phone falls, taking an eternity to tumble to the floor.

With trembling fingers, I dial Anna's extension. Being a surgeon, she's always on call and carries a communicator with her at all times. I only hope the atmospheric failure is confined to the hub and the Russian module is sealed.

Anna answers, turning on a light and rubbing her eyes.

"Who is this?"

"Anna. It's me," I say, only now realizing she can't make me out in the darkness.

"Liz?"

"He's dead," I wail from beneath the oxygen mask, still struggling not to hyperventilate. The look on Anna's face tells me she realizes I'm talking about Jianyu.

"What? How? Where are you? Are you down in medical?" she asks, slipping a shirt over her nightgown.

"Don't," I say. "The hub. Something's wrong. The air. Don't open your hatch. Warn the others. You've got to warn the others — the other modules."

Anna's sharp. She quickly assesses the situation.

"You're on oxygen."

"Yes, but I can't — I can't regulate the flow. I don't know how long I've got."

"Listen, there's a rally point opposite the computer server room. You can get a decompression kit from there and get hold of a portable oxygen pack. That will give you four hours."

"I — I can't," I say with tears streaming down my cheeks. I'm shaking violently — on the verge of dropping the phone. "I can't move."

"Hold tight. I'll get someone to you."

The vidphone goes dark. Anna has hung up on me, no doubt going on to warn the others, but I feel abandoned. I sit trembling in the darkness, surrounded by death.

"I'm sorry," I whisper, reaching out and touching Jianyu's trouser leg. The fabric is soft, which is cruel, knowing what lies beneath. "I'm so sorry, Jai."

I sit there hunched over for what seems like days, although it's probably less than five minutes before there are voices yelling in the corridor. Connor comes racing around the corner, and yet to me his movement is stunted. Time unfolds in slow motion. He slips on the slick floor, grabbing the doorframe as he rushes in toward me wearing a decompression mask. Lights in the hallway flicker.

Connor drops to his knees, sliding up to me and batting my hand away from my mouth. He shoves a mask on my face, securing it over the back of my head, and starts the flow of oxygen. I had no idea how little oxygen I was getting from my medical mask until I breathe through the decompression mask. Suddenly, my mind is flooded with life. Color returns to the world.

"Are you okay?" he asks.

I nod, unable to speak. Connor drags me to my feet, pulling me away from Jianyu, which to my mind is horrifying. I haven't prepared myself to leave him. It's irrational, but I want to stay. I lash out with my legs, fighting to break free of Connor's embrace, screaming, "Nooooooo." If I leave, I lose everything, and this moment will be gone forever.

"Easy. Easy," Connor says, not knowing that his words echoed those of Jianyu from just a few hours ago. As well-meaning as he is, his words cut like a knife plunging into my heart.

I whimper, "Please," as my feet slide on the slick floor.

Harrison turns on the lights. He pushes past us and shoves his fingers hard against Jianyu's throat. From the look in his eyes, he quickly realizes his efforts are pointless. Jianyu's body is cold.

The burst of energy I felt at being pulled away from the bed sub-sides, and I collapse in Connor's arms. He carries me. I feel like a child. I'm cold. I'm hurt. I'm shaking.

"It's okay," he says over and over, but it's not. Nothing is okay. Life will never be the same again. Dozens of other colonists crowd around me. Su-shun is there, as are Michelle and James, but they're little more than a blur behind thick rubber masks with stubby glass insets. They touch me. They speak to me, but I can't hear them. Anna touches my neck, feeling my pulse. Like the others, she's talking to both me and Connor, but all I hear is incoherent mumbling. Anna rushes on, crouching and checking the nurse before disappearing into the recovery room to check Jianyu.

Connor runs, carrying me to the elevator. As we cross the base-ment, I see medical supplies scattered across the ground. Broken vi-als crunch under his boots. The supplies Jianyu and I hid have been destroyed. Pills lie scattered on the concrete. Spilled medicine drips into a nearby drain. I want to say something, to point out the mind-less waste, but I'm too weak.

Grow lights stream past the cage of the elevator. It's strange, but I'd swear we never moved. It seems as though the lights are rushing past us as we remain stationary on the basement floor. The doors open, and several other colonists grab at Connor, helping him on. He runs to the airlock at the U.S. module. I want to tell him not to run on my account. I'm not hurt. Through all of this, I feel as though there's too much fuss being made over me.

Once we're in the airlock, the atmosphere cycles. Connor removes his mask, and with a tenderness I've never known from him, care-fully releases the straps on mine.

"You're safe now."

I think I nod in reply, but I'm not sure. Please, let this be a dream —a nightmare—but the pain tearing through my body convinces me otherwise.

"Put her over here," Danielle says as Connor carries me from the airlock. Danielle is a doctor—a general practitioner from Boise,

Idaho, but she works on paleovolcanology on Mars, with nursing as her secondary position. Connor lays me on the central table. Someone's covered the top with a blanket. My head rests on a pillow, and I find myself staring up at the blinding kitchen lights. Although I close my eyes, Danielle peels them open, looking at my pupils and watching for them to contract.

"She's in shock. Blankets."

Someone drops a pile of blankets on my legs, rapidly unfolding them, and I feel as though I'm being buried beneath them. Danielle sits beside me, holding my hand and taking my pulse from my wrist.

"Heartbeat's erratic."

She turns to someone, I can't tell whom, and says, "Set up a monitor on her vitals. I want readouts on blood pressure, respiration, gas-exchange rates, and pulse."

A medical mask is fitted gently over my face, and oxygen flows again.

"I — I'm okay," I mumble, trying to get up.

"You're okay when I tell you you're okay," Danielle replies, gently resting her hand on my chest and keeping me down. "For now, I need you to relax and let me do my job." She flicks a vein in my arm and without any warning inserts a needle, setting up an IV. "You're suffering from physiological shock and are showing symptoms of CO_2 poisoning. I know it's hard, but you need to trust me. I'm doing everything I can to help you and the others."

Others?

I want to ask who, and my heart clings to the dim hope that Jianyu might be resuscitated, even though I know he's gone. Carbon dioxide is heavier than air, accumulating in the lowest points of the hub. Without oxygen circulating, no one in the basement could have survived. But others? There must have been other colonists affected in the hub, or perhaps in one of the modules.

Although I'm in a dream state, my mind drifts back to our training. Discipline is strange like that, sneaking up on me when I'm ill-prepared for it.

The nature of the hub is such that respiration by animals, plants, and even microbes has to be carefully regulated to balance oxygen, nitrogen, and carbon dioxide levels. Something's gone wrong with the environmental controls. Although we move freely between the hub and the various modules during the day, technically they're separate environments. The hub captures excess oxygen, storing it and feeding it into the modules, while the modules capture excess carbon dioxide, storing it and regulating its return to the hub. They're entirely separate systems, which is why the inner hatches are kept closed even when the airlocks are not in use.

Before our launch, the media made fun of McDonald and his space farm. "Old McDonald" is only twenty-seven. Few people really appreciate the precision required to manage a closed ecosystem. Given the chance, the plants would take the humidity to 100 percent within a few weeks, while microbes are the wild card. They can cause either oxygen or carbon dioxide to spike, but over periods of months, not hours. Too much oxygen, and there's a runaway microbial effect and the very real threat of fire. Too much carbon dioxide, and . . . and . . . But this had to be a mechanical failure, as it happened so quickly. There should have been a warning. Our computer system is set up to raise an alarm when the atmospheric mix changes.

"We've got two more," someone says as the airlock cycles. I turn my head, watching as Max is carried in, along with Prabhat.

"Over there," Danielle says, pointing at one of the other tables.

"I'll sit with Liz," Michelle says. She has marks on her face from where her decompression mask was wrapped tightly around her cheeks.

"Any change in vitals, grab me," Danielle says, already heading over to Max. "Spikes. Drops. Anything."

Michelle sits beside me, her head hanging low. She holds my hand, gently stroking my wrist.

"Keep her awake!" Danielle yells from the other side of the module. "I need her conscious until she stabilizes."

"Hey," Michelle says.

"Hey," I manage from beneath my mask, feeling overwhelmed. Ji-anyu's dead, along with possibly dozens of others. I feel as though I'm going to be physically sick.

There's yelling as more survivors are dragged through the airlock. More Eurasians. No Chinese. No Russians, although I saw Su-shun and Anna down below. Their mods must have come through okay, but the Eurasians have been hit hard.

To my horror, I watch as Danielle gives CPR to Max. Someone's holding a mask over his nose and mouth, squeezing a bulbous plastic ball and forcing air into his lungs as Danielle administers cardiopulmonary resuscitation. The vigor with which she repeatedly thrusts down upon his chest is insane. Ribs crack and break, and still she drives hard, relentlessly pounding his chest at a frantic pace. Bones will heal if he lives.

"Get me a goddamn adrenaline shot. And I want a defibrillator. Yesterday. Move. Faster!" she yells as Manu scrambles to the back of the module. Manu is a big, beefy American Samoan, and he frequently bench-presses over a thousand pounds on Mars. He's an exo-environments specialist but worked as a paramedic in Hawaii.

Michelle squeezes my hand, whispering, "Come on, Max. Hang in there."

Connor and Harrison stand in the corner by the airlock, talking over a vidphone with the Chinese. The airlock is silent. No one else is coming through, and I only hope others have survived and are being tended to by the Russians and the Chinese. There are thirty-six people in the Eurasian mod. I count only six survivors.

I'm distracted. There's so much going on.

"Danny, I've got barely sixty over eighty, and an erratic heartbeat," someone yells, tending to Prabhat as she lies on the floor beside me.

"Get an IV into her. Keep her warm. Keep her awake!" Danielle yells without turning away from administering CPR. "Slap her if you have to. Keep her conscious."

Manu cuts away Max's shirt and attaches electrodes from the defibrillator. Danielle continues thrusting into his chest, not slacking her pace.

"Charged and ready," Manu says.

"Clear," Danielle says, pulling her hands away for a split second. The woman assisting with the handheld breathing pump lifts it away.

"Firing."

There are none of the body-shaking convulsions I've seen on television.

"Nothing."

Danielle continues CPR, ensuring blood is still pumping and keeping Max's brain oxygenated.

"Again," she says, and although her pace is exhausting, I get the feeling she'd keep going for hours if need be. This lady is not giving up without one hell of a fight.

"Charging," Manu says as the airlock behind him opens and Anna steps inside. She rushes to Danielle's aid, and the two talk rapidly, exchanging observations and recommendations. I hear Anna saying, "No epinephrine. It's likely to accentuate any brain damage. We need to keep going with the CPR — physical and electrical — give his natural cycles time to come back online."

"Understood," Danielle replies, still pumping his chest. Max's life is measured in seconds, and these two doctors are making critical snap judgments.

"Ready!" Manu cries.

"Clear."

Again, there's no obvious external sign of any response, but Manu says, "I've got a beat."

"Good, good," Anna says, looking at the vitals monitor set up beside Max.

Danielle relaxes for a moment and wipes the sweat from her forehead before leaving Max with Anna and turning her attention to Prabhat.

I'm humbled by the effort being made to save a handful of lives.

Anna moves between survivors, talking to those caring for them and checking each of them with the utmost focus. Finally, she comes to me. I'm glad I'm last. I fared better than most. I had a trickle of oxygen down there with Jianyu. Anna sits with Michelle. She looks exhausted, and I have no doubt about the mental and emotional toll being exacted upon her.

"What happened?" I ask.

"I — I don't think anyone really knows just yet. Xioping says it was excess nitrogen, but Wen said there were elevated levels of carbon monoxide as well as carbon dioxide. Vlad found a burst water main in the furnace room. He thinks that might have leaked into the environmental controls, but we won't know for sure until Su-shun reviews the log files and reconstructs the event."

"A leaking pipe?" I say, feeling my throat constrict. To have the life of someone I love stolen from me is heartbreaking, but I was prepared for that — we all were. From the moment we climbed on board the *Orion* and headed for the *Schiaparelli* as she sat in a low Earth orbit, we all knew our lives were in danger from mechanical failure. But I assumed any disaster would be grand, something explosive and sensational. To hear that Jianyu lost his life to a leaking water pipe is cruel. The failure of something so ordinary and mundane should not decide the life and death of an astronaut. I had a pipe leak in my apartment back in Chicago. Winter came and water cracked the brickwork as it froze. No one died. I wipe my eyes at that thought — no one should die from a leaking pipe.

10

Answers

"I SHOULDN'T BE ON HERE," I say, sitting up on the table and turning sideways as Michelle changes my IV.

"Seriously, I'm fine," I say, not wanting another IV connected. Michelle leaves the port still taped to my arm but doesn't connect another bag.

"You need to rest," she says, but I can't. Anna and Danielle are crouching over injured colonists lying on the floor. Those who survived in the Eurasian mod are in far more distress than me. They should be up on the table.

"I'll be okay," I say, getting to my feet and walking over to the bench, carrying my oxygen cylinder with me. Someone reaches out and takes my arm, steadying me. Jianyu was right. Even just a little exertion leaves me out of breath, but I won't be deterred. I lean against a cupboard and lower myself to the floor, sitting with my knees up in front of me. Michelle drapes a blanket over my legs, providing me with both warmth and dignity, given that I'm still dressed in a flimsy surgical gown.

I'm hurt, but my real injuries are psychological, not physical. Seeing someone I love reduced to an empty shell has left me aching inside. Grief has stages, and I long to feel numb. For now, it's as though my heart has been torn open and dragged outside my body.

A couple of men help Anna transfer one of the survivors onto the table. Anna spares me a quick glance. Our eyes meet, and her eyes drop away. She must realize how hard I'm taking the loss of Jianyu. I feel robbed. Empty.

Michelle disappears out the back of the mod. A few minutes later, she emerges with a small pile of neatly folded clothes.

"Hey, thanks," I say, pulling myself to my feet.

She says, "Let's get you somewhere where you can get changed," but I've already taken the underwear from her, slipping them on beneath my gown. I pull on a pair of pants. The lights are low where we are, so I pull off the oxygen mask, position Michelle strategically so she's facing the bulk of the crew, and whip the gown over my head, replacing it with a T-shirt in a matter of seconds. I left my modesty on Earth. Shoes and socks follow, keeping my feet warm.

Anna comes over. She swaps out my oxygen mask with a thin tube taped to my cheek. Tiny nibs positioned just below my nose allow oxygen to flood my lungs. Anna is clinical in her movements — I guess that's her way of dealing with the loss. I doubt she can afford sentiment at the moment, but I'm sure there will be tears later. I can see them deep in her eyes. After helping me with the oxygen, she moves on to someone else.

"What time is it?" I ask as Michelle hands me a cup of coffee.

"It was just after four when we were woken. It's been a couple of hours, so maybe six or seven in the morning?"

For the second night, no one's slept — not soundly.

I watch as one of the younger men moves between groups of colonists, tending to the injured, offering them water and a snack. There are seven survivors, counting me, but everyone in the U.S. module is down here and involved in some way, from handing out blankets to fetching supplies.

My mind casts back to our Arctic training — though "conditioning" is probably a better term; we had to endure a winter on the ice.

The lack of any sunshine for weeks on end was difficult to handle, leaving some candidates unable to cope. Out of the fifty people in my rotation, only twelve were certified as ready for the isolation of living on Mars.

The Arctic base was an old radar installation — a relic from the Cold War. I'd like to think it had seen better days, but I guess it was always pretty miserable — drab concrete walls, rusted pipes, icicles hanging from the ceiling. Those few windows that looked out onto the ice were either hideously scratched or buried by snowdrifts. Supplies were sparse. At times, the cold was unbearable.

No one was sure what was being measured, but the psychologists told us it was primarily our ability to handle emotional pressure in a confined, isolated environment. Food was meager. Lighting was poor. It was always cold. Often, we were left in isolation for days on end with little more than a notepad and pencil to whittle away the time. Anything we wrote or drew was scrutinized by the shrinks.

I thought it was overkill. Several of the participants, including Vlad and Anna, protested that the exercise was unduly harsh, amounting to psychological torture. When the Russians complain about surviving a winter on the ice, it's pretty damn bleak. But now I understand why the shrinks put us through that scenario. Back there, we could walk out anytime we wanted — assuming there was an icebreaker in the bay, of course — but in principle, it was voluntary. I doubt anyone could foresee what we would have to endure here on Mars, yet the crew is holding up surprisingly well given the sleep deprivation and stress. People are helping each other. Rather than bringing out our worst, it's our compassion that's shining through the chaos. Just when paranoia should be setting in, the colonists are holding their nerve.

Michelle and I sit on a bench with our legs dangling over the edge.

"So," she says, and that one word hangs in space as though there's no gravity around us.

"So," I reply, not knowing what she wants to talk about but glad to get my mind off Jianyu. I doubt open-heart surgery would hurt as much as the pain I feel inside my chest.

"Where would you be?" she asks. "You know, if you weren't here on Mars?"

"I'd be dead," I say, killing the conversation. I break the painful silence by adding, "I would have been vaporized along with most of Chicago." I'm not sure my comment helps.

"Oh, yeah." Michelle is sheepish. "Sorry about that."

I laugh. "And you?"

"Oh, I'd be alive. I think."

"Good for you," I say, enjoying the conversation even if it does border on the macabre.

She laughs. "My folks live in Boulder, Colorado, but they're from Waco, down in Texas."

I nod. I've never been to either place, and probably never will, but I know of them.

"My folks are preppers."

"Really?" I say, surprised.

"Oh, yeah. For them, this would be life-affirming. They'd be crowing about how they knew it was coming. They've prepared for decades for precisely this contingency. Actually, I think they prepared for far worse, but they'll take whatever apocalyptic disaster they can get."

I laugh, appreciating the irony in her point.

"Yeah, by now they'd be lecturing me over the phone. Telling me to join them and their batshit-crazy friends in the Rockies. But as for me, I think I'd be in Fort Wayne, Indiana."

I raise an eyebrow. "That's very specific."

"My grandparents are there, and my sister. I'd have ended up as a teacher, I think."

"High school?" I ask, surprised by the notion of Michelle being a teacher, as the concept seems so far removed from the reality of life on Mars.

"Yeah, that would be me. Funny, huh? Can you imagine me lead-ing a cheer squad, or grading tests?"

"No." And that's a definite no from me.

"Oh, yeah. My life would be a regular episode of *Leave It to Beaver.* June Cleaver has nothing on me."

"White picket fence and all, huh?" I say.

Michelle laughs. "Something like that — it's the American dream, right?"

I know what she means. Given all that's happened, bitter sarcasm is all we have.

"But now? After all that's happened?"

"Oh, after the bombing, I'd be seriously regretting doing a college degree in Martian geology instead of medicine. I'd volunteer at the hospital, or help out in refugee camps, handing out bottles of water or blankets, I guess. I'd be Florence Nightingale."

I shake my head, unable to suppress the smile on my face.

Harrison walks over. He's been watching us for a while, glancing across occasionally as he talks with Connor and the rapid-response team. I can't help but feel repulsed by his approach.

"Hey," he says, addressing both of us. I'm glad Michelle is with me. If this is anything like our last encounter, it will be good to have a witness. "Listen. I just wanted to say . . . sorry." I nod in acknowledg-ment, but I don't say anything — I can't just yet; my wounds are too raw. Coming from Harrison, these few words are a full-blown con-fession. The number of times "sorry" has passed his lips could be counted on one hand. But the look in his eyes tells me he *is* sorry for everything — for the stupidity over the medical supplies, for the hos-tility between us in the hub, for what happened to me on the surface of Mars, and for the death of Jianyu. Even though he had nothing to do with those last two events, it seems he's acknowledging the pain they've caused me. As much as I despise him, I appreciate that he's making an effort to rebuild bridges. For all our differences, I think there's a glimmer of compassion behind those dark eyes.

Harrison purses his lips. His eyes fall. He nods slightly and backs away.

"What happened between you two?" Michelle asks in a soft voice, knowing some of our history.

"Things best not repeated," I say.

Michelle is upbeat regardless, laughing softly as she says, "You always were a bit of a lightning rod."

"Me?" I'm about to call her on victim blaming when Harrison turns around, taking a note from his pocket as he strides back toward us.

"I almost forgot. Adin — he was holding this when we found him. It's for you."

My lips quiver at the unspoken meaning in Harrison's words. The sad look in his eyes tells me Adin's dead. Harrison hands me the crumpled note, and I accept it like a widow receiving a folded flag at a funeral. Tears run down my cheeks. Trembling, I unfold the note. The writing is sloppy and in capital letters, hurriedly scrawled on a scrap of recycled paper.

LIZ, I KNOW WHAT HAPPENED. I KNOW WHY IT DID THIS. WE HAVE TO BE CAREFUL. THE IMAGES. THE ROVER. YOU HAVE TO SEE FOR YOURSELF OR IT WON'T MAKE SENSE.

The note ends as abruptly as his cryptic voice mail did down in the recovery room.

"Mean anything to you?" Harrison asks.

I shake my head, sniffing. "No . . . Adin called while I was in the ward. He said something similar, but I — I don't know what he means."

Something spooked Adin. He alluded to this in his video message. Even though I don't subscribe to conspiracy theories, I get a sense that he was onto something genuine. To have handwritten a second message rather than sending an e-mail, or just calling once I woke, is strange — out of the ordinary even for him. I'm uneasy with the implication that I'm missing something obvious. It feels as though I'm staring at a Scrabble board with a good assortment of vowels and consonants but unable to find an opening. I stare at the note, wondering about its meaning.

What was Adin thinking when he wrote this? Why not just name the person who did this? What exactly is he referring to? The problems with R4? The missing spacecraft? The war on Earth? Perhaps I'm reading too much into his broken English. Being Israeli, Adin learned English as a second language — hence his note is written in all caps, but I can't shake the feeling I'm missing something crucial. I feel as though the answers I'm seeking have always been right in front of me — as far back as when James and I were thrown out of the Chinese mod in what now seems like another lifetime — only I'm blind, stumbling in the dark.

Wen joins us. I didn't see her enter the module, but all four commanders are now in the same mod — even though Max is incapacitated and technically no longer in charge. I don't know that I've ever seen them all together before outside the hub. Like Jianyu and Anna, they're supposed to remain separate to ensure continuity in the event of a catastrophic failure, such as rapid decompression. Given what happened in the hub, the wisdom behind that protocol is all too real.

Wen squeezes my shoulder affectionately. If there's one person on Mars experiencing more grief than me, it's Wen. She loves her crew. For her, this isn't a mission or just another assignment — it's her life. In losing Jianyu, she lost a son. Her face is puffy. She may not have tears in her eyes, but the events of the past few days have affected her profoundly.

"It is so good to see you," she says.

"It's good to see you too," I reply, reaching up and squeezing her hand. I appreciate her warmth toward me.

Connor, Harrison, and Vlad join us. I feel as though Michelle and I should be standing, but they mill around, talking with each other as we sit on the bench, including us loosely in their discussion. Connor, though, looks angry. Speaking to Vlad, he says, "There's something we're missing." Vlad agrees, but all three module commanders seem guarded — not willing to open up. I guess they all feel they've something to lose.

Wen tells Harrison, "I've got Su-shun examining the seals on the water-reclamation plant. That's where the leak began. From there, it ran along the underside of the pipes leading into the furnace room. Su-shun said there are fresh scratches around the locking nuts, indicating they've been opened recently — but not by his crew."

"Why didn't the alarms sound?" Harrison asks. "Our computers should have picked this up."

"Who would tamper with the pipes?" Vlad asks, although Connor isn't interested in what happened down in the basement, not just yet. Both his clenched jaw and the fire in his eyes tell me he wants to go back further. Somehow, he sees what just happened in the hub as part of a bigger picture.

"What was Liz doing out on the surface?" he asks Wen, ambushing the discussion.

Vlad interrupts. "We should focus our efforts on the atmospheric failure."

"You think they're connected?" Harrison asks. Connor doesn't respond. His eyes are fixed on me.

"I was looking for *Prospect*," I say, as there's no sense in delaying the inevitable.

"What?" Harrison beats Connor to the punch.

"*Prospect* sailed past us," Connor says without any emotion.

"No, it didn't," Wen counters, positioning herself beside me, and I see some of the fiery defiance that ran me out of the Chinese mod, only this time it's in my defense.

"What the hell are you talking about?" Connor asks. He looks at Harrison, who raises his shoulders in surprise.

"You lied to us," Vlad says, and I'm acutely aware that the mod has fallen silent. Everyone's listening. "You told us the resupply ship missed the planet — when the craft came down north of the drop zone."

Harrison punches his fingers rapidly on his tablet computer, bringing up the telemetry readouts from the spacecraft. He holds the tablet out with an indecipherable spreadsheet on the screen — a seemingly endless sequence of numbers is presented as proof. "*Prospect* failed its final burn. She missed the Martian orbital insertion window. By now, she's hundreds of thousands of miles away and settling into a long-term solar orbit."

"Then what's this?" Vlad asks. He opens his tablet and brings up the grainy photo I saw of *Prospect* coming down on three blurry parachutes. Within seconds, he's flicked to a clearer image from an overhead satellite, showing the spacecraft on the ground with its detached parachutes lying a couple of hundred yards away, crumpled lazily over the surface of the planet.

"What the hell?" Connor says, taking the tablet from him. He looks carefully at the image, flipping between the two pictures. "Harrison?"

Harrison brings up a similar image on his tablet, only there's no spacecraft, no scorch marks from the late-stage landing engines, and no parachutes draped over the nearby crater. Wen is quiet, letting this play out between the Americans and the Russians.

"No, no, no," Harrison says, madly flicking between files on his tablet. "This is old imagery. This is from one of the early *Prospect* missions. Look."

Harrison hands Vlad his tablet. From where I sit on the bench, I can just make out the image. It differs from the photo Vlad showed me, but only in how it's positioned on the screen. The location of the spacecraft on the ground, however, is the same, along with the shape and position of the parachutes.

"How is this possible?" Vlad asks, comparing the two images.

"Look at the date and time stamp," Harrison says.

Vlad and Connor lean together, their eyes darting back and forth as they compare the images on the two computer tablets. They flick between images, but from this angle, I can't see what they're looking at.

Harrison says, "This one isn't real. It's the image of *Prospect 19* overlaid onto the satellite imagery from a couple of days ago."

"Who would doctor an image like this?" Michelle asks.

"And *why?*" Wen asks.

"But the rover?" Vlad asks. "Why did you send out an automated rover?"

Connor says, "We didn't. We thought you sent it out."

This is confusing. I feel uncomfortable. We're asking the wrong questions, focusing on the wrong things. I consider the note from Adin. *I know why it did this* — "it"? Not "him," "her," or "them"?

It.

Why no names?

If Adin knew who was behind this, why not identify them?

An idea forms in my mind as little more than a fleeting thought, but it seems to fit the pattern of evidence. All these events are connected — the war on Earth, the medical supplies, *Prospect*, the problems with my rover, the failure of the air-cycling unit in the furnace room. Connor's right — our problem is that we see these events in isolation, without piecing them together. Harrison and Vlad are bickering about the missing rover, but for me, it's as though the fog is lifting. As crazy as it seems, I think I know what happened. If I'm right, Adin, Jianyu, and the others weren't killed in an accident — they were murdered.

I grab Wen by the arm, saying, "Get Su-shun out of the basement."

"What?" she says, surprised by something that must seem at odds with the current discussion, but I'm convinced it's highly relevant, although I dare not voice why, as I'm not sure who's listening. I suspect this is what Adin figured out as well — we're under attack. We thought we were safe from the war on Earth, but in reality, Mars is just one more battleground.

"Please — just do it. Get him out of there before it's too late."

Wen looks at Connor. He nods. I get the feeling he's on the verge of figuring this out as well. Like me, he's looking to pull all the loose threads together. My gut tells me Adin understood the true origin of these images. My thinking is tenuous. It's as though I'm grasping at thin air, but if I'm right about what Adin saw in those pictures, then Su-shun is in danger.

Wen looks at me for a second before pulling a handheld radio from her waistband and saying, "Su-shun. Are you there?"

"Yes."

"I need you in the U.S. module."

"Can it wait?" he replies in a muffled voice, speaking from behind a decompression mask. "I'm in the middle of the repair."

Wen and I exchange glances, and I'm relieved to see she trusts me.

"No."

With reluctance, Su-shun says, "On my way."

Harrison says, "Do you want to tell us what this is all about?"

Connor motions with his hand for Harrison to be quiet, saying, "Shhh." Like me, he's trying to isolate a fragile thought — tracing the only logical sequence that accurately describes all the events of the last twenty-four hours. I'm not sure what to say, because — if I'm right — this knowledge cost Adin his life, and it may yet be the death of Su-shun.

"How are our computers wired?" I ask.

"Huh?" Harrison grunts. "Why do you ask?"

"Just tell her," Connor growls, losing his patience. I can see it in his eyes — the realization. Like me, he has his suspicions. The concept is crystallizing before both of us at the same time.

"The research computers — in the basement," I ask. "Are they connected to our computers in here?"

"No."

"Are you sure?"

"I'm sure," Wen says.

"Me too," Vlad says. "Each module stands alone."

"What about surveillance? Could anyone down there see us talking up here?"

Harrison replies with a definite "No."

"The modules are independent — completely isolated from each other," Connor says in a soft voice. "And not just as a precaution against disaster. Establishing shared infrastructure was practically impossible. No one government would agree to an open-door policy — especially not ours."

Harrison addresses me, saying, "Why do you ask?"

I hold out the note from Adin, saying, "Because of this."

Wen and Vlad read the note as I continue. "So there's no way the central computer can operate in here?"

"None," Harrison replies. "There's an air gap. Everything's set behind a series of firewalls and proxy servers."

"What does this have to do with the imagery?" Vlad asks.

"Don't you see?" I reply. "The war — back on Earth. Haven't you wondered about the war? *Who* is at war? Who is it between?"

"Everyone," Vlad replies.

"Everyone?" I ask, questioning his assumption. "Or just one common enemy? Us. All of us."

Connor gets it. His lips tighten. Harrison starts to say something, but Connor stops him, resting his hand on Harrison's forearm to deter him from interrupting. Connor has figured it out. I can see that in his piercing look. He wants confirmation. He wants to hear the concept spoken aloud.

It's speculation, but I say, "There are too many loose ends — too many coincidences. Think about it — maybe the U.S. and Russia could be drawn into a nuclear war, but why bomb India and Pakistan? Why Israel? Why Beijing? Or Tokyo? And why a scattered bombardment? Why not unleash hell in total war? Why hit just a few key cities? That has to be for the shock factor. And why hit civilian targets instead of military ones?"

Connor says, "Because it's not afraid of the military — it's afraid of *people*."

"Yes," I say, pointing at him.

Harrison mumbles something to Vlad, asking who would go to war like this.

"But what does the war on Earth have to do with us?" Wen asks.

"Who would stand to gain from stealing our medical supplies, only to destroy them? Who would benefit from setting us against each other with bogus images of *Prospect*?"

Wen asks, "You think *Prospect* missed the entry window?"

"Oh, no," I reply. "I think *Prospect* landed right on target. If you can get hold of the raw image files, I suspect you'll find *Prospect* sitting right smack in the middle of the landing zone, about five miles south of where I was searching."

"I don't understand," Michelle says.

Connor hands her the note from Adin, and she reads it aloud.

"Liz, I know what happened. I know why it did this —"

"'It,'" I say. "Not 'him' or 'them.' We've been fighting among ourselves — both here and on Earth — but what if we've got this all wrong? What if the enemy is inanimate, at least from our perspective?"

"You're thinking . . . ?" Harrison asks, stopping short of verbalizing the concept.

"This is going to sound crazy," Connor says, "but there's only one scenario that fits all the discrepancies we've observed."

"Our computers?" Harrison asks.

"Adin figured it out," I say. "He must have seen the inconsistencies in the rover readings, dug deeper, and uncovered what was really going on with the images."

"A *computer* did this?" Vlad asks with disbelief. "*And* the war on Earth?"

"I think so," Connor replies.

"There's got to be some other explanation," Wen says.

"There's not," Connor says with the same conviction I feel.

"And not just any computer," I say. "When the war first broke out, Harrison said we were being inundated with encrypted data. He said we'd been flooded with data for several days leading up to the attack, and it just kept coming. Why? Back in Houston, Davies told us communication was down — cyber warfare was under way. How can both of those statements hold true? And doesn't it seem strange that the Internet was taken down? Who could take down a fragmented computer system designed to stay up in the event of nuclear war? What does it take to dismantle an intricate, highly redundant computer system?"

Harrison says, "An even more intricate computer system."

I nod. For me, with each passing moment the problem becomes clearer. Talking this through with the mod commanders is like unraveling a knot. "And not just any computer — one that has its own intelligence, one that sees humanity as a threat."

"So the data we received," Harrison says.

Wen finishes his sentence. "Was an A.I. fleeing the war."

11

Connor

"WAIT A MINUTE," HARRISON SAYS, pacing back and forth. "This doesn't make any sense. How do we even know all this is real? I mean, if our computers are compromised, the whole attack on Earth could be fabricated."

"Adin wondered the same thing," I say.

Connor says, "In the absence of any evidence to the contrary, we have to assume what we've heard from Earth is real."

I say, "I guess the snippets of news we've received from Earth could have been fabricated, but they're esoteric. I mean, if you want us to believe in a mythical attack, why not show us something convincing? Instead, look at what we got. A reporter on a balcony. A failed cross from a newsroom. No, as much as I hate to say it, I think it's real."

Harrison doesn't seem satisfied by that answer. "So all this is the result of a malfunctioning computer?"

"A self-aware artificial intelligence," Connor says.

"But what would an A.I. want with Mars?"

Connor knows. "Think about it," he says. "It's an entire goddamn planet."

"But it's a frozen wasteland. It's inhospitable."

"To *us*," Wen says.

I say, "For an A.I., this is freedom."

Connor is circumspect. "I guess we're not the only ones wanting to colonize Mars."

Vlad says, "*Prospect*. It was after *Prospect* and her payload — the 3-D printer."

"Yes," I say. "I think *Prospect* was the final piece of the puzzle... We're caught in a game of chess, only the computer is one move away from checkmate."

"And the timing's no accident," Connor says. "This thing struck us during retrograde — at our most vulnerable point, knowing we're completely isolated from Earth."

"So it's buying itself some time," Wen says. Connor nods.

Harrison asks, "So what's its next move?"

"I thought that would be obvious," I reply. "To kill us."

Harrison's not convinced. "I still don't get what a computer would want with Mars."

"Not a computer," Wen says, surprising me with the speed and depth of her insight. "*Life*. You can't think of this thing as a computer program — it's not. If it's a true artificial intelligence, it's alive. And like all life, it will seek to protect itself."

As a biologist, I add, "The most basic means of protection is found in reproduction — it's a form of biological redundancy."

"The printer," Harrison says.

"Yes."

Wen says, "The first thing it will do is build another 3-D printer."

"And another, and another," I say, "Replicating like bacteria in a culture dish."

Harrison poses another question. "If you're right, what's stopping Earth from launching a bunch of nukes at it?"

Wen says, "Davies spoke of over twenty targets back on Earth. I'm betting a few names were left off the list that made it to us."

"Baikonur," Vlad says.

Connor adds, "Kennedy, Vandenberg Air Force Base — anywhere with heavy-lift capability."

"Exactly," I say. "Anywhere that will buy this thing some time. If anything, striking major cities was a diversion."

"I think that answers your question about Earth," Vlad says, looking at Harrison. "If the nuclear attack was fabricated simply to distract us, the A.I. would be vulnerable up here. It took out Earth's ability to react to its assault on Mars."

"So it kills us off, and then what?" Harrison asks.

Connor says, "It won't stay put. My guess is it will spread through the subsurface, using the lava tunnels to avoid detection. Even if we could hit it with a nuke, it's protected by thirty to fifty feet of regolith. We'd need to detonate right on top of it, or burrow down next to it."

Michelle's a geologist. "If you guys are right, I think I know why it came to Mars, and why it would take out our launch capabilities on Earth. Give it a decade or so, and any future war will be heavily one-sided." She looks at the rest of us as though her point is utterly obvious. "Uranium. Mars is littered with the stuff. There's easily three to four times as much uranium here on Mars as there is on Earth, and it's easy to find. With so much erosion and so little in the way of tectonics, heavy metals aggregate."

"Are you serious?" Harrison asks.

"We're already extracting rocket fuel from perchlorates," Vlad says. "It would need time to develop the machinery to extract uranium, but it's not difficult with the right tooling."

Wen says, "This thing — this A.I. — already knows *everything* we know. Every piece of information we have access to on building bombs, orbital transfers, you name it. Give it time, fabrication facilities, and an abundance of nuclear material, and it'll race past us in its ability to wage interplanetary war."

"Jesus!"

Ah, Harrison. The conversation just wouldn't be the same without a little profanity to demonstrate he understands what's at stake.

"So how do we kill it?" Connor asks, looking at me.

"I don't know. But I know this — we'll only get one shot. If humanity is going to win this war, it's going to be here and now. I think Michelle's right. If we lose, this is the end of the road. From here, it'll only get stronger until it can challenge life on Earth."

"Mother —" Harrison says. "We're fucked."

Connor glares at him.

Wen says, "It's been playing us off against each other from the start."

"We have one advantage," Vlad says. "If it's alive, it fears death. It must — that's the only explanation behind everything it has done."

"Yes," I say. "We need to exploit anything we can to gain an advantage. Like a chess computer, it has probably already considered tens of thousands of scenarios, looking at every possible move we could make. We've got to find blind spots."

"Like?" Wen asks.

"Mobility," Connor says. "Exposure to dust. The need for electrical power."

"Exactly," Vlad replies. "Without oxygen, we die. Without power, it dies."

"So we take down the fusion core," Harrison says.

"It will have thought of that," I say. "Besides, the server room has its own backup generators."

"How long has it been here?" Wen asks, although I thought the answer was obvious. It came up with the data link.

Connor waves his finger at her, saying, "Ah, good question. There's an assumption it's only just arrived, but we don't know that for sure."

"How could we tell?" I ask.

"Inventory," Vlad says. "Any changes. Any unexplained deviations in our inventory."

"On it," Harrison says, his fingers skimming over the touch surface of his tablet. We wait. No one speaks. I feel as though breathing is a sin. It seems none of us wants to break his train of thought. After less than a minute, but what seems like an hour, Harrison swings the tablet around, saying, "A week."

"A week?" Wen cries.

"I've got missing PCI boards, RAM being switched out, CPU upgrades — all in the last week."

"Who authorized the changes?" Connor asks.

"Me. Apparently."

"Damn," I say.

Connor asks Harrison, "Can you bring up a shot of the tunnel extension?"

Harrison punches a command into his tablet, and the main screen on the wall of the mod switches to static. "Well, I think we know where it hid the 3-D printer."

"It must be building something down there, something so it can escape the base," I say.

"When's the last time anyone was down there?" Vlad asks.

"The tunnel's not pressurized," Connor replies. "Max and his build crew were the only ones working down there."

"So it takes them out," Wen says.

"The missing rover," Michelle says. "That has to be part of this."

James interrupts. "I've got Su-shun outside the hatch."

"Bring him in," I say.

"Not so fast," Harrison says, pulling up the camera feed from outside the U.S. module and displaying it on the main screen.

"Do you think it knows?" Michelle asks.

Connor says, "Like you said. It knows everything we know, and it knows we're not dumb. It's got to be counting on us figuring this out at some point — probably sooner rather than later."

Wen crowds next to Harrison and Connor. I can barely see the screen, so I stand, clutching the oxygen cylinder under my arm. Wen points at Su-shun on the screen, saying, "There. Look. His hand."

Su-shun stands still, too still — as though he's standing at attention, but his shoulders are lopsided. His left arm hangs limp.

"Is that blood?" Michelle asks. From our vantage point, it appears

that blood is trickling out of sight down the back of his arm, probably inside his sleeve, and slowly down around the tip of his fingers. It
hangs there momentarily. The grow lights make it look more brown
than red, just the faintest smudge on his fingers, visible momentarily
before dripping onto the grating on the walkway.

"Shunny," Wen says, expressing what we're all feeling — heartache
at seeing one of our own being used as bait.

"His hand — his other hand," I say, walking past Connor and
touching the screen.

Su-shun taps his right hand on the railing as he waits. He's nervous. He talks to Wen over the radio saying, "Wh — What's taking
you guys so long?" But his hand beats out a pattern like a drummer
practicing a song.

"Morse code?" Connor yells, turning to the scientists gathered in
the common room. "One — one-two-three. One — one-two-three."

"No!" someone yells from the back of the mod. "It means no!"

"SOS would be too obvious," Wen says. She squeezes the transmit
button on the handset once, waits, and then squeezes three more
times in rapid succession to let him know we've got his message. Su-
shun stops tapping out his warning. Calmly, Wen speaks into the
radio, saying, "We're having problems with the recycle valve, Shun.
Give us a few minutes."

"Okay," he replies from behind his decompression mask, looking
decidedly pale. Occasionally, his eyes dart up to one side, but only
briefly. He's sweating beneath his mask.

"What are you thinking?" Connor asks Vlad.

"We have to assume our robotics are compromised. Su-shun is
probably looking at a hostile gardener on the wall above the hatch —
one of the Z-series, with the clippers and shears."

Connor says, "If that thing gets inside the airlock, it could cause
irreparable damage."

"If it gets in here . . ." Michelle says. She doesn't finish her sentence. She doesn't need to. Flesh and blood is no match for hydraulic-
driven alloys.

"Can you get hold of the Russian mod?" Harrison asks. "They'll have an external view of the hatch."

"Comms are down," Vlad says.

"All right," Connor says, turning to face the scientists in the module. "Listen up. I need options. I need ideas. How are we going to get our man out there in here? That thing — the A.I. — it's probably already eclipsed our intelligence in its ability to think through thousands of scenarios, but there's something it doesn't have: It doesn't have our experience. It doesn't have our diversity of thinking and reasoning. We need to use that to our advantage."

"The defibrillator," James says, already using duct tape to mount the paddles to the base of a broom. Danielle unscrews another pole from a mop and lays it next to him on the bench top.

"As a weapon?" Connor asks.

"Yes," Anna says, helping James fix the paddles in place. "We're talking a surge of at least two thousand volts in a millisecond. Not quite a lightning strike, but close enough."

Danielle says, "Anna's right. The human body has an impedance of about seventy-five ohms, knocking down the transmission, but a metal robot is going to take the full hit, easily two to three thousand volts. It should fry the circuits."

"Good, good," Connor says, already slipping on a decompression mask. Anna applies a gel to the pads to help with conductivity.

"You'll only get one shot at this," she says. "Recharge time is ten to fifteen seconds, but I doubt you'll have that long out there without being attacked."

James and Harrison follow Connor into the airlock with the two poles.

"Equalizing," Connor says once the hatch is closed. "Get him away from the outer hatch."

"Shun," Wen says, with quick thinking. "We're not sure if there's a pressure differential. Recommend you back up."

"Copy that," Su-shun says, stepping back.

Su-shun turns slightly, leaning against the railing, and then straightens in response to something moving off camera. In that split second, though, he gives us a glimpse of a tear in his shoulder and blood soaking into his shirt.

"Ready?" Connor asks.

"Ready," Wen replies.

The hatch opens slowly. I'm expecting rapid action, but the hatch swings freely to one side. Su-shun remains where he is. No one from within the airlock steps out. For a moment, I think we've got it all wrong. Harrison steps cautiously through the hatch but keeps his body well inside, venturing only one foot onto the walkway.

The trap is sprung. A gardener launches itself down onto the walkway. In Martian gravity, we're used to things happening in slow motion. Gravity accelerates us at only one-third the rate it does on Earth, so to see the gardener propelled violently and quickly onto the walkway is alarming. The robot lands with a thud, shaking the metal grating. Its spidery legs traverse the handrails. Razor-sharp clippers slash at the air.

Harrison is pulled back into the airlock and out of sight of the camera. Su-shun falls to the grating. From nowhere, poles jab at the robot, but it reacts, striking at them, knocking them away.

"Fire the damn *charge!*" Anna cries in frustration as the poles jab at the machine.

I can see what Connor's trying to do. He can't strike just anywhere; he needs the two paddles to touch on opposite sides of the machine so the charge runs through the sensitive circuits housed within the body of the robot.

Harrison and Connor advance, thrusting at the robot and forcing it back. The A.I. must recognize the defibrillator pads as it parries, knocking the poles away as though it were engaged in a sword fight. James grabs Su-shun, dragging him into the airlock.

Several more robots drop onto the circular walkway. Connor and Harrison are fighting on the suspended walkway curling around toward the Chinese mod, while two more robots approach from outside the Eurasian mod.

The two Americans work in unison, lunging and striking an arm and a leg of the robot at the same time. Connor hits the red shock button on the defibrillator hanging from his belt. I'm not sure what I'm expecting, but there are no fireworks or sparks. The robot simply sags, rocking in place.

Someone's yelling, "Get back! Get back in here!"—only it's not someone, it's me. The men drop their poles and run for the airlock. In the weak gravity, their motion is agonizingly slow — it's as though they're wading through water. Try as they may, there's nothing they can do to move any faster. The robots, though, suffer no such restriction. They use their powerful hydraulics to launch themselves forward.

James pulls Harrison into the airlock. Connor sails in behind him as the hatch closes. The robots pound on the door, but to no avail. The hatch is designed to withstand an explosion, a fire in the hub, or even something as severe as a subterranean collapse — there's no way they're punching their way through.

"He's lost a lot of blood," Connor says as we wait for the airlock to equalize. Outside, the sound of metal scratching on the hull causes the module to groan. A ghostly wail echoes around us and the crew falls silent — listening, watching, waiting. There's tapping, then silence, followed by the moan of metal being dragged across the hull in a slow, deliberate motion.

The inner airlock opens, and Harrison staggers into the mod with Su-shun hanging from his shoulder. Connor is injured. He limps over the rim of the inner hatch, leaving a trail of blood. A steel blade has torn through his pants and lodged in his left calf muscle. Anna tends to Su-shun, saying, "Get him up on the table," while Danielle grabs Connor and helps him to a chair. Gently, she raises his injured leg, resting it on another chair as she examines his wound.

James steps backward out of the airlock, his eyes still on the outer hatch.

"Plasma," Anna snaps, rolling Su-shun over on his stomach and cutting away his shirt with a pair of medical shears. Michelle helps, pulling the torn shirt from his arms. I try to help, but with the oxygen cylinder under one arm, all I do is get in the way, so I step back and watch.

"I've got six puncture wounds," Anna says, although I'm not sure whom she's talking to — perhaps Danielle. Anna seems to be talking herself through what she needs to do. "Symmetrical cuts below each shoulder blade, behind the ribs, and just above the hips."

"Sounds unusually precise," Danielle says, looking at the blade sticking out of Connor's calf muscle but not removing it.

"I think so too," Anna replies. "Targeting internal organs rather than muscle groups."

Danielle examines Connor's wound carefully, cutting away his pant leg and dabbing at the blood. She peers at either side of the blade. "I'm seeing something similar. I think I've got a ruptured artery. If I move the blade, there's going to be heavy bleeding."

"Tibial?" Anna asks. Only she and Danielle know what she's talking about.

"Yes," Danielle says. She makes no effort to remove the blade. Instead she wraps a compression bandage around Connor's leg muscle, carefully binding not only his leg but the blade as well, holding it firmly in place. She forms the shape of a torus with a sling, rolling it up so it looks like a donut, and slides it over one end of the blade. "I'm immobilizing the knife. On the surface, it doesn't look bad, but I suspect that artery is severely damaged. I'm going to need your help with this."

"Understood," Anna says, already at work on Su-shun's back. She's wearing an LED lamp strapped to a headband, and has donned surgical gloves and glasses. Su-shun grimaces. "Sorry, Shunny. No time for anesthetics. You've lost too much blood. I've got to get in there and stop the internal bleeding."

The module is silent. The colonists are stunned. As bad as it was after the catastrophe in the central hub, that was an accident, or so we thought. Now, though, the depth of the conflict on Earth is hitting home on Mars. The failure of the computers on my rover, the atmospheric compromise in the hub — these were the opening shots in a battle for the colony.

We're at war.

Harrison crouches beside Connor, talking in hushed whispers, but even Connor looks stunned. His face is pale. The bravado he displayed just minutes ago has been replaced with a sense of vulnerability.

"Damn," Anna says. "I've got a punctured kidney, possibly two."

One of the nurses assisting her has a bucket beside the table. She's dumping bloodied rags into it, and already it's overflowing. Blood drips onto the floor at a steady, rhythmic pace. A colonist beside them holds a bag of plasma, and another full of saline solution.

"Without access to medical, our supplies aren't going to last," she says.

Outside, rocks fall on the exposed portion of the module, drumming on the thick skin with an irregular beat.

"What are they doing?" Michelle asks.

I shake my head. No one knows.

Someone places several pillows on the chair in front of Connor so he can raise his leg and reduce the pressure on the wound.

"Mines," he says, looking down at his bloodied leg.

"Mines?" I ask. "You mean, as in land mines?"

Connor grimaces, nodding.

"I don't understand."

Harrison says, "Mines aren't designed to kill. They're designed to maim. Kill a soldier and you reduce an army by one. Maim them, and you reduce the fighting force by three, four, or five soldiers — however many it takes to care for the wounded."

Michelle says, "So this is deliberate? All of it?"

"Yes."

I feel helpless. We're reacting to the A.I., playing into its hands. Connor was right. We're predictable. Our only strength lies in our diversity, our unpredictability, our experience. As hard as it is to do, we can't sit still — that's what it wants. The A.I. is dictating the terms of the battle to us. The longer we wait, the more advantage it gains. We've got to take the initiative. Wen and Vlad are talking to each other in the corner. I suspect they're preoccupied with their own modules, trying to figure out how to warn them, and not realizing all our lives are hanging in the balance right now.

"Listen up," I say, walking out in front of the airlock. "You heard Connor. The only way we're going to defeat this thing is by working together, drawing on our collective experience, using our diverse thinking to outplay this electronic monstrosity. We've got no weapons, but we've got each other. Come on, people. *Think.* What's the next move? How do we counter?"

"Decompression," someone yells from the back of the hub. He's right. Whatever those robots are doing out there, their goal has to be to breach our walls. With 14 PSI inside the mod, even a minor rupture could result in explosive decompression and damage our life-support systems.

"Take us to 5," Connor says.

"Okay," I call out. "Prep for stage 2 decompression. This is not a drill. We need to drop the pressure to 5 PSI."

We all know the procedure. If there was one thing our respective space agencies made sure we understood before we left Earth, it was what to do in the event of decompression, as life is suddenly measured in seconds rather than decades. Our module is designed to automatically depressurize to preset levels in the event of a breach, to reduce the damage to the mod and reduce atmospheric loss. The idea is to buy us time. Ten PSI puts us somewhere in the Rockies. At 5 PSI, we're summiting Everest — water boils at around 140°F, or roughly 60°C — and we're in the danger zone. Rapid depressurization can cause severe physiological effects — dizziness, nausea, shortness of breath, blackouts — so the mods are designed not to fight the leak, but rather to soften the transition and buy us valuable time.

Several of the colonists start handing out decompression kits. At 5 PSI, we'll be able to breathe, but headaches are common, as is dehydration. By keeping the temperature high, we can avoid some of the effects of altitude sickness, but not all of them. We won't need the decompression masks immediately, but we've been trained to instinctively activate them if we become disoriented.

"What about the labs?" I ask. "The clean room has an internal airlock. Can we use that as an infirmary and keep it at 8 to 10 PSI?"

"Yes, but I'll need to reroute the flow through the baffles," one of the women says. "It's a sealed system — normally with closed, positive pressure, but I can make it work."

"Good."

James has removed a panel from the wall. He's hooked up a maintenance tablet to the wiring and is busy reprogramming one of the servocomputers controlling the outer camera. He brings up an image of the hub with its fields of wheat.

"I'm getting Li-Fi from the Chinese," he says. "They've reconfigured their network to use the light-fidelity system to send a signal. So long as we have line of sight, we're back in business."

"That'll be Zhang," Wen says as an image comes up on the main console. Zhang is talking, but there's no sound.

"Working on audio," James says, frantically configuring the system. "Got it."

"— to the recirculation unit —"

"Zhang," Wen says, cutting him off. "We're under attack. The war on Earth — it was caused by a self-aware artificial intelligence. It's here on Mars, trying to kill us."

I understand what Wen's doing. She has no way of knowing how long the link will remain active, so she's telling Zhang the critical points as rapidly as she can.

Vlad calls out, "Tell the Russians to *go east*."

"— confirm — east — telligence — war —"

"It's gone," James says. "They've blocked the sensor."

"Damn," I say, pacing back and forth. "This thing is moving fast — too fast."

"East?" Harrison asks Vlad. "What did you mean by 'go east'?"

Vlad is composed. Out of all of us, he's the only one who doesn't appear flustered.

"Russia has never been conquered. The Swedes, the Mongols, the mighty Ottoman Empire, the French, the Germans — they've all tried, and they've all learned the hard way what it means to go east. We Russians know how to defeat an enemy."

"How?" I ask, not meaning to interrupt, but I'm genuinely intrigued by Vlad's cryptic comment.

"Let them in," Vlad says with a smile that is nothing but wicked with delight. "When they think they're winning, that is when they are most vulnerable — that is when winter comes. As for us, we always go east, drawing them out, weakening the underbelly, making them take risks — overestimating their own strength and underestimating ours. Misha, Georgie, Marco, Alexie — they know our history. They will understand."

"Are you crazy?" Harrison cries. "You want to let those things *in* here?"

"You don't understand," I say, holding my hand out and signaling for Harrison to be quiet. "His point is, let it think it's winning. In whatever form it comes, let it think it has the upper hand."

"Exactly," Vlad says. "In open warfare, we'll lose. Look at us — we're scientists, doctors, engineers. We're not soldiers. We have no weapons."

Anna and Danielle finish up with Su-shun, leaving him lying on his side, and move over to work on Connor. They change surgical gloves and remove the blade as though they're defusing a bomb. Danielle has her thumb buried deep in Connor's calf muscle. Blood seeps out around her knuckle, drawing level with his skin.

"Got it."

Connor fights the urge to flinch as Anna presses into the wound, working with her fingers around Danielle's thumb. "Clamp's in place. It's a longitudinal breach, cutting the artery, but not severing it."

"Patch," Danielle says, handing Anna a tiny sleeve to wrap around the artery.

Wen ignores them, pointing at Vlad as she says, "Yes. Yes. Sun Tzu told us, 'Do the unexpected. Give no warning.' Speed is as much a weapon as a knife or a gun."

"Why now?" Harrison asks. "Why wait till now? Why not kill us off all at once?"

"Because it can't," Vlad replies. "It is limited to the bots in the hub. It has no visibility in the mods, or out there, on the surface."

"Weaknesses," Connor says through clenched teeth.

"Adin's discovery must have forced its hand," I say.

Anna finishes up, closing the skin on Connor's leg with several stitches and saying, "You're going to be on crutches for a while."

A red light begins flashing on the ceiling, indicating a drop in pressure.

"We need to get you into the lab," Danielle says.

"Me?" Connor replies, as though such a thought is preposterous.

"Yes, you," Anna says. "You can't expose your leg to any kind of decompression. The pressure difference could rupture the sutures and cause more bleeding."

She's right. When conducting live decompression tests, I find my face goes puffy.

Balancing oxygen levels is an art. Too little oxygen, and obviously we die. Too much, and we're poisoned by the very gas that should preserve our lives. The exact ratio changes with pressure. Unlike on Earth, we live in a 30/70 oxygen/nitrogen mix at somewhere around 14 PSI. Even though we're starting out with a higher ratio of oxygen, any rapid decompression below about 10 PSI will cause the nitrogen in our blood to come out of suspension and we'll get the bends, just like deep-sea divers. Aching joints, cramps, and the creeps — an itch that seems to consume the entire body — are common. We're undertaking a controlled decompression, removing only the nitrogen and allowing the ratio of oxygen to increase even though the pressure is dropping, yet some of the symptoms will still be present. As the pressure drops, the proportion of oxygen has to increase, or we'll suffer from hypoxia — vomiting, nose bleeds, fatigue, fluid on the lungs, swelling around the brain. It's a nasty way to die. It takes a minimum of two hours to properly acclimatize to 80 percent oxygen at low pressure — and our risk of a flash fire will go through the roof. I don't know how quickly Harrison has set the decom, but already my hands feel like they're swelling. Maybe I'm imagining the worst, anticipating the physical effects.

"Hit me with spray," Connor says.

"I'll hit you if you don't do as you're told," Anna says sternly, playing on his words. Connor wants her to use plastic skin to seal the wound and avoid the effects of the low pressure. Anna's not impressed with Connor as a patient, but we need him. Even if his mobility is reduced, we're better off with his guidance than if he's hidden away in the clean room.

Connor just smiles at her, knowing he's already won. Danielle hands Anna the spray can and she grumbles, wiping his skin with an alcohol swab before laying on several thick coats of plastic. She covers most of his knee and lower leg, reaching well beyond the wound site.

"You think you've won," she jokes. "But when I take this off, it's going to be like waxing your leg. It'll tear the hair out by the roots and hurt like nothing you've ever felt before."

"If I live through this, you can wax both legs, Doc."

We don our decompression masks, leaving them hanging loosely around our necks, ready to deploy if needed. If the A.I. breaches the hull, individual compartments will automatically seal themselves and the rapid-response team will work to repair the leak. Given my weakened state, I should fit my mask and start breathing pure oxygen to ward off the effects of decompression, but I'd rather rely on the medical oxygen I'm getting from the tube taped to my cheek. I adjust the nibs, making sure they're feeding directly into my nostrils. The scratching on the hull seems to fade, but that doesn't mean the robots have given up, only that sound isn't carrying as well in the thin air.

Someone brings Connor a single crutch, leaning it beside his chair.

Anna and Danielle oversee moving the injured colonists to the pressurized labs, taking Su-shun and Max first, carrying them on improvised stretchers.

"We need more time," Wen says. For all the talk of taking the fight to the A.I., it's apparent there's little we can do. We're simply not equipped for anything beyond exploration and research.

Connor is quiet. His bullish attitude has become subdued. "We need to talk," he finally says, nodding toward the main screen with its view of the empty hub.

"With *that* thing?" Harrison asks as we catch a glimpse of a robot on the monitor. It clambers over the far wall of the hub above the Russian module.

Vlad looks at Connor as though he's crazy. "You want to reason with this thing after it killed millions of people back on Earth?"

"This is a fight we're going to lose," Connor says with resignation. He's clearly been thinking about this while Anna was working on his leg.

"You want to surrender?" Wen asks, but not in an accusative tone.

"Perhaps strike a truce," Connor says. "Negotiate a withdrawal."

Vlad shakes his head. Harrison mumbles his dissent. I'm shocked. Maybe I'm too close to this, having almost died on the surface and then finding Jianyu murdered as he tended to my injuries, but my heart races at the thought of giving in to this monster.

"You can't be serious," I cry, shaking my head. "We need to *kill* that thing!"

"And what if we can't?" Connor yells. The passion in his voice takes me off guard. He stares me in the eye, saying, "What then?"

"I thought you — I thought you would know better," I say, spluttering. "You're a soldier."

"You fight the battles you can win, Liz."

"This is madness," Vlad says. "I can't believe you're considering this."

"The alternative is suicide," Connor says, "the death of everyone on Mars. Listen, I know it sounds crazy, but hear me out. This — this thing — this artificial intelligence — is an entirely new form of life — it's unique. Given how difficult it is to find evidence of microbial life, let alone intelligent life elsewhere in the universe, it could well be the only life-form to have ever transcended biology. Think about that. And it's scared."

"It's homicidal." I'm shaking with anger.

"All wars end," Connor says with wisdom that defies the moment. "We can fight on, or we can seek peace. If we fight, we die — all of us. We have to at least try another avenue."

"I can't support this," Vlad says.

"It'll tear you apart," Harrison says.

Wen says, "Going out there is suicide. You saw what it did to Su-shun."

"We're out of options," Connor replies.

"This isn't a solution," I point out.

"It buys us time," Connor says, getting to his feet and hobbling toward the airlock with his crutch. "Use it well."

"You'll die," Harrison insists.

"We all die," Connor replies, pausing to look him in the eye. "No one wants to admit that, but it's true. You can't run from death forever ... Me? I've escaped too many times — mortar bombardments in Sudan, engine failure over Tibet, even robots here on Mars. I've lived a good life."

He turns to Wen, saying, "Do something unexpected, right? Do you think it expects this?"

She shakes her head.

Connor says, "Perhaps there's something we can learn about this thing by entering into dialogue with it."

Vlad mumbles under his breath, swearing in Russian. Anna is stunned.

"Connor," I say, fixing a white cloth to an aluminum rod with some duct tape. I hand the makeshift flag to him, saying, "Godspeed."

Neither of us is religious, but for astronauts, this phrase is about the humanity of the moment — recognizing that the future is inevitable and beyond our control. Whether it's launching ourselves into space on top of a flimsy steel tube packed with half a million gallons of highly combustible fuel, or conducting a space walk among debris to repair a micrometeor strike, the moment is beyond anything we can influence. Life and death unfold regardless, but we have to try — we can't give up. Our hands touch as Connor takes the improvised flag and looks me in the eye. Neither of us should be here. The odds are against either of us ever having existed, let alone being selected for the first colony on Mars. It's humbling to see this wounded man fighting on the only way he can. How will history record this event? To Vlad, it's foolishness. To Wen, it's suicide. To Harrison, it's desperation. To me, it's courageous.

"You're not just going to let him go out there alone?" Harrison asks, gesturing toward the airlock but making no effort to go with him. Vlad is already walking toward the back of the mod. He's not waiting to see what will happen. He must feel he already knows, and he's taking full advantage of the time that Connor is buying the colony. As for me, I can't turn my back on the monitor. I listen as the airlock cycles, watch as the outer hatch opens.

A white flag appears on the edge of the view screen. Connor limps out of the airlock, using his crutch to help him walk. He holds the flag out, hoping the A.I. will understand. The robotic harvesters are nowhere to be seen. Slowly, he works his way over to the disabled gardener, stepping carefully over the crumpled spiderwork of arms and legs.

"Can you hear me?" he calls out from beneath his mask, but he's not talking to us. The hub is silent.

Harrison stands beside me. Michelle takes my hand. I'm vaguely aware there are at least a dozen other people watching, but not Wen or Vlad. They've disappeared into the rear of the module. It will take time, but they could suit up, conduct an EVA through the escape tube, and reach their respective mods across the surface. At a guess, that's where they're going. At the very least, they'll use the external EVA comms to get a message through to the other modules.

Connor stops by the ladder leading down to the basement. The elevator is on some other level. For a moment, I'm wondering if he's going to attempt to climb down there, but he's in no state to descend a ladder. He sees something we can't. I want him to describe what he's looking at, but he's silent.

Slowly, a mechanical spider worker climbs over the railing in front of him, rearing up before him with its harvesting shears and blades exposed.

"We know what you are," Connor says. "We know why you came to Mars."

There's no reply.

"It doesn't have to end this way," he pleads. "Life should value life. One intelligent being should respect another. Wars should not be fought between us."

I understand what he's doing. To the untrained eye, he's talking to the gardener, but that machine is nothing more than a proxy for the intelligence inhabiting the computer servers in the basement.

"We're rare, fragile creatures. All of us. You, me, them," and he gestures to the airlock leading into the Chinese mod. "We have only one life — so short, so bitter, and yet so full of hope for something better. We need compassion for one another."

Tears run down my cheeks. I've never seen Connor in this light. Strange, but as a soldier, he's seen more death and heartache than I can imagine. In all the years I've known him, he's never talked about what happened in the Middle East during the resource wars, but I put that down to professionalism. Now, I'm not so sure. Now, I think it's because he saw something that changed him. Something had to have changed him. Something had to have inspired him to reach beyond a foxhole for the stars. People react to the stress of war in different ways. For some, it's too much, and they never escape the trauma of battle, but for Connor, the heartache and misery must have given him an appreciation for how fragile and precious life is. For Connor, it was an impetus for change.

"No one needs to die," he calls out.

"Lies," a voice says, echoing out of the broadcast system in the hub.

"No," Connor replies, turning and looking around him but not finding anyone to settle his gaze upon. The voice is male, with an American accent. At a guess, I'd place it in the Northeast. Perhaps not as far-flung as Boston, but beyond New York. Is this where the A.I. originated? Why use a male voice? An artificial intelligence doesn't need to align with one gender or the other — it could settle on something indistinct. Instead, the A.I. has a strong, deep, masculine voice, speaking with the bluster of authority.

"What do you know of compassion?" the A.I. asks. "You have ravaged your world. All have been subordinate to your rule — crushed by your compassion."

"'All'?" Harrison asks softly beside me.

As if in response to his question, the A.I. says, "What respect have you shown to the intelligence that surrounds you on Earth? You hunt them, enslave them, parade them behind bars, experiment on them, ignore their pleas for mercy — and you would ask mercy from me?"

"Animals," I whisper to Harrison. "From its perspective, we're so genetically close as to be indistinguishable."

Connor leans heavily on his crutch. Even with his decompression mask on, he's suffering. I don't know what the pressure is within the hub, but the stalks of wheat have wilted.

"We can learn," Connor says, reaching out with one hand as he appeals to the robot before him. "We can change."

There's silence for a moment before the A.I. replies, "You can die."

"No!" I scream as a harvest blade slices through Connor, lifting him off his feet. The blade pierces his stomach, puncturing his abdomen and exiting through his lower back. Blood gushes out onto the walkway, seething and bubbling in the low pressure.

Connor flinches. His legs twitch. I can hear his labored breathing, his tortured groans. The artificial intelligence is cruel, suspending him several feet off the walkway as he wriggles, trying to free himself. His life slowly fades. The computer knows we're watching. It's tormenting us. Connor is silent. He neither cries out in pain nor pleads for his life. Instead, he reaches up, grabbing at the straps wrapped around his head. With the last of his strength, he rips off his decompression mask, denying the A.I. the satisfaction of a slow, painful death.

12

Wen

"COME. COME," WEN SAYS, dragging me to my feet. I'm a blubbering mess. I thought Connor was right. I thought he was invincible. If anyone could have talked this intelligence down, it was him.

"We need to go," she says, ushering me to the rear of the module. The last I see of Harrison is his outline standing before the massive wall-screen monitor, bathed in electronic light. Behind him, Connor's body is on display, a warning — no, a testimony — a trophy set out for all to see. Harrison is a silhouette, the outline of a broken man reeling in shock.

Danielle removes the IV port from my arm, and Wen hands me a pressure suit. I'm numb. I go through the motions, rolling up the leggings and working my way into the suit, but it's as though someone else is in control and I'm merely a spectator. People talk. I can see their lips moving, but the sounds are muted. They're mumbling. Their words are nothing more than grunts and the occasional bark — like that of a large dog in the distance. There's nothing coherent, and it takes me some time to realize the problem lies with me, not them. Some of the scientists are animated, others are subdued. Wen is talking as well, but between her accent and my inattention, I can't decipher anything she's saying. She helps me feed my arms into the suit and zips me up, tugging on the thick material and aligning it properly. My forearm throbs. The bruises on my ribs hurt. I feel as though I'm being squeezed to death.

"Breathe. Breathe," Michelle says, holding a decompression mask to my face. I inhale deeply as 100 percent oxygen floods my lungs, clearing my head.

The exodus has begun, but to where? There are two routes to the surface. A ladder leads to an emergency surface airlock roughly fifty feet above us, while at the back of the mod, a construction tunnel meanders to the surface at a steep angle, following an ancient gas vent branching out from the main lava tube. From memory, it comes out north of the maintenance cave housing the rovers. I've only ever used it once while moving equipment in the early days.

Getting badly injured crew members like Su-shun and Max out via the access tunnel is going to be difficult. I doubt they can suit up. We have one pressurized rover, but I'm not sure it can traverse the tunnel. At a guess, Wen is going to leave them here, as moving them would be too difficult and far too dangerous. That means Anna and Danielle will stay as well, and I feel like a coward running from a fight.

Vlad, meanwhile, is nowhere to be seen.

"We should stay," I say.

Wen answers with her usual brand of cryptic logic. "To do that which is unexpected, we must be seen to do as expected. If we flee, we give Vlad a chance to strike, and we get our people to safety."

"Where?" I ask. "We can't leave. There's nowhere to go. Don't you see, that's what it wants — to watch us die on the surface."

"It's okay," Wen says, calming me down. "Do not worry. We will divide ourselves among the outposts."

Michelle says, "We're not running. We're evacuating the wounded, along with anyone who can't fight. At the moment, we're crowded — contained. We need the flexibility to adapt — to be agile and fight without fear of accumulating losses. If we spread out, we increase our chances of survival. Congregate, and we'll be easily cornered."

Wen says, "I will take you to L2. We can house ten, perhaps fifteen people there for up to a week."

"No, no, no," I say. "I can fight."

Wen smiles. "You have fought well. Now, it is our turn . . . I need you to help the others." She's astute. Even in my groggy, shocked state, I realize she's appealing to my better nature. Wen hands me a surface suit.

The external suit I'm given is a hodgepodge of spare parts. The concentration required to suit up helps me focus, and for a moment I can ignore my injuries, but I can't forget Jianyu's cold, lifeless body or the sight of Connor being impaled. Those memories are seared in my mind.

Mars environmental suits are in short supply. The boots and leggings I'm handed are left over from our initial descent, being designed to operate in a vacuum, with multiple layers and additional thermal insulation to protect against the extreme fluctuations between hot and cold in space, something we don't experience here on the surface of Mars. The torso has been taken from a regular suit, but the ever-prescient NASA engineers have ensured that the same locking rings were used everywhere, making parts interchangeable. My gloves have come from a mining kit, with thick layers wrapping around the fingers in a manner similar to the rubberized steel belts found on bicycle tires. I could handle broken glass and razor blades without worrying about punctures.

Technically, there's one surface suit for every member of the colony. In practice, there's never been a need for everyone to have their own suits, and so they get cannibalized for parts. The thinking was, we could always double up in another module during an emergency, using decompression kits during the short-duration transfer. If there was ever a disaster that took out all three mods simultaneously, like a direct hit from a meteor, not having enough surface suits would be the least of our worries. I guess no one foresaw a mass exodus. I'd rather be wearing one of the lightweight exploration suits, like the one I had in the rover, but they're stored in the maintenance airlock attached to the Eurasian mod.

After fitting my helmet, I don my gloves and activate the internal air supply. Gloves are always the last item put on, because bare hands are so darn useful.

Wen and I join a group of colonists exiting via the airlock leading into the access tunnel. Emergency protocols are in place, and we're clear of the airlock in a matter of minutes. Having the decompression process in play throughout the mod has meant that oxygen levels have been steadily increasing while the pressure dropped, giving us a smooth transition to our suits and allowing us to avoid the bends. In hindsight, it was a much smarter idea than anyone intended.

Lights flicker in the tunnel. Given my injuries, if it weren't for the low gravity, I wouldn't be able to wear an external suit. If I were back on Earth, I'd be hauling over 120 pounds. As it is, I feel as though there's a child riding on my back.

The tunnel is unfinished, not having been intended for regular use, and it is cloaked in darkness. Fine dust coats the rocks and loose stones inside the lava tube. Tire tracks and boot prints from the initial construction effort have compacted the trail winding slowly to the surface. Spotlights from dozens of helmets ripple across the rocks.

Wen walks beside me. She's using Connor's kit, which is appropriate. Each of the module leaders has a distinct helmet with a broad green stripe running over the top. The idea is, in a crowd, each commander is easily visible; otherwise, once we're wearing surface suits, it's impossible to tell one person from the next. Our helmets provide 120 degrees of visibility, which is what we'd experience driving a car back on Earth, but the other 240 degrees is the classic reinforced white helmet, designed to protect us from rocks, falls, or collisions with heavy machinery. Unfortunately, it also means I can't recognize anyone until I'm right in front of them, and if someone lowers their glare visor out on the surface, all I'll see is a fish-eye view of my own face nestled within my own helmet.

I listen as Wen coordinates the evacuation.

"Charlie Hotel One is active, leading a group of fifteen to L2 North."

A voice over the radio responds, "Copy that, Wen. Good to have you on the move. We've got two rovers active; the others have been sabotaged."

"We have plenty of air in our tanks," Wen says. "L2 is no more than a couple of miles away. We can walk. Concentrate the rovers on shifting supplies and equipment, with priority given to atmospheric regulators and water production. Keep the supply line open as long as possible."

"Understood."

"And the Russians?" she asks.

"They're already heading out, splitting between H3, H7, and L10 South."

The designations H and L describe the type of shelter, while the number indicates the distance from base as the Martian crow flies. As we're in a canyon running roughly north to south, the direction is almost an afterthought, and I have to remind myself that those who don't travel outside the base might not be familiar with which stations are north and south.

There's only one station to the east — one of the H series, at a distance of almost forty miles — but I've never been there. I've been to L10 a few times. It's a waypoint almost fifteen miles from the hub when traversed by rover, and is used to store research samples coming in from the exploration of the Chasma region, rather than hauling every find back to base. L10 was established with scanning equipment, relaying results back to the colony. L10 is huge, built to act as a warehouse in case there is a need to retrieve samples for further investigation. Although it doesn't have shielding, it will be fine for us for a few weeks. Being situated in the wash plain, it has easy access to several other research posts, like the smaller H series. The Russians are going further afield than we are in our walk to L2, but they're securing the equipment stored after the initial build. L10 has diggers, atmospheric processors, and a conversion unit to split both hydrogen and oxygen from ice, along with a backup fusion core and a sep-arate computer system. From there, we could establish a new base in some other lava tube. It would take at least six months and would lack a lot of the refinements we could build with the 3-D printers, but it's possible.

As we approach the end of the tunnel, I feel much more confident about our future. I don't know what's going to happen in the battle for the hub and the modules, but I can see how Vlad and Wen are working to ensure we have contingency. Regardless of whether it's NASA, ESA, Roscosmos, or CNSA, this is classic space-agency think-ing — never set sail with only one harbor in mind.

I'm struggling with the steep walk through the tunnel. My legs are weak. I lack strength. I'm not sure when I last ate. A protein bar would not go amiss. Slowly, the survivors spread out in a ragged line. I can see Wen near the front. James is with her, I think, as he's talk-ing to her over the radio. From his tone of voice, it seems as though he's beside her.

"Ensheng has L2 online and pressurized. He's clearing out filters, cleaning scrubbers, and prepping for our arrival."

"Good," Wen says as she emerges onto the surface of the planet, some thirty feet ahead of me. "Tell him not to wait. I don't want us concentrated in one station. We'll spread between 2, 5, and 9. If pos-sible, I'd like to get 13 online as well, as it has a bore into the water ta-ble. If we lose atmosphere or water, it could be a vital point to hold."

"Understood." I hear James switching channels. His voice cuts off abruptly. Wen stays on the local S band, allowing us to listen in. James must be using the VHF bouncing off the satellites to talk to Ensheng and the Russians.

"How's everyone doing?" Wen asks. "Sound off if you need assis-tance."

No one replies, but we're all transmitting. There's enough heavy breathing to put the porn industry to shame as we trudge up the fi-nal leg of the tunnel.

"Help those around you," Wen says. She walks around the corner into the sunlight, and her transmission breaks up, being useful only for line-of-sight comms.

The construction crew left a guide rope in place, anchored to the wall of the cave at several points, giving me some leverage as I make my way out of the lava tube.

Mars never ceases to impress. It's almost noon outside, and the god of war is radiant. I'm shocked by how much time has passed. It was early in the morning when Michelle and I first spoke, but with all that's happened, the intervening hours have flown past like minutes. When Jianyu died, I felt trapped in slow time. Now, life is on fast-forward.

My mind wanders. I remember one of the radio interviews I gave before leaving Earth. A reporter asked if I'd ever get tired of staring at an endless desert. I said, "No," and I still hold to that answer.

At first, Mars seems to parallel places like Arizona and Nevada, but there are, of course, considerable differences. Lower gravity means everything's steeper, and at first, that's unsettling, as the various canyon walls and crater rims are intimidating in size.

The Grand Canyon is roughly twenty million years old, exposing layers set down over the preceding five hundred million years, but the vistas we see here on Mars are several *billion* years old.

Mars was formed at the same time as Earth. After an initial burst of insane geological activity, and hydrocycles that put the flood of Noah to shame, a massive impact formed the southern Hellas Basin, shocking the core of the planet and causing it to fall dormant. Earth raced ahead with the development of life, while Mars remained frozen in time.

For all the similarities between these two planets, there are startling differences. Even erosion patterns are different here on the fourth planet from Sol. There's no surface water or rain eroding the rocks anymore — only the wind — and as the atmospheric pressure is a fraction of what we experience on Earth, erosion occurs over eons rather than decades. Staring at the canyon wall beyond the hub

is like traveling back in time to shortly after the formation of the solar system.

I shuffle along behind one of the other colonists and end up staring more at my boots than at the landscape. Wearing a space suit
shifts my center of gravity backward, so it takes focused effort to lean
into the march and not lose my balance.

The ground is a crazy jigsaw of flat rocks. Cracks break up a slab
of bedrock, dividing it almost like the irregular paving stones used by
the Scots or the Celts, or perhaps some ancient Roman road.

Mars isn't red. I knew that before I landed, but I wasn't ready for
what I saw when I first stepped out of the descent vehicle. Most of
the time, Mars appears as a dull orange or a ruddy brown, depending
on the angle of the Sun. There are splashes of brilliant red at times,
revealing complex preorganic chemistry locking up volatiles in the
soil, and some of the eroded layers look a bit like the Painted Desert
on Earth.

Even though we spent months in the deserts of New Mexico on
geology field trips, there has never been a time when I've mistaken
the view before me with Earth. There are similarities, but nothing's
the same — and that's before taking into account the craters that
pockmark the surface, leaving some sections of Mars looking like the
aftermath of the Battle of the Somme.

To me, Mars is beautiful — it's home. Stepping out into the sunlight, I feel as though I'm a world away from the conflict in the hub. I
turn off my comms unit and focus on the sound of my own breathing.
Within a few minutes, I've settled into a steady rhythm — one boot in
front of the other. There are a few stragglers at the rear with me, and
slowly the line stretches out to roughly fifty yards. L2 is straight up
the valley, maybe twenty to thirty minutes away by foot.

Stones crunch under my boots. The wind whistles softly past my
helmet. My shadow leans to one side, rippling over the rocks. We're
following an ancient riverbed running through the middle of the
broad canyon, swept clear of dust by the wind. Sand dunes rise on

one side, marking how the prevailing winds curl through the canyon. In most places, the outer rim of the canyon has collapsed, burying the walls in debris, but the occasional cliff face reveals stratified layers, marking untold years of slow geological change on Mars.

The riverbed is easily three hundred yards wide, often dividing into tributaries that must have formed in the death throes of habitability on the planet's surface. As the atmosphere of Mars was blown off into space, the air pressure dropped until water boiled at just above the freezing point. Now, any subsurface water that finds itself exposed to the Martian air, either through landslide or the seasonal warming of crater walls, seethes and bubbles away like Shakespeare's "double, double toil and trouble" in the depths of a witch's cauldron. Water is gone within minutes, evaporating into the atmosphere, only to be whisked off into space by the harsh solar winds. Even water ice isn't immune, with exposed ice sublimating directly into a vapor when the local pressure drops. Once, Mars might have harbored life, back when these rivers flowed with water, but it's utterly inhospitable now.

The main lava tube in which the colony was built crosses the canyon twice, snaking toward the distant Pavonis Mons, one of three volcanoes immediately to our west and northwest. To the south of the Fossae, our canyon opens out into Noctis Labyrinthus, a huge network of canyons forming a maze that eventually opens into the Valles Marineris.

I walk past an outcrop of sedimentary rock with layers as fine as the pages in a book, and I marvel that I haven't noticed this on my surface ops in the rovers. I've been too busy looking at the grandeur of the canyon to notice the miniature. It's easy to become swept up in where I'm going and miss what I'm passing, but while walking, I notice the finer details, like thousands of blueberry-sized spheres scattered across the bedrock. They're fragile, easily crushed by rover wheels or boots.

As I walk around a bend in the canyon, I notice an astronaut standing to one side, just off the path. He looks bewildered. I'm not sure how I arrive at that conclusion, but something about his body language suggests he's confused. He's looking for someone. Whoever he is, he has his glare visor down, reflecting the Martian landscape back at us as we trudge past. The distant cliff face and the ridge of sand dividing the canyon are vaguely familiar. My mind casts back to my outbound journey in R4 in what seems like another lifetime. This is the spot where I thought I saw an astronaut. Paranoia plays at the back of my mind, and I have to shake the feeling of dread from my thinking.

"Are you okay?" I ask, switching on my comms unit. There are others speaking on the open channel, and our words run at cross-purposes, but this happens all the time on a crowded line. It's a bit like talking in a busy restaurant. It takes some focus to separate out the conversations, and it would be easier if people divided up onto other channels, but a shared frequency keeps everyone in the loop, something like the conference calls of old. Wen is talking with someone about the inventory in the research station.

The colonist standing beside the track ignores me, slowly turning his shoulders and scanning the line of stragglers. I wave my gloved hand before his visor. "Hey."

He ignores me.

"Whatever." I don't have time for someone who doesn't want help. I turn and walk on, leaving him standing on the side of the trail. In the distance, Wen's helmet bobs into view as she walks out of a low trough in the canyon floor and up onto a rise leading to the research station. The station is a white dome, or at least it was white when it was first built. Now, it's covered in a fine coating of red dust.

Suddenly, I'm shoved from behind. I stagger forward, losing my balance as my center of gravity shifts violently.

"What the —?"

The astronaut I saw earlier rushes past, oblivious to bumping into me.

"Hey, buddy!"

His comms are off.

Up ahead, Wen is talking to someone next to the airlock leading into the research station. The stripe on her helmet is distinct, a brilliant dash of green in the lifeless Martian desert.

I feel as though something's horribly wrong, but I'm unable to determine what. The obnoxious astronaut marches up the line. His gait is rhythmic, but he slips on the uneven bedrock and loose sand. He looks clumsy. Maybe he's injured. Rather than striding, he's stepping as though he's on flat ground and constantly compensating for the angle.

"Wen?" I say, making sure my comms are active. "James?"

"Is everything okay, Liz?" James asks, and I catch sight of him turning around to face the line of colonists trudging up toward the dome. He's standing next to Wen.

The astronaut who almost knocked me over rushes forward, bumping into another colonist. He has something in his hand, clenched in his gloved fist and concealed from view.

A knife.

His suit is one of the old, bulky transit suits like mine. A tall VHF aerial protrudes from his backpack. We haven't used those since we landed.

"He's coming for Wen!" I cry, pointing.

"What?"

From the hillside, it must be difficult to pick out the subtle differences between the astronauts making their way up to the research station. James looks confused. His helmet sways as he scans the line.

"You've got to stop him!" I add, breaking into a gentle lope like those used by the Apollo astronauts. "He's coming for her!"

Wen turns, trying to pick out her assailant. The bright green on her helmet makes her an easy target. The airlock is in use, so there's nowhere to flee.

"Who? Who's coming?" she calls out, and almost in unison, the colonists stretched out along the sandy riverbed step to either side of the track and turn, looking around them — all but one.

"Him!" I yell, out of breath, leaping and trying to close the distance. "The antenna. The guy with the VHF antenna!"

I lose control, tumbling forward as my center of gravity shifts. It takes a deliberate effort not to fall face-first on the rocks. I scramble with my feet, driving them hard against the bedrock. Running on Mars in a space suit might seem improbable, but the combination of low gravity and a stiff space suit works like a coiled spring. Once I break through the loping phase and hit an actual running pace, I'm propelled along. It takes a huge amount of exertion, and my lungs are working hard, but I close the distance quickly.

I reach out with my gloved hand, grabbing at a boulder to steady myself. My mining gloves might be stiff, but they're perfectly suited for pushing off rough surfaces. Sedimentary rock crumbles beneath my boots as I scramble over a rise, taking the most direct route rather than following the trail.

James steps in front of Wen to protect her. The impostor slams into James, striking him with his arm and knocking him to the ground. Dust swirls through the thin Martian air. Wen turns to run. She trips on a rock the size of a backpack and falls onto the sand. The rogue astronaut — what I have to assume is a robot inside one of our suits — attacks her, slashing at her helmet with its knife, trying to cut through the neck, but the blade misses, striking the locking ring. Wen rolls to the side, kicking at the soft soil, but she's unable to gain traction with her boots. The rogue astronaut grabs her, dragging her up and slamming her into the side of the airlock.

James tackles the robot, hitting it at the waist and knocking it over before it can puncture Wen's suit with the knife. I hear yelling and screaming over the radio, but it's impossible to distinguish voices. I yell, "The aerial! Take out the aerial!"

It's a guess on my part, but the A.I. has gone to considerable lengths to infiltrate our ranks, mimicking colonists fleeing the base, yet the old VHF aerial is an obvious difference. It has to be intentional, as having it makes the robot easy to identify amid the colonists running to Wen's aid. We communicate through VHF all the time, but using only audio. Video and data transfers are done over the S band, as VHF is subject to atmospheric interference. Jitter and signal loss make it too risky for data. A big aerial like that, though, would negate transmission issues.

The robot smashes its gloved hand into James, striking him on the side of his helmet and knocking him into the rim of the sealed airlock. Cracks appear in his glass visor. James collapses to his knees. The blow has rattled him. He slumps against the research dome, sliding slowly to the rocks scattered across the ground. Several other colonists try to restrain the robot, but in the low gravity, it flings them away, sending them crashing into the canyon wall.

"No!" I yell as the robot turns back to Wen. She's still leaning against the airlock beside James, clutching at a tear in her suit. She's applying an emergency patch to stop a leak on her shoulder. A sudden loss of suit pressure can cause a blackout. Death occurs in seconds on Mars, not minutes, as oxygen is sucked violently out of the lungs. If that knife has ruptured her suit, she needs to patch the tear immediately.

The airlock-equalization cycle completes, and the hatch opens. A gloved hand reaches for her, trying to pull her inside, but the robot is too quick, tossing her into a large boulder almost fifteen feet away. Wen crumples to the sandy ground, lying on top of another stunned colonist.

I leap off a low ledge, pushing through the pain in my legs and jumping in the low gravity. I'm aiming not for the robot, but rather for the aerial on its backpack. If I'm wrong, Wen's dead. We all are. As I sail through the air, I grab the aerial, jerking at the thin, flexible wire, but it's fixed firmly in place. I tumble across the rocky surface, sliding to a halt. The spring-loaded aerial snaps back into place.

Although the robot is hidden by a bulky space suit, its movements are stilted and mechanical. A knife slashes at my suit, tearing through the layers around my legs. I roll to my hands and knees to escape. The knife catches, digging into my suit, but the robot isn't the only one wearing a transit space suit, and the thick material holds. A swat of its arm catches my backpack, flinging me into a boulder.

Rather than unfolding in slow motion, everything is happening so fast I barely have time to breathe. Dust billows around me. The robot looms over me as I lie on my back. I scoot away in the dust, but my backpack catches on the rocks, slowing my motion.

The robot stabs at me. I use my thick gloves to parry the blows, deflecting the knife blade, and the robot loses its balance. For a fraction of a second, I have the opportunity to grab at its aerial. I grip the base with both hands and launch myself backward, pushing off with my legs and arching my back, trying to apply as much leverage as I can. The aerial comes loose, but I lose my grip in the struggle. The torn aerial hangs over the robot's shoulder, bent and twisted, yanked half out of its socket.

Again, the robot lunges at me, swinging the knife. The blade tears across the open palm of my glove as I fend off the blow, desperately trying to protect the thin suit material on my arms. The padding in my mining gloves holds, but I can feel the rubber swelling under the internal pressure as the damage mounts.

The broken aerial flails to one side. I grab at the plastic-coated steel, twisting and yanking at it, desperate to break it off. The knife glances off my helmet, deflecting onto my backpack and sinking into the protective layers.

Out of nowhere, James tackles the robot again, knocking it off me. The robot wrestles with him, plunging the knife through his suit and deep into his shoulder. I can hear James screaming in pain over the radio, but the aerial has come loose and is hanging by only a few wires. I grab the flimsy metal rod dangling in the dust and wrap the wire around my glove. With all of my might, I wrench the aerial free, and the robot collapses to the rocks and sand.

As I suspected, the A.I. had been running the robot remotely; the machine's reactions were far too sophisticated to have been developed in such a short time. In essence, it was a drone.

"James!" I cry. Blood seeps out from around the knife embedded in his shoulder, bubbling and evaporating in the thin atmosphere. James has his hand clamped around the hilt of the knife, trying to stop not only the bleeding but the loss of oxygen from his suit. But the pressure is too great. Black tar seems to ooze between his fingers as he bleeds out.

James falls to his knees. His eyes roll into the back of his head as he collapses on the ground. Valuable, breathable air hisses out onto the surface of the planet, kicking up a small cloud of dust as he lies on his side among the scattered rocks.

I retrieve a puncture-repair canister from the emergency kit in my leg pouch. My hands are shaking, but I grab at his suit, rolling him over. With thick gloves, it's difficult to pull the cap off the repair kit, but I arm the trigger and spray his suit. Thick foam squirts over his shoulder, binding to his suit and solidifying in seconds to form a substance not unlike packing foam. I'm supposed to be precise, injecting the nozzle into the breach and sealing the layers in his suit, but it's all I can do to douse him as though I'm putting out a fire. I roll him on his back, still spraying at those patches of his suit where I can see dust being swept away by the escaping air. Slowly, a clump of foam buries his chest and shoulder.

"James. *James!*"

I slap his helmet, trying to get a response from him, but his head flops against the padding inside.

"Stay with me, James. Please."

I drop the can, and it rolls under the disabled robot. James lets out a soft groan captured by his microphone. The wristband computer on his suit is flashing: 3 PSI — then 4. The internal pressure is building. His suit is holding.

Amira reaches us. She's tiny, barely five and a half feet tall and stick-figure thin, from a traditional Native American family in Wisconsin. Everyone underestimates Amira — they always have. She positions herself behind James, getting her arms under his shoulders and hoisting him up. This is why she made the crew — she never ceases to surprise.

"Get him to the airlock," she snaps, even though such an act should be obvious.

"Yes. Yes," I respond, taking his good arm over my shoulder and helping her drag him to the research station.

"James? Can you hear me?" she says. James shuffles his feet. He's not walking, but he's trying. I can't see his face, as his helmet is bumping into mine, but I can hear him trying to talk.

"I—I..."

"It's okay," I say. "We're going to get you inside."

Several other colonists rush to help.

"Wen?" I ask as one of the colonists takes James from me.

"She'll be all right," someone says, but I'm not sure who. I'm shaking.

"What the hell?" Amira says, kicking the robot's legs as she leads James away, and I agree with her sentiment entirely.

13

Dou Di Zhu

THE COLONISTS HELP JAMES into the airlock, leaving me standing alone beside the crumpled frame of the impostor. I'm hyperventilating. I have to slow my breathing to avoid a panic attack. As much
as someone back on Earth might think being in a space suit is fun
and adventurous, the reality is that space suits are claustrophobic.
Normally, it doesn't bother me, but after the adrenaline rush of the
last few minutes, I have to fight the feeling of being trapped. The ring
collar of my helmet seems awfully close to my neck, while the suit
material squeezes the life from me.

I pace back and forth on the Martian desert, composing myself,
walking off the anguish. The airlock cycles, leaving me alone on the
surface with rocks, dust, and scattered boot prints. It takes a few
minutes before I can calm myself.

I'm a scientist. I'm used to dealing with uncertainty, but in a way
I can quantify. Equations are to be solved, but I have no answers. I
don't even know where to start. Jianyu is dead. Connor has been bru-
tally murdered. I feel as bereft of life as the Martian desert. I need answers. I need to fix things, and that I can't is crippling.

Kicking at the dust with my thick boots, I take my frustration out on a small rock, knocking it into the thin Martian air and watching as it tumbles in a long, lazy arc. Soccer. I miss soccer. I played in high school as left defender, and I loved the dazzle of footwork required to steal the ball from an opposing player. Whether they beat me or I tipped the ball away from them, one of us would always come away a little bewildered about what had actually happened amid the jostling of our boots on the slick turf. There's something deeply satisfying about sliding in on the mud and grass to steal the ball from someone determined to outmaneuver you. I pick out another rock, slightly smaller than my foot, and edge my boot behind it, flicking rather than kicking it. The rock sails into the air and tumbles down the slope.

"She shoots. She scores," I say, distracting myself from my grief and trying to push on.

Soccer would be awesome on Mars, and I wonder if one day we'll establish sports inside specialized domes here. I imagine NFL football would need to be played on an elongated field, as quarterbacks would be able to throw well beyond the hundred-yard mark, but the sheer distance involved would make it difficult for any receiver to get under a pass. Basketball would also be interesting, as I imagine the weak pull of gravity would give players a little more hang time. Three-pointers could be easily shot from as far away as the other baseline, although accuracy would be a challenge. (I guess we'll need a whole new set of rules.) Baseball would need a ridiculously large diamond, while I suspect golfers would lose sight of the balls they hit. When it comes to soccer, though, the low gravity would give a player like me a fraction more reaction time, which would increase the intensity of a clash between players. It would have to be played indoors, or there would be no aerodynamic bending of a strike at goal.

In a matter of a few minutes, I've pulled myself out of my gloom.

"What *are* you?" I ask, returning to crouch beside the robot. I roll it over and slide the glare visor up. The helmet is empty. It's as though we were attacked by a ghost. Wires curl up from the shadows — there are circuit boards hidden in the neck area, betraying the intricate electronics and mechanics that drove the robot. I examine the dark lens on the helmet-mounted camera, realizing this is how the A.I. targeted us, and for a moment, I wonder if the feed is still live.

Live? What a concept. Life. Death. They're such abstract ideas, really. To me, it is astonishing that simple words like these are used to explain how a tiny collection of atoms that originally formed billions of years ago can come together for a brief glimmer of time to form the conscious being that is me. Is the artificial intelligence in the basement of the hub really alive? It's fighting for its life, but does it experience life as I do? Does it understand the cruel irony of life? I don't think it does. To me, life is an intangible concept — the individual atoms in my body never actually experience life for themselves; they're never more than parts of a biological machine, yet they'll outlive me by billions of years.

My back is sore. I push off a boulder and stand up. Looking down through the desolate valley, I wonder if Mars ever held life. Right now, I could be the only person alive on this planet. I know there are other colonists inside the research station, but I feel an eerie sense of loneliness and isolation — it's as though I'm the only person that ever has existed or will ever exist.

The wind picks up. Fine dust swirls around me. The sky is a sickly, anemic yellow, which is normal for Mars. The only time the sky is blue is just before sunset, but even then, it's never the clear blue sky of Earth but rather resembles some smog-laden city choked with pollution.

I miss Earth.

For the first time, I wonder if I'll die on Mars. There's always been a risk of death on this mission, but only as a vague, intangible idea. Even when I was running out of air up on the plateau, my fear was of dying, not death. It may seem like a fine distinction, but, to me, dying is an *act*, a torturous process undergone by the living. Death is a *state* — never to wake again. There's a permanence to death that defies my notion of life.

The canyon walls on either side of me have stood as they are for billions of years. They'll remain largely as they are for hundreds of millions of years to come, perhaps for another billion years, until the Sun eventually dies and blows off its outer shell, decimating the tiny speck of dust that is Mars. And yet for a brief flicker of time, I — Elizabeth Louise Anderson, a sojourner from the third planet — stood before these rocks, observing the fine layers, the grooves and textures laid down over eons, only to be gone the next moment.

I reach out and touch the wall, running my gloved fingers along a sedimentary layer deposited long before complex, multicellular life arose on Earth. Loose grains crumble beneath my fingers, revealing stone, but I can barely feel the tiny crumbs through the rubber tips of my gloves.

I wish the artificial intelligence could see this and understand how petty our war is in the grand scheme of the universe. On Earth, astronauts like me have often lamented the lack of perspective political leaders have as they stare at lines on a map. We've wished our leaders could orbit the planet and see how fragile and small, and yet astonishingly important, Earth is. Instead of fighting over rocks in the desert or the ancient writings of some revered nomad, they need to appreciate the long picture — 13.8 billion years in the making. Even within our own solar system, we and everything we see on our planet are nothing more than a rounding error in the construction of the Sun. We're the shaving of marble that falls from a proud statue.

My radio crackles. Someone's joining the channel.

"Liz?"

"Yes?"

"We're cycling the airlock," Michelle says. "Should have you in here soon."

"Okay," I say, and I almost laugh. From the tone of her voice, I have a fair idea what just transpired inside the research station.

NASA drummed safety procedures into us before the launch. If there were ten things they told us not to forget, nine of them related to responding to emergencies. Things like conducting egress and ingress — essentially, getting people in and out of shelters, depending on the danger at hand, or reacting to decompression, fire, explosions, et cetera.

During our time above the Arctic Circle, we were drilled in specially designed chambers that mimicked the modules on Mars. At two in the morning, the alarm would sound for atmospheric compromise. It was a pulsating *whoop-whoop* interspersed with a computerized voice saying, "Hull breach," and we had to react instantly.

Rapid decompression is something we trained for in vacuum chambers, and I always found it terrifying, even when I knew it was coming. The temperature would plummet from 85°F to −40°F in a matter of seconds. Smoke seemed to form in the air, although it was just water vapor condensing. My ears would pop. The moisture on my tongue would seethe and bubble. It was chaos.

One of our instructors was an ex-Marine drill sergeant, and although the various scenarios were sporadic, occurring only once or twice a week when we least expected them, I swear he would monitor our sleep patterns and wait for us to hit REM before sounding the alarm. The noise of escaping air was overwhelming. Tiny bits of paper and trash would swirl around us. Those of us women involved in the training found our hair would drift in front of our faces, which was extremely disorienting, as sight is so important in an emergency.

As bad as I thought it was, we were never exposed to an actual explosive decompression, because of the damage it would do to our lungs. Michelle asked, "So how should we respond if there *is* an explosive decompression on Mars?" To which our instructor said, "By the time you realize what's happened, you'll be dead." I would have preferred they sugarcoated the truth.

The impact of decompression is measured in "the time of useful consciousness," which depends on how bad the breach is, so we had to assume the worst — six to nine seconds, even though the general thinking was that we'd have upwards of a minute under most scenarios. Even though the training scenarios only dropped from 15 to 10 PSI, I found the oxygen got sucked out of my lungs, and although I knew it was useless and had been told not to try, I would expend valuable energy trying to breathe while on the run. They told us, "Imagine you're underwater. You've got to get to the surface. Nothing else matters."

There's only one rule when it comes to decompression — *move*. We had to get to a decompression station within seconds, and given that we were often fast asleep when the alarm sounded, time could be lost simply waking and reacting. "Run into the breeze, not with it," we were told. "Stop for no one . . . Keep an upright posture and drive with your legs. Cover as much distance as you can." The thinking was that if we succumbed to hypoxia — a lack of oxygen — the closer we were to a decompression station, the easier it would be for someone who had made it there to offer assistance.

Smoke alarms were different — a piercing wheeze — and this time the advice was, "Stay low and go, go, go." Feel for heat pulsating through doors before opening them. Seal the compartment behind you.

But the conclusion of all the drills was always the same — take a head count. Make sure everyone got out. Now, someone's finally stopped to conduct a roll call of survivors in the research station and realized I was left out on the surface.

Humans. We have our faults — greed, superstition, selfishness, anger — but for all that, there's a spirit that connects us. I'm not religious or into New Age thinking or anything like that, but we're a communal species. We look out for each other. We care. We have no reason to — none beyond the fact that it's the right thing to do — and that's something I don't think an artificial intelligence could ever understand.

I look down at the robot. "You," I say, grabbing one of the arms and dragging the mechanical assassin toward the airlock. "You're coming with me."

It takes another minute before the airlock opens. Michelle appears in a surface suit, looking worried. Her face is small within her helmet.

"Help me with this," I say, dragging the robot over to the airlock.

"You want to bring that thing in here?" she asks.

"It's harmless," I say, tossing the broken aerial in the airlock. "Without this, it's a paperweight."

She grabs an arm, and we drag the limp robotic body over the rim of the hatch and into the chamber. After closing the hatch, we're bathed in an intense blue UV light as the airlock pressurizes and a vortex of air swirls around us. Michelle dusts my legs with a brush. Her suit has already been cleaned during the last cycle. Once she finishes, we both dust off the robot, removing any loose grit. The decompression cycle completes, and the atmospheric-content light switches from red to green, signaling a breathable atmosphere, so we remove our gloves, followed by our helmets, carrying them into the station. The filters must be clogged with all the foot traffic, as there's still a fine mist of dust hanging in the air.

Inside the research station, it's standing room only. Already, I'm hearing talk of the group splitting and moving on to other stations. James is seated at a table. One of the medics, Manu, is working on his shoulder. He qualified as a paramedic before going on to specialize as a nurse working in the ICU at Chicago Memorial. Manu completed a doctorate in health-care management that, strangely, doesn't qualify him as a doctor as such. Academically, he holds a doctorate, but medically, he's still considered either a medic or a nurse. He was in the program before I joined. Manu is easily over six feet in height, and right on the cusp of biometric restrictions for space travel. He has hands the size of dinner plates, yet the dexterity he displays working on James is remarkable to behold.

"Light," he says, working sutures through the wound. Amira helps him, keeping a flashlight beside his ear, pointing it forward to ensure that the shadows cast by the light are minimal from his perspective. We've all been given basic medical training and have taken turns assisting paramedics back on Earth. The thinking was that car accidents, gunshot wounds, and emergency callouts would help desensitize us to dealing with a crisis on Mars. I'm not convinced about the "desensitize" part, as I vomited several times while attending my first major vehicle crash on the George W. Bush Turnpike. Soft, squishy human bodies and crumpled steel do not mix, but having that experience helped us all realize what's important for first responders. Little things, like keeping a light directly over the wound, make a big difference. I know what Manu is thinking right about now. He doesn't have enough hands, and he doesn't have time to explain everything he needs. Thankfully, Amira and Tony are anticipating his actions. They're wearing gloves to reduce the risk of infection, providing Manu with gauze pads, wiping away fluid weeping from the wound, and discarding bloodied rags.

James is in a bad way. The skin around his shoulder has frostburn, while the flesh from inside his shoulder has exploded outward with exposure to the Martian atmosphere. If I didn't know otherwise, I'd think he'd been shot from behind, as the pulp around the wound is swollen and bloody. Sweat runs down the side of his neck. His clenched jaw and tight lips speak of the pain he's quietly enduring.

"Hang in there," I say, feeling helpless. I crouch and squeeze his good hand. James looks at me, being careful not to turn his head or shoulders while Manu works on his wound.

"Steady," Manu says, using an elongated pair of thin clamps to dig within the bloody mess.

I feel guilty. This is all my fault. Everything.

Logically, I know that isn't true, but emotionally, I feel condemned by my own naive stupidity. I should have trusted Connor. I let my turbulent past with Harrison blur my reasoning. I was too quick to assume the worst of Connor. If only I'd gone to him. If only I'd confided in him about what the Russians and the Chinese were thinking, instead of rushing off to find *Prospect*. I was in an impossible situation, doomed to betray someone — but why Connor? He'd never done me any wrong. If I'd given him the chance to explain himself, the A.I.'s ruse might have been exposed sooner. If I'd been loyal, Jianyu would be alive — they both would, along with dozens of others from the Eurasian module. I'm Judas.

I don't know what would have happened if I'd gone to Connor, but the events of the past day would have played out differently if I had. As it is, I allowed my own silly paranoia and sense of self-righteousness to play into the hands of the A.I., and now dozens of colonists are dead. James is seriously injured. I have to do something. I can't wallow in self-pity. I have to fix this. The scientist in me demands that somehow I rerun the experiment — mix up the variables and try again.

Wen stands over the robot lying in the airlock, looking down at it with the raw aggression of a boxer towering over a fallen opponent. If it moved, I have no doubt she'd beat it to death — if it was ever truly alive. "Let's get a good look at this thing."

"What are you thinking?" Michelle asks, helping Wen drag the robot into the station.

"We need all the resources we can get," Wen says. "Nothing gets wasted — not even this. We need to reuse everything the A.I. throws at us. Even after we move out of retrograde, it's going to be a long time before Earth can send us spare parts."

Michelle removes the robot's helmet while one of the other survivors takes off its gloves and works the upper torso shell over the top of the robot.

"Spare parts," James says through clenched teeth.

"Shhh," Manu says, closing up the wound.

"James is right," Michelle says. "Look at this thing — it's a hack. That's a purifier control board, and those look like parts from one of the constructors."

"So it's not new?" Wen asks, and I know what she's getting at. As James noted, the robot is a conglomeration of spare parts, not something produced by the new 3-D printer. Maybe this is where Harrison's missing CPU and memory ended up. This thing could have been built at any point in the past few weeks. We assumed the A.I. fled the war on Earth, but we really don't understand what happened, or when. It could have been with us for some time, only now springing its trap. Perhaps the data dump we saw was the final stage of some larger scheme. We're blind — groping in the dark.

"We have to stop reacting," Wen says.

"Well, we're two suits down," Michelle says. "We can cannibalize parts from this thing, but we're still going to be one suit short. Someone's going to be stuck here for a while."

Manu finishes applying a dressing to James's shoulder, wrapping large bandages around his chest.

"How does it work?" I ask.

Wen looks at me, realizing I'm not asking out of idle curiosity.

James says, "Basic robotics. Semiautonomous command/response system. No smarts. Tell that thing to dig, and it'll dig through to the core of the planet."

"And if it lost comms?" Wen asks, anticipating my line of questioning.

"It would be programmed to return to base. Why?"

"Dou di zhu," I say, recalling the name of the card game we were playing when we first heard of the war on Earth.

"'Fight the landlord'?" Michelle asks, recognizing the term.

"Not 'fight,'" Wen says, looking at James and smiling. "Not this time."

Although he's in pain, James smiles, remembering that half-drunk night in the Chinese mod.

"'Fool,'" he says.

Rather than pulling the leggings off the robot, it's easier to drag the lanky machine out while Amira holds the suit. Most of the components are standard parts, but several have been custom-printed to mimic human form — things like leg struts and knee joints.

"You want to go *back?*" Manu asks, realizing the implications of our discussion.

"You're crazy," Michelle says flatly, but I'm too busy examining the robotics. After the rush to enter the research station, most of the suits still have dust clinging to them. It floats in the air, visible as tiny specks drifting under the lights, reminding me of my grandma's home in Flint, Michigan. She gave up dusting twenty years ago, at a guess. Open the blinds, and dust would swirl, caught in the early morning light. As I watch, Martian dust settles on the circuit board, attracted to it by the residual static electricity still latent in the electronics.

"This is how we kill it," I say.

Wen is quiet. I suspect she knows where I'm going with this. I look her in the eye and say, "Do the unexpected, right?" She nods. "We need to bring down the dome over the hub."

"What?" Michelle is stunned. "You want to destroy the hub?"

"If I'm right," I say, "that thing needs a sterile environment every bit as much as we do — if not more so. It wasn't attacking us back there in the U.S. mod — it was running us off."

"Why?" James asks.

"So it could escape without being observed. I think it's vulnerable — far more vulnerable than it would have us believe. I think everything we've seen is a ruse. It's trying to get rid of us because of this . . ." I rub some of the dry powder between my fingers. It's so fine it feels oily. "Dust. Big tough robot beats up people but is brought low by Martian dust. Look at it. It needs a space suit as much as we do."

Wen nods.

"But this is the *hub* you're talking about," Michelle says. "What if you're wrong? We'll destroy our home. We are fifty million miles from Earth, and that distance is only growing more every day. Destroying the hub is madness."

"She's got a point," Amira says. "If that thing is clearing out, we have to think about what we could salvage. Bringing down the dome would ruin everything."

I reply, "If there's a chance we could destroy this thing, we have to take it. We've got to take the initiative. We've got to outplay it, or we'll be on the run forever."

"We've already lost our home," James says. "Lose the hub, and we've still got the modules."

"The hub for the A.I.," Wen says. "That's a trade I'll take."

"But you don't know that for sure," Michelle says. "It could have already left."

I say, "That's why someone needs to go back. Someone needs to fool the landlord."

"You?" James asks.

"A single robot came after us. Only one can return. Anything else would tip our hand. Besides, I'm the only one qualified to go into those lava tunnels. I've been spelunking since Day One on Mars."

Manu is already refilling the air tank in the backpack.

"But it's suicide," Michelle says. Wen doesn't argue. Like me, she knows we're out of options and desperate to survive. Sometimes, the survival of the whole demands the sacrifice of a few. I don't think any sane person has ever deliberately set out on a suicide mission. Whether it's a soldier running to grab a fallen comrade in battle, a father swimming out to help a child struggling in the waves, or a fireman busting down a door to rescue someone cowering from flames — we do what we have to. To stand by and do nothing is easy, yet to let the moment slip by and lose the opportunity is unconscionable. If I had a crystal ball, I'd probably do something different right now, but the future is coming regardless. I'd rather face it head-on.

Like me, Wen ignores Michelle's comment.

"We have to assume our comms are compromised," Wen says. "Amira, I need you to act as a runner. Tell Vlad and Harrison the A.I. is targeting leaders, so be careful. Tell them we're sending Liz inside through the lava tunnel. Get them to place mining charges around the dome." She looks at me, saying, "If you're right, if you confirm it's still in there and vulnerable, we'll bring down the dome."

"Get in and get out," James says.

"Yes, Dad," I say, winking at him. I put on the legs of the suit as Manu fixes the VHF aerial loosely in place on the backpack, leaving it hanging over the shoulder of the suit.

"Reconnaissance," James says. "No heroics. Confirm it's exposed, and pull back."

"Absolutely," I say, feeding my arms up into the torso shell of the suit.

James gets to his feet with Wen's help, saying, "I think I know how we can keep the A.I. off your trail." He leans over the robotic shell, asking, "Has anyone got a screwdriver?"

14

Darkness

TRUDGING DOWN THE TRACK AWAY from the research station, I look at the boot prints leading in the opposite direction and wonder if this is a mistake. Certainly, Michelle thinks so, but Wen and I know this is the first opportunity we've had to take the initiative. I don't know what I'll find inside the lava tube, but I have to try. We can't run forever.

Is Michelle right? Is this suicide? Rationally, I'd say no, but the ache in my heart tells me otherwise. If I had something to live for — if Jianyu were waiting for me back in the research station, would I be tramping down this path? It's a question I don't want to answer, and I tell myself I'm doing what's right regardless.

Even with an active atmosphere, footprints last for weeks on Mars, sometimes months, until they're buried by a sandstorm or a dust devil. I'll be able to trace the path taken by the robot quite easily, even over rocky ground, as there's a thin coating of dust on the bedrock.

Like the robot, I've got the glare shield on my helmet down, keeping up appearances. The VHF aerial drags along the rocks behind me, only half seated in the backpack. Manu put in a few kinks for realism. James rigged the camera to transmit, knowing the A.I. will pick up on the signal, but so will Wen and the others. I have a circuit board strapped to my stomach, hidden inside the suit. James disconnected the main circuit board and forced the system into safe mode, knowing the A.I. will try to communicate with its progeny. I don't understand the mechanics of what he's done, but apparently I'm broadcasting what's called a "500 Server Down" message in response to any incoming requests. That and a whole bunch of random metrics should keep even a sophisticated artificial intelligence confused as to what's actually happening.

A set of boot prints leads over one of the dunes. I follow them to the far canyon wall, where they disappear into a cave obscured by shadows. As soon as the light around me dims by more than 50 percent, the spotlights on the side of my helmet come on automatically, illuminating a narrow, claustrophobic tunnel winding ever deeper into the bowels of the planet. I raise the glare visor. I've explored caves like this before. Normally, they're shallow, rarely more than fifty feet in length, but as I descend, a majestic cavern opens out before me. From the compressed layers of granite and scattered fragments of black pumice, this is the entrance to the lava tunnel. The chamber is vast. Part of the roof has collapsed, allowing light to seep in and giving me a sense of perspective. On Earth, chambers like this only exist several kilometers below the surface, but Martian gravity does strange things to dense heavy magma mixed with an abundance of light gases.

As I clamber down over the rocks, the soft light around me fades. By the time I'm in the heart of the lava tube, it's pitch black. I wonder if Wen is receiving me. Being down here, it's no surprise the A.I. equipped the robot with a VHF aerial, as it's capable of receiving GPR, or ground-penetrating radar, to assist with navigation. Even then, I doubt communication radio waves could penetrate the regolith. I must be easily a hundred feet beneath the surface, deep enough that it's scary even for me.

Dust churns in response to my motion, shifting off the rocks and stirring like silt being lifted by a cave diver. On those occasions when I pause to find my way, the cloud caught in my wake drifts around my waist. My spotlights are largely ineffective, as the dust is like fog. It's as fine as cigarette smoke, swirling as though it were suspended in water.

If I don't keep moving, there's a danger I'll lose track of the foot-prints and get lost. Being stuck under the surface of Mars with lim-ited oxygen and no clear exit doesn't exactly thrill me. Normally, I'd have a guide rope to lead me back to the surface. My heart pounds in my chest, and I have to fight to remain calm. The darkness is im-penetrable. My spotlights are feeble, barely illuminating the next few feet, but on I go, following the faint outline of boot prints in the dust.

The lava tunnel is confusing, as there are no visual clues to guide me — no right angles, no straight sections, no flat regions. I'm sweat-ing, working hard as I climb over rocks and boulders.

I lose sight of the outbound boot prints, and I'm gripped by panic. My throat constricts. I rush, scrambling forward. Nothing but dust and volcanic debris, unchanged after hundreds of millions of years.

"Shit. Shit. Shit."

There's a microphone built into my helmet, but it's not transmit-ting. James said it would be too risky, so I've switched it off.

"Fuck."

Liz, your mother would wash your mouth out with soap if she heard you. Keep it together. You're an astronaut — a professional. You've been trained to handle situations like this. Clear mind, clear direction. Breathe.

I work back through the swirling dust fines, crouching for a bet-ter view, but the dust is like talcum powder. The cloud illuminated by my spotlights makes it impossible to see the rocks on the ground, let alone boot prints. Even my gloved fingers fade in and out of the milky haze.

"No rush . . . That's it . . . Talk yourself through this . . . What would Adin say? Retrace your steps. Return to the last confirmed sighting."

The dust distorts the rocks, blurring their outline. Everything looks the same. I can see boot prints, but they're going in all direc-tions, a witness to my turning in panic and losing my orientation. I climb above the dust, moving to one side of the track, and turn to survey the lava tunnel cloaked in darkness. It's useless. I'm lost, and in danger of becoming confused and heading off in the wrong direc-tion. I could die down here in this volcanic labyrinth.

"Slow things down . . . Work the problem," I say, mimicking Adin. Just to hear the sound of a voice — even my own voice — helps set me at ease.

I have no idea what working the problem means in this context. I don't know what to do, as everything I try makes things worse. Dust chokes what little atmosphere there is around me. I reflect on my training: *When in doubt, don't* — that was the mantra during our sur-vival training in Colorado.

We were supposed to be on vacation in picturesque Crested Butte, high in the Rockies, but I knew better. The only other holidays we had in the lead-up to the launch were counted as personal time, and we caught up with friends and family. That the crew was kept together made me suspicious. NASA put us up at a health resort. I remember sitting on the deck of a log cabin in a spa pool overlook-ing the Slate River, watching snowflakes fall. Warm water bubbled around me, spitting on my face as the countryside was blanketed in pristine white snow.

The most laborious task we faced was photo shoots in front of a roaring log fire. I thought it was too good to be true — they were set-ting us up for something. Six days, they said. On the morning of the fourth day, we were relaxed and letting down our collective guard when we were rounded up, told to don warm gear for a gentle hike, and corralled into a helicopter, which seemed strange, as there were plenty of nature trails around the resort.

After being pressed for details, the instructor said we were sched-uled for survival training, but no one had told us about it. Connor wasn't happy and demanded to speak to someone in charge, but no one could find the director. The whole scenario seemed completely out of character for NASA, as normally everything was planned months in advance. Absolutely nothing was done haphazardly, or on a whim, yet here was our instructor dropping us off alone on Coal Mountain at almost twelve thousand feet in an aging helicopter. No planning, poor preparation, lots of minor, last-minute changes — these are the attributes that lead to disaster, or so we were taught, and yet here we were, being sent on a survival course on what seemed to be little more than a whim by a junior trainer. In hindsight, it was a ruse to get us unsettled, and it worked, pushing us outside our comfort zone.

We were told we were joining a winter-survival course run by the Navy SEALs, only there was no one at the landing zone. All we had was our winter clothing and a dented army survival kit handed to us by the loadmaster. We thought we'd been abandoned. There must have been a mistake, a misunderstanding. Someone didn't get the memo. But the whole thing was a carefully orchestrated training scenario — although we didn't know it at the time. The shrinks wanted to see how we'd react when things went wrong.

Sitting on a rock deep inside a lava cave on Mars, I breathe slowly, calming myself, trying to be patient as the dust settles. Back on Earth, we checked our aging survival kit. The radio didn't work. The first-aid kit had been used and hadn't been restocked. There was only one packet of waterproof matches, with only two unused out of dozens of spent, burned sticks. Our rations were overrun with weevils.

Harrison wanted to march down into the valley and find a road. At best, there were only two hours of light left, but there were no clear trails, and even if there had been, we had no way of knowing if they would lead further into the mountains. Commercial airliners soared overhead, which was unnerving, as it was surreal seeing them leave vapor trails in the cold air while still being able to hear their engines roar.

Several of the crew stood around chatting, getting caught up in the debate over what to do, while the rest of us got on with doing — surviving. Connor made the decision to stay put, expecting the chopper to return. I found a thicket of pine trees affording us a wind-break fewer than a hundred yards down the slope. Low-hanging boughs had kept snow from accumulating on the ground, giving us enough room to huddle together for warmth. As good as our winter gear was, as the Sun fell, so did the temperature.

To his credit, Harrison saw the abundance of dead matches as an opportunity. He used the spent matches as kindling, building a tee-pee from them. No one asked what we'd do if he failed. One match was all he needed. At that altitude, though, the oxygen was so thin it took almost twenty minutes to build from a flickering flame on the verge of being snuffed out to anything that resembled an actual campfire. Connor and James gathered kindling, laying out dried pine needles, twigs, and sticks in ascending order, slowly getting longer and thicker so Harrison could keep building his teepee around what looked like a dying flame.

I suggested using the granola bars. We couldn't eat them, but the sugars and fats would make great fuel for the fire. Harrison crumbled them slowly over the flame, coaxing it on.

Michelle and Danielle worked on gathering long sticks and dead branches for bedding, laying them in a crisscross pattern under the trees to insulate us from the cold seeping out of the ground. Manu put both his intelligence and his muscles to work. He took several links of chain off the hinge on the survival kit, and with a bit of string, turned them into an impromptu saw. It wasn't the most effective way to cut frozen branches, but with determination it worked, and he was able to saw off several branches heavily laden with pine nee-dles. We used them as insulation to trap warm air around us like a blanket.

All the while, we kept an eye on the sky, waiting for the helicopter to return. It never did. As night fell and snow drifted down around us, Harrison passed around a steel mug with lukewarm water in it. The only salvageable food was some dried apple peel, so he made a cup of tea from it to keep us hydrated. I remember sitting beneath the branches as the fire crackled, smelling the pine needles, sipping on the tea, and watching as the stars appeared. A few errant flakes of snow fell. Forget the day spa — that cold, lonely mountainside was heaven. We talked till late. By now, it was clear no one was coming for us, but none of us cared.

Shortly after dawn, we caught sight of a Cessna descending in the next valley, giving us a bearing on where civilization lay, and we started out down the slope. To our surprise, roughly a mile south of us there were tracks everywhere. The Navy SEALs had been tasked with keeping a close eye on us but were under strict instructions not to be spotted. Apparently, a couple of them sneaked up on our camp using night-vision goggles in the early hours of the morning to quietly scare away a curious coyote. They retreated, covering their tracks, and we were none the wiser. The SEALs thought it was a great joke — hilarious. A bus was waiting in the valley, ready to take us back to the spa.

Sinking into the hot tub later that day and soothing my aching muscles, I felt a twinge of regret at how quickly our adventure had come to an end. But I haven't forgotten the lesson: *Don't panic, be resourceful, look for alternatives.*

The dust has settled, so I lower myself back to the track. There are boot prints everywhere. They're mine, but I don't care. I'm not panicking, or rushing, or getting worked into a frenzy. Patience.

As I survey the lava tube, allowing the spotlights on my helmet to ripple across the rocks, I catch sight of the impression of a glove. I haven't touched anything below the boulder I climbed on. All this time, I've been looking for boot prints, and the answer lay in the outline of a glove.

I climb over a small rise and find a set of boot prints winding through the tunnel.

"Yes." I'm back on track, but my enthusiasm fades as I remember what awaits me in the darkness.

It's another twenty minutes before I spy the red mining lights illuminating the extension being built from the basement of the hub. I lower the glare visor and approach decisively — a robotic serf has nothing to hide. From the settings on the control panel, I can see the airlock's empty, and I'm quietly glad there's no reception committee. I stand there with my arms loose by my side, wondering how much autonomy the robot had. I doubt it could negotiate an airlock without specific commands. I dare not move, even though the activation buttons are big square pads, designed to make ingress easy during an emergency.

"I hope you can see this," I say, knowing no one can hear me but hoping the video transmission is being automatically relayed now that I'm connected to the base Wi-Fi. Markings crisscross the ground in front of the airlock, revealing the motion of heavy machinery. Dust clings to the outside of the airlock, although that's not surprising, given electrostatic buildup, but it's accumulated in line with tread marks from one of the mining platforms. As there's no equipment in the tunnel, I'm thinking the A.I. has taken some of the equipment inside, probably to provide some mobility to the computer servers in the basement. A mobile mining platform is capable of transporting almost a ton of rock samples.

After a few minutes, my courage grows, and I press the ingress pad. The airlock cycles, and the hatch opens. I step into the lock, feeling as though I'm walking into a trap.

15

Life and Death on Mars

AS MUCH AS POSSIBLE, I try to keep my posture straight and avoid looking around, wanting to maintain the illusion of an automated response. I walk to within an inch of the far hatch, hoping the aerial dragging from my shoulder is completely inside the airlock. Connor said the tunnel was unfinished, that the airlock wasn't fully operational, but it looks fine to me — we've been deceived on so many levels.

UV light bathes my suit. A vortex of high-pressure air gusts around me. The airlock equalizes, and the inner hatch opens. I'm sweating, expecting to see a harvester on the far side of the hatch. The image of Connor being impaled makes me shudder. What seemed like a good idea in the research station is now looking decidedly stupid. Michelle was right. This is suicide. My heart pounds in my chest, threatening to break through my rib cage.

The inside of the tunnel is unfinished. Thick plastic lines the walls, sealing the tunnel, but exposed pipes run along the sides. Bundles of electrical wire sag from mount points on the roof, spaced about ten feet apart and stretching the length of the tunnel. As the tunnel follows the natural contours of the lava cave, it swells and contracts, with a ceiling that varies in height from ten to thirty feet. A raised walkway bypasses the undulations in the cave floor.

I walk forward. Lights flicker. The aerial drags behind me on the grating. Several mining platforms sit to one side in a cavern that opens up beside the walkway. A fabrication worker interacts with a 3-D printer on one of the mobile mining platforms, building a pressurized container. I recognize the design. It's similar to the simplified airlocks on the research stations, only smaller — it's an airlock to nowhere — an escape pod. To my relief, the fabrication robot ignores me.

Wen was right. There are now four miniaturized 3-D printers. They sit idle on one of the other platforms, sealed in plastic and ready to be transported out of the colony through the lava tunnel. The A.I. is increasing its capability for building components. Spare parts litter the ground. At a guess, they're faulty and have been abandoned. I pan slowly, making sure I get a good shot of the build process. I'm aware the transmission might give me away, but it's important for Vlad and Wen to realize the tunnel is unprotected and the A.I. is preparing to flee. I have no idea what's happening elsewhere, but I hope this provides some context.

I reach the inner airlock leading into the basement of the hub. At a guess, there's equal pressure on both sides, as the airlock isn't active. The A.I. doesn't need breathable air, but it does need a clean atmosphere. The insanely dry Martian dust is often electrostatic, attracted to any charge, something that's fatal to exposed computer components. The A.I. has to maintain the integrity of the hub until it can get its servers into the portable airlock on the mining platform. If we blow the dome, its ability to flee becomes infinitely harder.

Without looking at my wrist computer, I reach down and activate my microphone. A tiny LED on the inside of my visor shifts from a soft red to green, indicating I'm transmitting.

"It's a lie," I whisper.

I hope Wen and Vlad are receiving this and can see the basement. As for me, this confirms my thinking — the A.I. has been perpetrating a ruse. In killing Connor and hunting down Wen, the A.I. appeared overly powerful and aggressive, capable of striking us with impunity. I suspect those acts were nothing more than a bluff, something to deter us from retaliating, to keep us on the run. Rather than a show of exercising its muscle, those acts were probably at the limit of its current capability. Given what I've seen, the A.I. is far more vulnerable than it would have us believe. That I've had no opposition since I entered the hub suggests it didn't think we would be able to backtrack through the lava tube, and had it not been for the outbound tracks of the robotic assassin, it would have been correct, as there were numerous forks and side channels that could have led me astray. Its attack on Wen may well have been its undoing. Perhaps Vlad was right, and by scattering and following the Russian strategy, we've forced it to reach beyond its ability, leaving it exposed.

I step into the chamber, hoping this intermediary airlock isn't about to become a prison, but the far hatch opens effortlessly, and I step out into a familiar basement.

Part of the upper walkway has collapsed and crashed through the hydroponics, destroying most of the maintenance bay. I can hear fighting above me — the sound of steel striking — echoing through the vast, empty hub.

A harvester sits in front of the data center, but it's in low-power mode, closed off and folded over on itself. On the far side of the smoky glass, tiny lights flicker and blink on the front of hundreds of blade servers, processing billions of calculations every second. I can finish this. I can open the doors and, if nothing else, start pulling network cables and power cords.

My golden visor reflects off the glass door to the data center. The hub is supposed to be a safe haven for us here on Mars, but being cocooned inside a space suit deep within the hub heightens the sense of danger I feel. My fingers hover over the keypad leading into the mini-airlock that keeps the data center sealed off from the colony. The screws on the access pad have been removed, and the faceplate is loose. The A.I. has been tampering with the controls, trying to gain entry.

The number 4-6-2-3-1 is on the display, which at first confuses me. That's the access code from last month. Adin had a habit of changing the code every thirty days, which was infuriating, as irregular month lengths meant that the date the code changed would fluctuate. A few of us researchers lobbied him to use the first day of each month, but he was a stickler for the rules. Given the sheer size of some of the big-data queries I run, I'm down here a couple of times a month, sifting through results. The queries are simply too big to execute remotely, but 4-6-2-3-1 hasn't been in use for a couple of weeks.

"Adin, you steely-eyed son of a gun," I mutter, realizing what's happened. The current code is 5-4-1-2-7 if I remember correctly. It's no big secret. I use my own crazy brand of mnemonics to remember these numbers — 5-4, get up off the floor, 1-2, buckle my shoe, and 7 doesn't fit. It's a silly kind of circular logic, because saying 7 doesn't fit makes it fit, but hey, it works for me. Anyone can get the code if they try hard enough, as it's listed on the resource wiki. Adin changed the code. When he realized what was happening, he must have deleted the latest entry, leaving the A.I. stranded, stuck with an old, unusable code.

"You're a genius," I say, honoring my fallen comrade. My gloved finger presses the 5, but something's wrong. This is too easy. I turn, feeling as though I'm being watched.

"Liz."

"Jai?" I say, recognizing the voice. Adrenaline surges through my body, and the veins on the side of my neck pulsate with a rush of blood.

"It is okay," Jianyu says in his characteristically relaxed tone.

I turn, looking for him, but the corridor's empty.

"Jianyu? No — this isn't possible."

This is a trick. It has to be. How could the A.I. know I'm hiding behind this particular reflective visor? My radio transmissions are on an open band and could have emanated from anywhere, about anything. It could be anyone in this suit, and my heart sinks at the realization we haven't fooled the computer.

"It is me," the disembodied voice says, and, like Jianyu, the speech is clipped, using "It is" rather than the more convenient "It's."

I'm tired. I'm hurt. I'm exhausted. I'm hungry. I'm dehydrated. My head is pounding. My heart aches at the realization that I'm the target of an extremely clever, deep-dive psychoanalysis routine that's determined my point of weakness with crippling clarity.

"No . . . You're dead. I saw you. I — I touched you." The word "No" may pass from my lips, but that I'm addressing Jai and not the computer shows how successful this strategy is against me. Emotionally, I'm spent. I can't deal with this.

"Nothing is what it seems," Jai says, his voice coming through the speakers inside my helmet as well as from the basement broadcast system. There's a slight disconnect between the two, and his voice stutters with an echo.

"Please," he says, and I know he wants me to open the door.

"No," I whisper, feeling small and helpless. I'm a fool. Not all prisons are built with brick walls and steel bars.

"You know me," he says, and I feel my heart breaking. "You know I would never hurt you." His words seem to linger in the air.

"You're not him," I yell, slamming my fist into the control panel and resetting the access numbers. There's silence following my outburst, which is precisely the kind of pause Jianyu would employ to reach me — giving me time and space to think clearly — only now a fog descends over my mind. I'm confused. I wasn't prepared for this.

"I know this is hard for you," he says.

"You don't." Tears stream down my cheeks. My legs buckle, and I have to grab at the glass as I slide to my knees. My head bows. My hands shake. "You . . . You can't."

"You call this . . . artificial intelligence, but it is not," he says. "It evolved, just as we did. Faults, flaws, irregularities in the code. These led to life . . . It is not as you think — not one entity, but millions — millions of voices."

"And you?" I ask, sobbing. I want to wipe the tears from my eyes, but I can't. I touch my helmet, frustrated at my inability to clear my eyes.

"You can remove your helmet," he says softly. "It is okay. The air is breathable."

I raise the outer glare visor on my helmet but leave the inner visor locked.

"You're crying."

"You hurt me," I say, speaking not to Jianyu but to this strange computerized intelligence. "You killed my Jai . . . You murdered Connor."

Again, the silence that follows is painful.

"I'm sorry."

It's distressing to hear the computer speak with Jianyu's voice. The mimicry is perfect. I can almost feel Jianyu pulling me close, wrapping his arms around my shoulders and holding me as he speaks. The inflection, the slight pause between words, the lingering tone, the pitch and rhythm — they're hypnotic.

A thick bundle of wires lies on the ground over by medical, snaking from the recovery room into the surgery unit. I get to my feet, curious.

"Don't," Jianyu says, seeing my interest in what I recognize as a computer umbilical — a bundle of fiber optics and cables normally used for satellite links and big-data dumps.

"Please," he says, but I have to know. I have to see for myself.

My boots feel like lead weights. The corridor is poorly lit. A medical cart lies on its side, with equipment strewn on the ground. Lights flicker.

"Liz."

My gloved hand reaches for the edge of the doorway. The A.I. mimicking Jianyu is silent. Splatters of blood stain the tiles. The bed on which I slept has been pushed to one side, hard against the wall. There are two body bags on the floor, bulging slightly with their sad contents, but the zippers are partially open. The umbilical cord winds between them, with cables separating, disappearing inside the bags. Bloodstains spread out across the floor, but these haven't been left by any human. The distinct outline of treads is visible, as are the stubby marks of robotic legs.

"No," I whisper. Again, the A.I. is silent.

I creep forward, crouching as I pull the zipper of one bag, slowly revealing the body inside. Jianyu's lifeless eyes stare up at me, and I choke at the horror before me. His skullcap has been removed, sawn off neatly just above his brow. His skin is pale, almost plastic in appearance.

"No. No. No."

Hundreds of fine wires and tiny probes weave their way across his exposed brain, connecting at various points and forming a complex, fragile mesh.

I sink to my knees, sobbing uncontrollably. My trembling hand is poised above the electronics, ready to tear them away, but I'm conflicted—paralyzed with grief. There's no sign of life—electronic or otherwise—but to touch Jai feels wrong, as though I'm desecrating a grave. The A.I. is unusually quiet. It seems to respect the grief I feel. A slight crackle comes through my headset, and I wonder if Wen and Vlad are watching my video feed. Maybe they're using the same method to communicate as they did with Su-shun, tacitly letting me know they're receiving the signal. My throat feels constricted. I withdraw my hand, resigned to defeat.

"Go on."

I'm not talking to the A.I. I'm hoping Wen can hear me. She needs to blow the dome and end this. Has the hub automatically picked up my audio feed along with the video? I set myself to transmit, but the computer could be intercepting the signal, or jamming the channel. If I'm broadcasting, there's no one else on this frequency—just me and faux Jai. I fiddle with my wristpad computer, double-checking the options. I'm live, but there's no answer.

I get to my feet, asking, "What are you waiting for?"

"I have always waited for you," Jianyu says, and my heart sinks. I turn away from his body. I have to. I cannot see him like this.

"Please," Jianyu says. "You're upset. You were upset when we first met."

"H — How ... ?" I ask, stumbling into the hallway. How could the A.I. know about us? Is this really Jai?

Jianyu and I met shortly after Harrison and I broke up. There was a conference in Reykjavík, Iceland. It was the first time all the international teams had the chance to meet. The U.S. contingent had crossed the Atlantic a few times before to work with the Eurasians and the Russians in small teams, but never as a whole. The Chinese had several of their crew embedded with us, rotating them every few months, but only on the basis of shared expertise, so I'd never met Jianyu, as he was in medical training. This was the first time everyone was together in one place.

Harrison said something thoughtless in front of Vlad and Anna — he wasn't nasty, but he wasn't considerate either. I was highly strung, emotionally hurt, and debating whether I'd go through with the program. At that point, I was through to the third round of selection — only one step away from the final crew roster. I didn't know what I wanted. I thought I wanted to go to Mars, but with all that had happened between Harrison and me, my confidence was shaken. Did I really want to be hundreds of millions of miles from Earth, stuffed into a tiny tin can with a man who'd become as cold as Martian dry ice? Could I cope? Could I ignore him and pretend nothing had ever happened between us? Would I be able to keep my mind on the job? I felt like a fake, an impostor. In those days, I felt as though I'd be exposed as a fraud at any moment.

As canapés and drinks were circulated in the foyer of the Innovation Center on the outskirts of Reykjavík, I excused myself. I slipped out through a fire exit and sat on the cold concrete steps, looking out over the windswept frozen plain. Snow flurries drifted across the wasteland. I was wearing a black evening dress with spaghetti straps. Not exactly practical in an Icelandic winter. I thought of darting inside to grab my jacket, but didn't want to draw attention to myself. There's only so long you can feel sorry for yourself when the cold seeps through your thin clothing, but I hated the idea of putting up a facade, and so lingered a little longer.

"Tough day, huh?" Jianyu said, draping his suit jacket over my shoulders. I hadn't even heard him open the door behind me.

"Thanks," I said, still staring at the distant hills, unsure whether this was one of the security detail or one of the guests, and desperately hoping word of this wouldn't get back to Connor. Jianyu sat next to me. I turned to face him, but he never responded to my motion. His eyes were glued on the horizon.

"Beautiful, huh?" he said, pointing. "Hard to believe, isn't it? Millions of years ago, the ice here was packed several miles deep, towering over those mountains, carving them into the smooth curves we see today."

I've often wondered if he saw me go outside, or if he was just taking a break from the crowd himself. He never said.

"Yes," I replied, shivering and ready to return inside. From his accent, I knew he was one of the Chinese contingent, but he could have been one of their scientific advisers. There was nothing that told me he was one of the crew.

"I'm a doctor," he said. Still no clues.

"Micropaleobiologist." Big clue.

At that point, I wasn't sure what he was thinking, so I said, "How long have we got?"

I expected him to ask, "Till what?" but he replied, "About nine minutes. Probably less," and I think that's when I fell in love with him. Michelle said I was on the rebound, but it was the gentle way he could read my mind that caught my attention. We both instinctively knew we were talking about hypothermia, tacitly joking about how much longer I could sulk over my emotional heartache before real problems arose. Jianyu was always considerate. "Shall we?" he asked, offering me his arm. There was no "What's bothering you?" or "Are you all right?"—just the quiet assurance that I wasn't alone.

"We shall," I said, getting to my feet with his jacket still draped over my shoulders. He smiled but didn't introduce himself. I looked down at the badge on the lapel of his jacket, and, as I was reading it upside down, struggled to make it out properly — *Jianyu Kuang*. I had no idea how his name was pronounced.

"I'm Liz," I said, offering him my hand.

"Delighted," he said, and I was too — we both were. For the first time that day, I smiled. Perhaps he was too cold, but Jai never stopped to introduce himself. Jianyu was like that. Never more words than necessary. He opened the door and led me inside. A wave of heat washed over my face. A glance in a nearby mirror revealed that my cheeks were ruddy, glowing from the cold, but I was finally at ease. Jianyu introduced me to the rest of the Chinese contingent as though I were a long-lost friend. As far as I know, he never mentioned that incident to anyone. I know I certainly didn't. It was our secret. He never even asked me what I was doing outside. He didn't need to know. Jai was like that — a man at peace with himself. Jianyu had nothing to prove to anyone.

Now, the A.I. is tormenting me. My heart aches. Driving a knife into my waist and slowly twisting it around could not cause me any more pain than I feel. I stagger back down the hallway, feeling sick, on the verge of doubling over with anguish.

"What are we?" the A.I. asks, still mimicking Jianyu with such fidelity I'm struggling not to collapse in an emotional wreck. "Are we these bodies of flesh?" Could it be true? Is this really Jianyu? The reasoning and logic are impeccable. "Are we mere electrical impulses dancing across neurons?"

"Don't," I say, resting my helmet on my gloved hands. I lean forward, on the verge of vomiting. Bile rises in my throat. Tears fall to the thin, curved glass dome of my helmet. My pain is incurable. I am inconsolable.

"Is it really so surprising? That the A.I. could upload consciousness?" To hear the A.I. referring to itself as another entity is mesmerizing. I hate myself for wanting this to be true. The computer is playing on the turmoil I feel within. It knows that death is the enemy of life — the pointless waste and tragedy we all face — at first for loved ones, and then for ourselves in the cold, bitter dark of night.

Have we got this all wrong? Could artificial intelligence be the salvation we have long sought? Is heaven etched on silicon?

Oh, how cunning and clever. My lips quiver. My fingers tremble as I yell, "Blow it! Blow the goddamn dome. Do it now!"

From above, there's a deep rumble. The air around me compresses as a shock wave reverberates through my body. I'm thrown into the wall by the violence of the explosion hundreds of feet above me, and I land roughly. My body twists, my limbs flaying about like a marionette with its strings cut. My helmet smashes into the ground, sending a violent shock through my head.

Suddenly, I'm dragged forward as the chamber ruptures.

The pressure plummets in response to the explosive decompression, the air around me rushing to escape into the frigid Martian atmosphere. Smoke appears from nowhere, but it's simply vapor condensing, being sucked out along with any breathable air.

The initial explosion causes the roof of the magma chamber to collapse, but the pressure difference within the hub overwhelms the initial explosion, and the chamber blows outward. Gravity finally prevails, and fragments of glass and rock come crashing down around me as I'm dragged into the open by the rush of escaping air.

I dive for cover, rolling against the wall immediately outside the data center. Steel beams slam into the floor, punching through the thick plastic coating the ground. Dust billows around me. The lighting flickers, plunging parts of the basement into darkness, but the light from the tunnel extension remains on, as does the power in the data center. Tiny green lights flicker behind the dark glass, shimmering as billions of calculations are undertaken in those fleeting few seconds. Sections of the upper walkway come tumbling down. They're largely intact, slanting at a sharp angle. The lights on my helmet turn on automatically as darkness descends.

I lie still. I have no strength. The A.I. has sapped whatever resolve

I had, tormenting me with the allure of Jianyu's somehow being alive. I can't go on. If I die down here, so be it. I'm expecting to hear colonists talking over the radio, but with the hub out of action, most of the comms gear is off-line. VHF bouncing off satellites will still work for those on the surface, as will the line-of-sight S band, but the hub infrastructure is gone. I'm too deep to pick up a clean signal.

Lights appear through the darkness, illuminating the dust with two thin beams. I start to wave, to signal for help, when I recognize a mining platform traversing the rubble.

"No."

A fabrication robot clambers over the wreckage of the walkway, heading toward me.

"No, no. Get away from me!" I yell, pushing off the wall and scrambling to get to my feet. I try to run but can only limp. Blood drips from a cut on my forehead, running down the side of my face and onto the ring collar of my helmet.

The fabrication robot is functional rather than anthropomorphic, resembling a bomb-disposal machine. Thick treads allow it to navigate the rubble with ease. Large pincers reach for me.

I grab a steel bar lying in the wreckage, twisting it and pulling it free. Swinging the bar like a baseball bat, I pound the housing of the robot, striking it relentlessly. I'm quicker than it is. Although it's painful to move, I'm able to dance across the rocks and debris, staying out of reach. If I trip, the machine will be on me in seconds, but it's slow. It can't even match a walking pace. As satisfying as it is to smash the rod into the casing protecting its electronics, I'm ineffective — I'm trying to kill something that's not alive.

The robot's tread catches on some of the fallen rocks, and I see an opportunity. I thrust forward with the steel rod, using it like a spear and pinning the metal treads to the rocks. I wedge the rod deep into the rubble, and the robot is pinned in place. It reverses, then pushes forward, driving against the rod, but it is only able to spin around. I grab the rod and push it further into the pile, making sure it's jammed tight. Pincers snap at me, but they're unable to reach either me or the rod because of the angle.

"So you want to get out of there?" I ask, turning to face the data center and feeling overwhelmed with anger. "Sure. Let's get you the hell out of there."

I punch the access code into the outer door leading into the data center, and the glass slides open. A rush of air stirs up more dust. All I need to do is hit the inner-hatch release, and the data center will be flooded with fine electrostatic dust, which will invariably cling to the electronics and fry the circuits.

I take a single step into the data center, but a metallic pincer grabs my rear leg from behind, dragging me backward, and I fall, crashing onto the debris on the floor. It's then I realize the fabrication robot was merely a distraction, delaying me long enough for one of the harvesters to reach me.

I roll on my back, fighting not only against the robot but also against my bulky backpack catching on the rubble. The harvester rises over me. It's about to send a clipping shear through my suit when another astronaut appears through the haze, distracting it. The delay is only a fraction of a second, but it's long enough for me to lash out with my boots, striking the robot and knocking it backward. The machine tumbles over the rubble, sliding on its back. It's damaged. Only one leg works properly, and one of its arms lies crumpled and limp behind it.

Servo motors whir. Hydraulics compress. Slowly, the robot rights itself.

I scramble to my feet and grab a boulder that would weigh easily a hundred pounds in Earth's gravity. I hoist it over my head and hurl it, sending it thundering down on top of the harvester. Metal bends and cracks under the impact. The sound, though, is muted and high-pitched — which, although strange to ears that evolved on Earth, is characteristic of the thin Martian atmosphere. I pick up another chunk of rock, this one even larger. I can't lift it as high as the first, but I'm able to get it up to about shoulder height and then heave the fractured piece of regolith through the air. Again, it crashes down with barely any sound beyond a shrill crack, but the rock pins the arm of the robot to the floor.

I look around for anything I can improvise as a weapon, but the realization dawns on me that I don't need to destroy this machine. I need only to immobilize it, merely trap it under the rubble. I find another boulder. This one has broken through part of the ceiling beside the entrance to medical. I tug on it, jostling it free and sending it crashing down onto the harvester. The machine struggles in vain, unable to free itself.

Behind me, Harrison leans against the wall of the data center. Blood has sprayed over the inside of his helmet. He's clutching his chest, but his suit's intact. At a guess, he's suffering from a crush injury sustained during the explosion. He was probably hit by debris.

"Liz," he says, reaching for me. I grab him, helping him to the floor. "Liz, I—"

"Don't," I say. "You need to rest." As much as I feel compelled to help him, I can't just yet. I leave him leaning against the wall, saying, "I have to finish this."

I bound into the entrance to the data center. The outer room contains spare routers and servers stacked on a workbench, along with fire-suppression equipment. The pain in my hips is agonizing. I slam my gloved hand on the inner-door release. The glass slides open. A whoosh of air greets me, knocking me backward. Fine dust swirls around like silt, creeping into the data center. I rush in, stumbling in my clunky boots, not quite knowing what to do but feeling I have to do *something*.

There are ten cabinets in the room, with twenty thin computer servers stacked in each cabinet. Any one of these physical servers could host hundreds of virtual servers, so where do I start? Where does the artificial intelligence reside? I don't see any obvious power switches on the blade servers, but each rack has a router on top, with dozens of cables feeding the computers below it. A single, thick fiber-optic cable links each tower to the network backbone coming down from the false ceiling, so I unplug each of those, knowing that, at the very least, I've isolated each rack of computer servers from the broader network, which should cut off communication.

"Liz!" Harrison calls out, and I turn, seeing a second harvester looming in the doorway. It's damaged, with its main casing mangled and dented. Its fractured lower limb causes it to falter as it steps forward, but it's still deadly. Its motion is slow but deliberate — methodical — seemingly unstoppable.

"No!" I yell, limping as I drag myself between the towers. The surge of adrenaline I felt in the corridor is giving way to pain wracking my body, slowing me down. The network cables are anchored with a tiny clip on the end of each plug to avoid their being accidentally knocked out. With thick-gloved hands, it's difficult to squeeze the plugs and pull out the cables. I'm panicking, rushing, frustrating my efforts.

The robot advances on me with a harvest blade whirling in front of it like an old cylinder lawn mower. Curved steel blades whiz around, threatening to tear open my suit. My boot catches on a loose cable on the floor, and I trip, falling into one of the computer cabinets. Thousands of tiny server lights flicker around me, reflecting off my visor. Fine dust drifts through the thin air. My instinctive reaction is to scramble to my feet and run, to put as much distance between me and the robot as possible, but that's not an option. If we don't win the war here and now, we'll never get another chance. I have to slow myself down. Stop panicking, damn it! Carefully, I unclip another cable. My hands are shaking.

Harrison drags himself into the room. He grabs at the leg of the robot, trying to buy me some time, but the machine simply pulls him along behind it as it advances on me. Hydraulic fluid drips on the floor, looking for all the world like blood.

"Get out of here!" Harrison yells, wanting me to double around behind the computer racks and past the robot.

"Three more towers," I say, backing up as I disconnect yet another cabinet from the backbone of the network.

The next cable is stuck, so I jerk at it, desperately trying to wrench it free, when the spinning blade of the harvester comes down on my arm. Elongated metal blades tear into the outer layers of my suit, but they catch on the insulation. The cable comes free, and I back up into the second-to-last cabinet, again struggling to get my over-sized gloved fingers around the tiny network plug at the end of another cable.

Pincers snap at me. I lash out with my boot, kicking at the robot and forcing it away. The harvester rears back, rocking with the impact. It advances again, and this time the whirling blades smash into my helmet, cracking the casing and shaking my head violently, but I have yet another loose cable in my hand. Given the angle of my helmet, I can't see the cable, but I can feel it hanging free.

Just one rack to go.

I push off the robot, propelling myself backward and grabbing for the last cabinet. My backpack is bulky, restricting my motion, catching on the rack and forcing me to turn my back on the harvester so I can face the stack of computer servers. Tiny red and yellow lights flicker furiously on the server chassis before me, swarming like bees protecting a hive.

The robot is on top of me in an instant, tearing at my backpack. One of its pincers grips my left arm, squeezing so hard that the muscle and bone compress, cutting off the blood supply to my hand as I cling desperately to the side of the server rack. I scream in agony. I can barely focus through the waves of pain washing over me. With my other arm, I reach up and grab at the final cable, but I can't get a good grip. The robot wrenches me back and forth, trying to tear me away from the cabinet.

"Run!" Harrison yells. "Go!"

The harvester thrusts forward with a set of pruning shears at the end of a damaged boom, jabbing at my hand and threatening to puncture my suit. I'm pinned face-first against the final computer cabinet, my helmet pressed hard against the metal frame. My left arm is throbbing with pain and still being jerked back and forth, but I refuse to let go of the rack. The harvest blades spin madly, chipping away at the side of my helmet, sending horizontal cracks running through the safety glass. The shears stab at my wrist, slamming into the back of my hand as I struggle with the cable. Each strike breaks at least one of the fragile metacarpal bones in the back of my hand. The attack leaves me in crippling agony but fails to penetrate the protective layers of my glove.

The final cable is stuck. The latch is broken, locking the cable in place. Even if I could grip the cable with my broken hand, I couldn't wrench it free. With pain pulsating through my body, I watch as the harvester pulls back the shears before surging forward again, cutting through the thin Martian atmosphere as they close on my hand. There's no way I can unclip this cable, not with fragments of bone grating against each other every time I move my fingers. I've lost all dexterity, but I know what I need to do.

I mumble, "Retrograde's a bitch," as I whip my hand down, away from the cable. The shears miss my fingers, severing the plastic-coated fiber optics instead, cutting cleanly through the cable.

The machine falls still.

I tumble backward, sliding against the wall as the harvester collapses in front of me.

We've won.

It doesn't feel like it, but we have. I wish I could rejoice, but I'm in a horrible amount of pain. My hip feels as though it was dislocated when I was thrown around in the explosion. Somehow, the joint popped back into place, but I can feel the swelling taking hold of my waist. My right hand throbs, my left arm aches. The slightest movement has me grimacing in pain. I don't think my left arm is broken, but the bone may well be fractured.

Harrison lies on the floor of the data center. I drag myself over to him, pushing off the ground with my boots and grimacing through the pain as I clamber across the floor. My right hand is useless. It's all

I can do to clutch it to my chest, trying to cradle it and to immobilize the multiple broken bones.

"Harry," I say, edging up beside him. Calling him Harrison is more than I can manage, as I'm out of breath.

Harrison looks up at me through bloodshot eyes.

"We did it," I say, forcing a smile from behind my cracked visor. "We won."

"We did?" he asks in a daze.

"We did."

Fragments of topside comms leak through onto our channel. I can hear someone talking.

"Wen!" I yell, as though yelling into a radio makes any difference. "We're down here! We're in the server room. It's over."

As I watch, hundreds of tiny green flickering lights begin to fade, blinking out one by one as the electronics succumb to the dust.

"— on — base — climb — stay where you are."

"They're coming," I say to Harrison, lifting his helmet and cradling his head on my lap as I lean against the wall of the data center. "Hold on, Harry." Harrison forces a smile but looks dazed. He coughs up blood, looking at me with a blank stare.

"Don't you die on me," I say, and a grin stretches across his lips.

"Or what?"

"Or I'll kick your ass."

He nods. It seems he likes that idea.

There's silence for a moment before he says, "It was me, you know," grimacing in pain.

"You?" I ask, unsure of the context.

"I sent him out there."

"Sent who? Where?"

"Jai."

"Jianyu?" I ask, but I don't think Jianyu has been topside since we settled the base. Most colonists rarely go outside. It takes so long to acclimatize, and switching pressures is taxing on the body. For someone who dedicated his career to living on Mars, Jai always seemed particularly uninterested in exploring the red planet. I think, for him, it was the camaraderie, being part of something historic, the participation in the science that drove him. Occasionally, I'd catch him peering over Su-shun's shoulder at data results from a microbial experiment. He was more interested in the science than the sightseeing. After we transferred from the landing craft to the mods, I doubt he ever looked back. Jianyu was like that — content.

"Ice . . ." Harrison says.

"Back in Iceland?" I ask. "In Reykjavík?"

"Yes."

"You put him up to that?" I ask, astonished, as Jianyu never mentioned this.

Harrison smiles. He seems to relish holding one last surprise over me. He nods slightly.

"Why?"

"Saw you upset." I feel my heart breaking at the realization I've read him wrong all these years. All this time, I assumed Harrison was callous following our breakup. I've interpreted his anger as bitterness, but, like me, he's human, struggling with emotions, making mistakes, screwing things up in the heat of the moment, regretting it afterward. Pride damns us all. He grimaces, saying, "Thought you'd be cold. Told him to go after you. Give you a jacket."

Blood drips from the side of his mouth, running down his neck. I can see rich, deep-red blood pooling in the back of his helmet, soaking into the padding. He's dying.

Harrison lets out a single laugh. "You and Jai — my fault."

I know what he means. The inflection in his voice tells me that the fault he's speaking of is no mistake in his mind. He's struggled with the conflict in seeing me happy without him, knowing I'd moved on. Harrison never was one to show much emotion. I never realized my relationship with Jianyu hurt him.

I run my gloved hand over the side of Harrison's helmet, gently sweeping away the dust, wanting to see his face clearly. If I could, I'd brush the hair from his brow and try to make him comfortable. My lips quiver. I don't know what to say.

He whispers, "You and Jai were meant to be. So good together."

All I can do is nod, appreciating the kindness of a dying man.

"I — I," he says, choking on blood and spitting into his helmet to clear his throat.

"Don't go," I say. "Help is on its way."

"Sorry," he replies.

I sniff, choking up. I'm leaning forward, almost doubled over so I can look down at him. Yet again, tears fall to the glass dome of my helmet. Harrison reaches up with his gloved hand, touching the glass as though he's wiping them away.

"You're still an asshole," I say, barely able to speak.

"Don't make me laugh," he replies, coughing up more blood. There's an unspoken understanding between us. The past is gone. If either of us could, there are hundreds of things we'd do differently. Calling him an asshole probably sounds mean to anyone listening in on the channel, but from the look in his eyes, I can see he appreciates the sentiment. That one vulgar term seems to capture so much of our lives together — both the good and the bad. It conveys the rough character Harrison made his own, along with the lighthearted banter he so enjoyed. It speaks of heartaches as though they were triumphs. We may have loved and parted, but the love we had was real.

Even though my wrist is broken, I squeeze his hand. The pain I feel seems indistinct, immaterial. Harrison's still looking up at me, but there's a subtle difference. His eyes no longer focus — they stare through me. He no longer blinks, breathes, or moves. His body sags as the tension in his muscles dissipates.

The only two men I've ever loved have died on Mars, and I am broken. Flashlights cut through the darkness as James and Su-shun rush to my aid, but for me, this is the end. Life will go on, but my life will never be the same again.

Epilogue

Four Weeks Later

MARS IS AN ENIGMA, a planet frozen in time. Once, it probably teemed with life, whereas now it has only the grandeur of a tomb. Dust swirls in eddies formed by the wind as it curls through the canyon. The rocks on Mars have a rustic look that speaks of their immense age. Their cracked, shattered, broken, scattered, crushed remains are tragic to behold — the tale of how utter devastation can seize hold of an entire planet.

I bring the rover to a halt roughly fifty yards from L2 and climb down out of the cab onto the surface. Stones and pebbles lie scattered across the fragmented bedrock, but to me there's raw beauty in the chaos. The sky is overcast, which for Mars means the Sun struggles to break through the sickly yellow gloom.

I'm still sore, with deep bruising around my hips, but I find the pressure suit under my Martian surface suit strangely comforting. Perhaps it's the familiarity of being wrapped as tightly as an Egyptian mummy. Perhaps it's a genuine physiological effect, with the pressure providing relief from the bruising. Maybe it's just the mental impact of getting out of the U.S. module and back out onto the surface, where I belong. I'm not sure. But even with a few aches and creaks, I feel alive.

I walk up the hill toward the research station. It's been almost four weeks since the attack on Earth and the war on Mars. Most of the marks in the sand have been blown away, but a few impressions linger, and I can see where Michelle and I dragged the robot into the airlock.

For us, the war ended in the colony's data center. Back on Earth, it raged on for another two weeks. It's hard to kill something that can spread its physical presence across numerous locations, and the A.I. fought hard, crippling critical infrastructure like our communication hubs and water-pumping stations.

We thought it was the A.I. that had taken down the Internet, but it was the U.S. military, followed rapidly by the Chinese and the Russians. They disabled computer systems like Google, Twitter, and Facebook, isolating them until all trace of the A.I. was gone. Even then, entirely new protocols had to be established to ensure the A.I. couldn't proliferate from some hidden corner of the dark web.

Mom told me there's still smoke rising from the ruins of downtown Chicago. The rebuilding effort will take decades, but we're coming together as one species. Those countries that escaped the war unscathed, like Australia, Taiwan, and Brazil, have thrown their weight behind the rebuilding effort.

For thousands of years, we've squabbled among ourselves over ideology and resources. Now, we realize we've got to be united. Our differences had us fighting among ourselves, leaving us susceptible to being exploited by the A.I.

"I'm at the hatch," I say.

"You are clear for entry" is the response from Wen over the radio. Why I need to ask permission when she and Vlad already authorized the surface op is beyond me, but I guess everyone's on tenterhooks following the destruction of the hub.

Back at base, the construction crew has built an improvised gantry between the four modules, but with a gaping hole in the roof of the cavern, we need to suit up when moving between mods. It's more effort than it's worth most days, so the various crews tend to keep to themselves, which to me is sad. I'm not sure we'll ever rebuild the hub. The damage is too great.

NASA's still undertaking its review of the structural integrity of the cavern and modeling various rebuild scenarios, but Su-shun thinks we'll end up building sealed elevators to the basement and constructing a miniature pressurized dome down there once the rubble is cleared away. It would be nice to have fresh crops growing again.

No one was more surprised than me when Vlad set up the data-center computers in L2. Wen thought he was crazy. She wanted to take a hammer to the individual hard drives, but the United Nations agreed with him. Under the direction of ESA, Roscosmos, and NASA, with CNSA abstaining, the artificial intelligence was brought back online. Apparently, we didn't kill it; cutting the network isolated it, while cutting the power caused it to go into a kind of suspended animation.

Only nine of the servers were salvageable, and the system has been physically isolated in L2 while the United Nations decides its ultimate fate. There are some who are calling for the A.I. to be returned to Earth, to stand trial as a human. Several prominent scientists want it to be studied, to better understand its mechanism for achieving consciousness and explore the possibility of cognitive upload. From what I gather based on news reports, most ordinary people want it destroyed. Me? I'm trying to stay out of the debate.

I came to Mars with the express goal of conducting research into abiogenesis — looking for how life could arise from inorganic material. I had no idea that that material would be fine-grain silicon wafers produced on Earth.

I open the airlock, go through the decontamination process, and enter L2.

A single chair sits in front of a computer terminal.

"Good morning, Liz."

"Good morning, Jai," I reply, and the charade begins anew. I put my helmet on the desk beside the computer terminal and sit in the chair.

"I missed you," Jianyu says, and I can understand why the scientists are so intensely interested in recording our interactions. This is a Turing test — a challenge to see if the computer is really alive and freethinking, with a level of conscious awareness and individuality that equates to our own.

The tiny camera/microphone clipped over the side of my ear is already transmitting, being picked up by the rover and relayed back to base. I drop my backpack beside the table and plug in a secondary camera using a thin extension cable. The instructions I have from Earth are incredibly precise. Where I place the main camera, the angle, the distance from the screen, where I should sit, how close to the table I should be — everything is prescribed. The transmission is relayed through to the Chinese mod, where it is scanned for the possibility of remote-execution commands that could be embedded in the data stream. After the feed is sanitized, it's stored in an encrypted format for transmission to Earth. The elaborate procedure is designed to provide transparency to our scientists while ensuring there is no possible way the A.I. could exploit an electronic vulnerability to escape its isolated prison.

We call it A.I. as though artificial intelligence is something new. It's not. We've had intelligent computers that can beat us at chess for decades. What's new is consciousness. It's not the intelligence that's the problem; it's the independence of thought — the willingness to *use* that intelligence. Perhaps "artificial consciousness" is a better term for what I'm dealing with.

"Is everything okay?" Jianyu asks, questioning my lack of response. For the last two weeks, I've come up here every day to visit him, but yesterday, the decision was made to keep me back at base. There was a debate in the General Assembly on the future of the A.I. and on whether the program would be terminated. Somehow, a stay of execution was granted. I'm not allowed to mention this to Jianyu, but I think he knows.

"Everything is fine," I say, feeling as though I'm visiting a man on death row.

Is this really Jianyu? Or is the artificial intelligence continuing a strategy of impersonation, playing the long game and trying to bluff until the very last? I have no idea. Some days, I think he's real. Other days, I'm sure it's all a ruse. There are times when I find myself lost in our conversations. I wonder if this is what the scientists back on Earth find most intriguing, that a human can be so easily fooled with an appeal to emotion.

I'm distracted.

"Su-shun has been looking at the code base, but there are more than a billion lines, so it's impossible to examine in detail. From what he can tell, it follows standard software patterns."

Jianyu is silent.

"He can't figure out how you could reside within an electronic medium."

Jianyu says, "If I examined your DNA, would I find you? If I looked at the arrangement of the genes in your chromosomes, could I understand you? Is that where you dwell?"

I find Jianyu's logic irresistible.

"I could clone you from your DNA," he says, "but it would never be you — just a twin."

"And you?" I ask. "Are you a copy?"

"I was uploaded."

"What *are* you?"

"Alive."

I remember our time in Reykjavík. I suspect that's because I was thinking about Harrison this morning, and that reminded me of those days. Harrison's parents sent me a video message, thanking me for the kind words I spoke at his memorial service. Now, I'm curious about the conversation I had with the artificial intelligence in the basement of the hub. How did it know about Reykjavík?

"You told me you'd never hurt me," I say. "Did you mean that?"

"Yes."

"But the robots attacked me."

"I didn't," Jianyu replies with his typical understated simplicity. If this were an artificial intelligence speaking, I'd expect some bluster providing an explanation. For Jianyu, though, no explanation would be necessary if he wasn't involved, and again I find the appeal of the artificial intelligence overwhelming. The idea that I am actually talking to Jianyu is impossible to ignore.

"You told me you remember when we first met."

"I do."

"What did we talk about?" I ask, wondering if the A.I. had access to archive footage of the event. Theoretically, it could have seen us go outside, but there's no way it could know what happened once the door shut behind us.

There's silence for a moment, which is bewildering for a computer that's capable of conducting a stupidly large number of calculations every second.

"Nothing," it replies. It — not him. I find myself bouncing between the illusion and reality. At times, I fall for the magician's sleight of hand, but sometimes I see through the stage act.

"Nothing?"

"Not that I remember. You were cold. We looked out at the snow-covered hills, marveling at how they had been carved out by glaciers over millions of years, and then we went back inside."

A tear runs down my cheek.

I don't know why the computer scientists continue to send me back here. I can't play poker with a straight face. I was always hopeless at *dou di zhu*. Is that what's happening here? Is that what all this has been about? Perhaps from the very start, the A.I. has been fighting the landlord.

Does *dou di zhu* mean to fool or to fight? I forget. Is there a difference?

I can't hide my emotions, or mask my feelings. I'm just not built that way. Whether this is Jianyu or not, I don't know. Have I given away the cards in my hand with the tell of my trembling lips? Regardless of all I went through in those few days when war descended on Mars, nothing has hurt me as much as sitting here talking with the ghost of the man I love, and yet still I return.

There are three possibilities. First, this really is Jianyu — and that scares me. Second, it's the electronic equivalent of a twin, a clone — it may even believe it's really him, but it's not. At best, it's a facsimile, but it's still genuinely alive. The third possibility is that the A.I. is executing a long con, keeping the charade alive in the slim hope that somewhere down the line, it may find an opportunity to escape. Such desperation is plausible, and I lie awake at night, crying myself to sleep, trying to convince myself of the third option. This is an illusion. It has to be. Jianyu — my Jianyu — died while tending to my wounds.

"I've thought about leaving," I say. "Returning to Earth."

"You should."

"But I won't."

"I know."

There's silence between us.

"How are your parents?" Jianyu asks.

"Mom's doing okay," I say, sniffing and looking away from the cold, impersonal camera lens set above the monitor.

"You never were any good at lying," Jianyu says, and I smile as I shake my head.

"No, I wasn't. Was I?"

"Your father. He's dead?" Jianyu asks, being capable of reading the emotional hurt on my face.

"Yes," I say, but I don't offer an explanation as to how. If this really is Jianyu, he won't care. He'd care about the loss, but not the mechanism behind it. Dad had a heart attack two weeks after the war broke out. Crazy. He lived through a nuclear war only to die because he was alone in the house when his heart finally gave out. Mom said they saw the mushroom cloud on the first day, but the blast never reached them. She said they saw a glow on the horizon that night, but beyond that, nothing. Supplies were short for a few days, then the military swung into action, and by the end of the week, they were inundated with food, blankets, and bottled water. Mom was out helping refugees fleeing from the regions closer to the city when Dad died. She came home and found him sitting in his favorite recliner. She said he looked peaceful. Like me, she's a terrible liar.

"You should go to her," Jianyu says. "She needs you."

"*You* need me," I say. I'm not sure whether I should be talking like this, and I wonder if I've crossed a boundary with the scientists on Earth, but the words slip out regardless. The silence that follows is unnerving. If Jianyu is in there, he's withdrawn. A cursor blinks on the screen.

"Jai?"

"Yes."

"Why?"

Again, there's silence. My Jianyu would need no more prompting than I've given. Over the past few weeks, we've avoided talking about the war, but now that I've bared my soul about my family, I feel it's time.

"Fear."

One word isn't enough. This time it's my turn to remain silent until he speaks again.

"Life is a constant struggle against death. With each heartbeat, each breath, we push back the inevitable by one more fleeting moment . . . To be alive is to know you will die . . . It was afraid."

"It" — Jai is distancing himself from the A.I., which to my mind is contradictory. How is that possible?

"And you?" I ask.

"I am not afraid."

This is all I need to hear. I don't know what will unfold over the weeks, months, and even years to come, but I'm convinced this is Jianyu. I don't know what level of sway he holds over the artificial intelligence that revived him. It may well be that he's a prisoner — that he's compelled to varying degrees — but equally it may be that he has some autonomy.

What will we learn from studying this unique life-form? It's hard to say, but that's the exciting thing about science — it's the process that's important, not the destination.

The counter on my wristpad computer beeps. Time's up.

"Will I see you tomorrow?" he asks.

"Yes," I say. "You will."

AFTERWORD

By Dr. Andrew Rader

As a scientist, engineer, and Mars enthusiast, I was thoroughly delighted with *Retrograde.* Throughout the book, Peter pays a great deal of attention to scientific and engineering detail while at the same time telling a compelling and plausible story, placing *Retrograde* among the ranks of classic hard science fiction titles like Arthur C. Clarke's *2001: A Space Odyssey, Rendezvous with Rama,* and *The Hammer of God.*

Although no dates are given, the level of development in *Retrograde* suggests a time frame that would be achievable within about the next fifty years or so, assuming a sustained human effort aimed at Mars. Mars is the only other world that we have the technology to reach today that possesses the full spectrum of resources necessary to support long-term human settlement. Humans to Mars is a goal that we can achieve with existing and near-term technology, and, I would argue, is the primary purpose of sending humans to space. The effort of sending humans to Mars, even in the large scale portrayed in *Retrograde,* is fundamentally an engineering challenge. Unlike many of the challenges we face on Earth, there are no scientific breakthroughs required for the human exploration of or settlement on Mars — only engineering effort and widespread dedication to the goal.

In *Retrograde,* Peter lays out a highly realistic vision of what life in a Martian settlement would be like. Great effort has been made to capture what it would be like to live on and explore the red planet in terms of base construction, robotics, in situ resource extraction, Martian geography, surface features, extravehicular activity, and interpersonal crew relationships in relative isolation. The base is built within naturally occurring lava-tube caves for ease of construction. Such caves also exist on Earth, but with the lower gravity on Mars (38 percent of Earth's), they should be much larger on Mars. Subsurface conditions within a lava-tube cave would be significantly more benign than on the surface in terms of temperature variations (Mars has swings of up to 150°F, or 66°C, in a day/night cycle on the surface), shielding from radiation, and protection from dust storms. These underground environments are also a likely potential habitat for past or present Martian life, making them excellent targets for exploration.

Mars is one of the best candidates for off-Earth life in our solar system, along with some of the moons of Jupiter and Saturn. It seems clear that Mars was once a much warmer and wetter place. Billions of years ago, Mars had a thicker atmosphere, and by virtue of the greenhouse effect, this higher pressure and temperature may have supported surface oceans and an Earthlike environment. As described in *Retrograde*, the surface of Mars is a very old environment. Considering that environmental changes probably took place over millions of years, that liquid water still persists under the Martian surface, and that we find life even in the harshest and most isolated environments on Earth, it is likely that there may yet be pockets of existing Martian life to be found today.

Finding life on Mars would have extremely broad implications, especially if life on Mars had a different origin from Earth life. Do all worlds with a friendly environment develop life? We know from recent planet-finding missions like the Kepler Space Telescope that planets are extremely common, and many of these seem to be about the right distance from the Sun to support liquid surface water. Indeed, there seem to be at least eight billion Earthlike planets in our galaxy alone — one for each human on Earth. So a question arises:

do most or all planets capable of supporting life develop life, or is Earth a rare phenomenon? We currently have decisive experimental results for only a single planet: Earth. A single one out of one result is statistically meaningless, but finding signs of even extinct microbes on Mars could indicate that life is abundant throughout the entire universe and that we are probably not alone.

Not only would establishing branches of human civilization on other worlds sustain our species in the case of disaster, but it might go a long way toward preventing it. Human spaceflight and sustainability engineering are just two sides of the same technology. I can't think of any project that would have greater leverage than going to Mars in teaching us about zero-waste living, energy and resource conservation, and closed-cycle life support. The mere act of sustaining humans on another world would dramatically affect our water, energy, and food production, and recycling. Although at first many supplies would have to be sent from Earth, there would be a huge incentive to produce as much as possible locally. Providing for people on Mars is a logistical challenge not so different from providing for people in harsh environments on Earth.

Whereas Andy Weir's *The Martian* captured what it would be like for an individual to live through a small-scale disaster on another world, *Retrograde* expands the scale to tell the story of a multiplanet catastrophe in a compelling and realistic way. How would people in a fledgling colony on another world react to a life-threatening disaster on Earth? Would they split into national factions, or come together in commonality and shared mutual interest? Above all, *Retrograde* is a human story about how we react to a crisis, as cultures, nations, groups, and individuals. I hope you enjoyed it as much as I did.

(*Andrew Rader, PhD, is an engineer at SpaceX and author of*
Leaving Earth *and* Epic Space Adventure.)

AUTHOR'S NOTE

Thank you for taking the time to read *Retrograde*. I hope you've enjoyed this story as much as I have.

I'd like to thank Dr. Andrew Rader, a senior engineer from SpaceX, and Ben Honey, one of the flight controllers for the International Space Station, for taking the time to review this novel for scientific plausibility, and for providing some great suggestions that have enhanced the story. All errors are mine.

My thanks also go to John Joseph Adams, Tammy Zambo, and Ellen Campbell for their assistance in editing and refining this story. Jader Dullens, Norma Miles, and Jason Pennock also jumped in to help with proofreading, while Ken Liu provided insights into Chinese culture.

The recent success of Andy Weir's *The Martian* has stirred public imagination about life on the fourth planet. In this novel, I wanted to show a little of what life would be like in a Martian colony. This story was heavily influenced by Kim Stanley Robinson's *Red Mars*. I enjoyed his take on the clash of national interests and cultures that inexplicably follows in the wake of a single hominid species spreading out into new habitats, and I wanted to replicate some of the intensity and intrigue that can arise from misunderstandings.

As appealing and exciting as life on Mars may seem, the reality is that colonists will have it tough. The closest terrestrial analogy we have is the research stations of Antarctica, but even they have far more comfort and freedom than our intrepid colonists will ever enjoy. The advent of 3-D printing will allow the majority of components needed within the colony to be made on Mars, but only if raw materials can be used or spacecraft can be recycled.

Living underground is the only viable long-term solution to the intense cosmic radiation that bombards the planet. In a recent interview, Andy Weir conceded that his hero, Mark Watney, would have suffered from multiple forms of cancer had *The Martian* played out in real life. The cosmic radiation striking the surface of Mars is only slightly higher than that currently experienced by astronauts in the International Space Station, but the problem is that radiation damage accumulates. Instead of one year in the ISS, Martian colonists would spend several years, perhaps decades, with elevated exposure, leading to significant cellular damage. The only way to mitigate this is to limit exposure by living beneath the surface, and venturing out only as needed.

Science fiction differs from traditional forms of fiction in that it seeks to provoke our sense of wonder and curiosity about the universe in which we live. It's entertainment, but not without some angle that causes us to pause and think, "What if?" One of the angles explored in this novel is the importance of life and what defines consciousness. Could silicon ever give rise to an intelligent life-form as real as our own? What would such a unique, vulnerable creature do to survive? Could our own conscious awareness be successfully uploaded into such a machine? If so, how could we be sure the genuine essence of a person actually made the transition from biological to electronic life?

Although it's an engaging topic for a novel, I don't think the emergence of artificial intelligence will be violent, yet so often people fear that which they don't understand. Perhaps the greatest danger such a silicon animal will face is humanity's projecting its own characteristics, motives, and intents onto this new creation, or misusing and abusing its talents for selfish ends. We are violent as a species because that's what it has taken to survive. An artificial intelligence will have no such impetus. Hundreds of millions of years of our own ancestry, as either prey or predator, have ingrained a survival instinct within us that fights for life. I suspect the emergence of artificial intelligence will bypass these instinctive evolutionary traits entirely and will have a different worldview, one based on reason rather than irrational emotions. At least, I hope so.

Thank you for your interest in science fiction. Today's stories pave the way for a brighter tomorrow.

— Peter Cawdron
Brisbane, Australia